If you're a fan of historical cozy mystery books, especially those set in the WWII era, you'll love **Deadly Broadcast.** The strong characters, well-paced plot, blackout, and mystery make **Deadly Broadcast** a must-read for cozy mystery lovers! *Christy's Cozy Corners*

Sure to be enjoyed by cozy fans in general but especially those that like historical cozies. *Books a Plenty Book Reviews*

Hair raising moments, untrustworthy suspects, and a despicable dead man make **Deadly Broadcast** a gripping page-turner. *Cozy Up With Kathy*

This was a page turner. It kept me reading later into the night than it should have...I enjoyed the investigation part – who wanted Kennedy dead? There seemed to be an overwhelming list. I also enjoyed reading the historical aspects of the book. *Reflections on Days Gone By*

Also from Kate Parker

The Deadly Series

Deadly Scandal

Deadly Wedding

Deadly Fashion

Deadly Deception

Deadly Travel

Deadly Darkness

Deadly Cypher

Deadly Broadcast

Deadly Rescue

The Victorian Bookshop Mysteries

The Vanishing Thief

The Counterfeit Lady

The Royal Assassin

The Conspiring Woman

The Detecting Duchess

The Milliner Mysteries

The Killing at Kaldaire House

Murder at the Marlowe Club

The Mystery at Chadwick House

Deadly
Rescue

Kate Parker

JDP PRESS

This is a work of fiction. All names, characters, and incidents are products of the author's imagination. Any resemblance to actual occurrences or persons, living or dead, is coincidental. Historical events and personages are fictionalized.

Deadly Rescue copyright © 2022 by Kate Parker

ISBN: 978-1-7367923-9-1 [print]
ISBN: 978-1-7367923-8-4 [e-book]

Published by JDPPress
Cover Design by Lyndsey Lewellen of Llewellen Designs

Dedication

To Jennifer, who introduced me to Denmark and is
always up for travel.
To the readers on the Lovely Ladies Swim Team.
To John, forever.

April 4, 1940

Chapter One

"What do you mean, drop everything and rush off to Denmark?" I stared at Sir Malcolm Freemantle, British counterintelligence spymaster, with a fury I wasn't trying to disguise. He'd told me three months before that he wasn't going to drag me into any more investigations. At least not until the war started in earnest. Probably.

But as dusk was falling over London and blackout curtains were closed for the night, he'd called me to his office to tell me he had a new assignment for me. In neutral Denmark, of all places.

"There's no fighting going on in Europe. At least not anything to bother Britain. Why are you sending me on another investigation, Sir Malcolm?"

"Do you know who Admiral Wilhelm Canaris is, Olivia?"

I shook my head.

"He's chief of the Abwehr, German military intelligence. And today he has informed the Danish and Norwegian governments that the German army will attack on Tuesday, 9 April." He studied me without expression.

I felt anything but calm hearing that news, and I know I showed my fears. That would mean the Phony War was coming to an end, and once more, my husband, Adam, would be in great danger. "Why would he warn them? Hitler will separate his head from his shoulders for giving away their battle plans."

"Canaris is no fool. He wouldn't have done this without Hitler's approval. Personally, I think he did it so the Danes and the Norwegians will have time to surrender without anyone getting hurt. Less expenditure of arms and fuel by the German military. Two countries conquered on the cheap."

"All right. It's now Thursday night. On Tuesday morning the Germans say they will attack." This was insane. Why would Canaris tell anyone? Why would Sir Malcolm tell me? "Why are you telling me? I don't work for you anymore."

"You signed the Official Secrets Act. I can call you to duty at any time until this war is over." His satisfied smile said it all.

"The war begins in earnest on Tuesday, and I need you to get back to work. Your holiday is over." He studied me from beneath his bushy eyebrows. "I need you to fly to Denmark in the morning."

"And do what? Stop the invasion?" I asked him.

Sir Malcolm's office was cheerless at the best of times. Now with blackout curtains and lower indoor lighting to save on fuel used to make electricity, monsters could, and probably did, hide in the shadowy corners. And Sir Malcolm, sitting at his desk in the middle of the room, was the biggest monster of all. "Get Olaf Jørgensen and his research out of Denmark and on Monday's ferry back to England."

"Why can't he do that himself?"

"He's conflicted." Sir Malcolm gave an exasperated sigh.

"And I'm supposed to convince him to come with me? Why would he listen to me?"

"He won't. That's why I'm sending Mike Christiansen with you. He speaks Danish and has some understanding of chemistry."

"Chemistry?" I studied modern languages at university, not science of any sort.

"Jørgensen won the Nobel Prize for chemistry in 1928."

I shook my head. We were way out of my depth now. "I'm probably not the best—"

"The point is, Olivia," Sir Malcolm said, one hand up as if to stop me, "Olaf Jørgensen won't leave Denmark without his wife, Ailsa. Ailsa is in a wheeled chair and won't leave without their daughter, their only living child, Katrine. And once upon a time, Ailsa Jørgensen and your mother, Phyllida Harper, were close friends."

The shock of hearing my mother's name, here of all places, made me drop into the nearest chair without paying any attention to protocol or decorum. Someone who knew my mother. Someone who might talk to me about her. When I again noticed who I was speaking to, I said, "I don't remember Mrs. Jørgensen, and I doubt she'd remember me."

"But she'll remember your mother." His dark eyes held me with his stare. "And we need you to help get her back to England so Jørgensen will come along."

"Back to England?" I emphasized the word "back." Was that where she'd known my mother?

"Jørgensen was a lecturer and researcher at Cambridge in the early 1920s. He and Ailsa lived here with their baby. Katrine."

"But my mother was dead by then."

"Before the war, your father was posted to Copenhagen. He and your mother lived there for two years before your mother returned home to have you. Once you were born, the two of you returned to Copenhagen. Do you remember the city?"

"No."

"I'm not surprised. You were only two when the war broke out and your father was sent—elsewhere, while you and your mother returned again to England."

"So my mother lived in Copenhagen for nearly four years." Something else I hadn't known about her.

"Yes, and during all that time, she and Ailsa Jørgensen were close friends."

Here was a chance for me to learn more about my mother. I could barely remember her. My father rarely mentioned her, leaving me with a roomful of unanswered questions.

Did I have her smile? Her writing talent? Her inability to boil water? Most women knew that much about their mothers. I didn't.

If I was going to get this chance to learn more about my mother, I'd have to show more interest in the rescue mission Sir Malcolm wanted to send me on. "Katrine. How old is she?"

Sir Malcolm looked through the folder on his desk. "She was born in 1918."

"And she's single?"

The look on Sir Malcolm's face told me that was a problem before he said, "She's romantically attached to a chemist, an assistant at her father's institute. A German postdoctoral assistant."

"And the Germans are taking over on Tuesday." He certainly wouldn't want to leave at that moment, with the Germans marching in, which would mean Katrine wouldn't want to, either.

"Exactly."

"Her father's institute? Is the ownership going to be a problem?"

"Actually, he's the head of the Danish Institute of Applied and Theoretical Chemistry outside of Copenhagen. It's not really his, so that's not a problem." Sir Malcolm brushed away any problems with a swoop of one hand.

"It belongs to Denmark?"

"Yes."

"Is anyone there besides Olaf Jørgensen and this German postdoctoral assistant?"

"Yes. There are five postdoctoral assistants working with Jørgensen including the German, plus a few technicians and cleaning staff. All paid by the Danish government."

Five assistants, all of whom could create problems for us trying to get Jørgensen out of Denmark. And at least one was German and the beau of Jørgensen's daughter. "You mentioned flying over. Do we leave from Heston Airport?"

"They closed that down to civilian aircraft last September at the start of the war," he reminded me. Then I remembered reading that in the *Daily Premier*. "Neutral countries are flying into Shoreham Airport in West Sussex. You'll leave there on a Danish plane after breakfast tomorrow and get to Copenhagen in time for lunch. On the way back, you'll travel by train and ferry. We don't know how voluminous or how heavy Jørgensen's research will be or how much Ailsa and Katrine will bring with them in terms of luggage. And then there's the wheeled chair. All too much for an airplane."

This sounded as if it were becoming more of a logistical nightmare by the moment. Even if Ailsa was willing to talk to me about my mother, and I really hoped she would, I didn't see how I could be of any use. "You really want me to do this? I haven't seen Mrs. Jørgensen since I was a baby. There's no reason to think I'll be of any use. Plus, I don't have any nursing background. How do I care for someone confined to a wheeled chair?"

"You're smart. You'll figure it out. It's not as if I'm asking you to solve a murder or hold off an invasion."

"I'm sure you're using this Mike Christiansen for that. Who is he?" From Sir Malcolm's smile, I knew I was sunk. I might as well learn as much as I could before I had to dash to Sussex.

"He went to Oxford. His mother is English and he spent plenty of time here as a child. His father is Danish and he speaks the language fluently. He's been a useful agent. Well trained. He's single, resourceful, and headstrong. He won't come back from Denmark without Jørgensen. That means you have to be on the ferry on Monday."

"Tuesday will be too late?"

"Tuesday, the Germans will see it doesn't sail. You must be on the Monday ferry, no matter what." He emphasized the "you."

"And I have to make sure that Mrs. Jørgensen comes with this chemist so he'll go willingly."

Sir Malcolm smiled that "I've trapped you now" smile. "That's the plan."

I knew how often plans went awry.

Chapter Two

In the too-early hours the next morning, after calling the newspaper and leaving a message for my editor, I left a note on the table for Adam in case he should return on leave before I got back. Then I took off for Victoria Station to catch a Southern Railway train to Shoreham Airport.

The train was crowded, even at that time of the morning, as all trains were in those days. I bought a first-class ticket so I was assured of a seat. I had no idea how Christiansen would travel.

I'd had Sir Malcolm show me his picture so I'd know who I was working with. He was blond, quite tall from his statistics page, and, while I was barely under thirty, he was a year or two on the other side. I didn't see him in my carriage.

After inhaling diesel fumes that came through the leaky windows for the entire train ride, I alighted at the Shoreham Airport station. The early spring dawn was lovely, but bitterly cold. I was glad I'd worn my winter coat, hat, scarf, and gloves over my gray wool suit. I still didn't see Christiansen anywhere.

At least the Jørgensens should speak English since they'd lived in England. I had my doubts about the rest of their country.

And I knew no Danish. I might be able to pick out a few words since Danish had its roots in German, but when spoken at the speed native speakers used, I'd be hard-pressed to understand anything.

We were led out onto the grassy tarmac to an airplane with *Det Danske Luftfartselskab Danish Air Lines* painted on the side of the shiny metal exterior. The winter dry grass around the airplane was damp with dew, making it slick. I was in the queue to board, stepping carefully, when a man's voice behind me said, "Ready to fly, Mrs. Redmond?"

I turned around and found myself looking at a man's neck and shoulders. Looking up, I found a tall blond man, a Viking in modern dress, looking down at me. His beard and mustache were neatly trimmed, and his eyes were icy blue. He wasn't smiling. I was sure his ancestors raided and pillaged.

"Mr. Christiansen?" I held out my hand, my elbow at my side.

"Yes." We shook hands. "You understand the importance of reaching the ferry Monday morning?"

"Yes." Did he think I was stupid? I was the only one of us without connections to Denmark.

The queue moved and I turned back and moved with it. We didn't speak again until we were on board and out of the wind and cold.

We found our seats next to one another. Leaning into each other and whispering was our best chance of getting any privacy. Once he was seated and stretched out his long legs, setting a folder on his lap, Christiansen said, "You understand the vital importance of what we are doing?"

"Apparently he's a brilliant man."

"Not just apparently. Your task is to convince his wife, and his daughter if necessary, to travel with us. Otherwise, he will be stubborn, and that will only benefit the Germans."

"Perhaps he wants to help them."

I could have been singed by the look he gave me. "No. Good Danes want nothing to do with the Nazis." Then he frowned. "In this case, they don't get a choice. The land is flat. There's no way to launch a counteroffensive. The Danes can't resist without a massive slaughter. But they don't want to help them."

"Has Jørgensen said he wants to come with us?" That seemed to me to be the most important point.

"Yes, as does his wife. It's the daughter, and her friend. The mother doesn't want to leave her behind, the same as any good mother. That is where you come in."

"What exactly am I supposed to do?" I didn't know the family, their country, their language. What could I do?

"Convince them to be on the eleven p.m. train from Copenhagen central station Sunday night. It is the last one that will get us to the ferry on time Monday morning."

"There's no ferry running from Copenhagen to England?"

He shook his head. "The ferry runs from Esbjerg, on

the west coast of Denmark, to Harwich. We have to take the train to reach it."

Wonderful. More complications.

We rumbled down the surprisingly smooth field and were airborne quickly, the engines becoming louder with the strain of takeoff until conversation was impossible. Once in the air, we were gently rocked from side to side as we headed over a patchwork of fields on our way to the coast.

This promised to be quite an adventure, moving people between countries who might not be willing to leave. When I'd done this for Sir Henry, the people I'd helped had all wanted or been willing to come to the safety of England, their fear of Hitler speeding them along. "Do you have any idea how I'm supposed to convince women I've never met to pack up and leave their homeland on a minute's notice?" I raised my voice, not certain if he could hear me.

"They've already had notice," Christiansen shouted over the now-deafening noise from the motors. Then he stared out at the waters of the North Sea beneath us. I could feel the greater turbulence of the winds outside our windows, although I knew we hadn't traveled far offshore.

"Besides, Mrs. Jørgensen knows you. Knew your mother," he added.

"Apparently so, but as I was a baby, I have no recollection of our meeting." He seemed to expect more miracles from me than even Sir Malcolm did.

Then Christiansen opened his folder and after a glance around us to make sure no one was listening, as if they could over the engine noise, handed me the first document. "This is the Jørgensen family."

The photo was of a middle-aged man, apparently gray-haired and portly, standing next to a thin woman in a wheeled chair. She was bundled up so that you could only see her face. On the other side of the chair, keeping a short distance away from them, was a young woman in her early twenties, tall, fair-haired, and fashionably dressed.

"And this is the staff of the institute." He handed me a second photograph.

This photo showed six men standing in a row. Olaf Jørgensen was in the center. On either side were men, all in their late twenties. One was small and dark, one quite fair and stocky, one who was blond and tall the same as Christiansen, one with what must be brown hair but again tall like Christiansen, and one who was fair and wore an eye patch that made him look as if he were a pirate in a children's book.

"You'll meet them all when we get to the institute," Christiansen said. "In the meantime, you can read about them here on board. After coffee and strudel," he added, shoving all the papers and photos into the folder as a steward brought my tray.

* * *

Despite some attempt at heating, the cabin was cold throughout our flight and my hands and feet were numb by the time we came to a bumpy landing in a field. Exiting the plane, I found the late morning air at Kastrup Airport just south of Copenhagen was even colder than that in England. I walked slowly across the dry, crackly grass, following the queue into the terminal with Christiansen behind me carrying his folder.

He came up behind me in the queue where officials examined passports and put his Danish one next to my British one on the table. He spoke in Danish and after a cursory check, we were handed back our documents.

Then we picked up our baggage from the pile. Mine was a standard case. He was carrying a sack such as sailors used. I suppose it emphasized his Viking heritage.

Walking out together, once my ears had popped, I murmured, "What did you say to the officials?"

"We're traveling together, visiting my parents this weekend."

"Do you have a British passport, too?"

"At home." He had the ability to speak softly without mumbling.

We walked toward the nearby train station under a brilliant blue sky. The train waited for us at the platform, where we hurriedly entered our carriage to get out of the cold and wind. Inside, it felt equally chilled, but thankfully not breezy.

"We should arrive in Copenhagen in time for lunch at the institute," Christiansen told me.

I hoped my stomach would be ready for food by the

time we arrived. The constant swaying of the plane had left me with a lingering nausea.

It was already Friday noon. We'd have less than two and a half days to spend at the home of the Jørgensens. If we were lucky.

"Where are we going to stay?" I asked.

"At the institute." Again, his tone said, why was I saddled with a dim child?

"They know we're coming?"

"Yes."

"Have you been to the institute before?"

"Yes."

Now, why wouldn't he expound on that?

I stared at him until he looked at me. "What?"

"Why were you there?"

"I did a few months' study there when I was at university."

"So, you know the Jørgensens? Anyone else?"

"None of the five doctoral assistants. They're all new, from after my day. Some of the staff may still be there from my time at the institute."

"Where do the Jørgensens live?"

"In a large house on the grounds of the institute. I believe two or three of the assistants live in a wing of the institute building itself. Where I lived when I was studying there."

"And the others?"

"The married ones would live with their families in

nearby cottages on the grounds." He grinned at me. "We won't be in the middle of nowhere. And the entire grounds are fenced in. The whole place is quite secure."

He might believe this was close to everything, but I felt as if I were a million miles from home.

We reached the central train station, finding ourselves in the middle of a beautiful, red-brick arched building. The top of the soaring roof rose in a glassed-in peak along the length of the station. It looked, in general terms, similar to the Victorian train stations in central London.

We wandered through the vast area crowded with travelers to the ticket office, where Christiansen bought our tickets and then directed me to a numbered arched exit.

Once through the arch, we went downstairs to a different platform with its own glass-roofed peak to transfer to another local train, which sped us toward our destination.

We were alone enough that I felt I could speak. "You're familiar with the institute, the people there, the language, but this is all foreign to me. If I'm going to help you, you're going to have to help me."

Christiansen considered for a moment and then said, "You're right. I'll translate whenever I can. The institute is owned by the country but run by Dr. Jørgensen. He does his own research, teaches a few select students, and oversees the research done by the chemists. And please, call me Mike."

He held out his hand.

I shook it. "Livvy."

We alighted at the stop Mike indicated, which left us in what felt as if it were a sprawling village. After a five-minute walk from the small brick station with the wind in our faces, we came to wrought-iron gates in eight-foot brick walls that opened into a small grassy park. Within the park was a huge stone-faced building, three stories tall, that sprawled across the grounds. Beyond it was a graceful brick mansion worthy of an aristocrat.

Christiansen pointed out the huge building as the institute as he headed for the house and I followed.

We rang the bell, which was immediately answered by a maid. She said something and Christiansen translated it as, "Set your case down and follow me."

I set down my luggage and followed them down a wide corridor with deep red and silver patterned wallpaper and then around a corner, where the maid opened a door for us. Christiansen walked in, speaking in Danish, and then moved away from the doorway so I could enter.

There was a gasp, and then someone said, "Phyllida."

Everyone was staring at me. Phyllida was my mother's name, and I didn't think we looked much alike. "No, I'm Olivia. Phyllida's daughter."

Chapter Three

A woman in a wheeled chair, thin and fragile-looking with very white skin, a long nose, and sparkling blue eyes, pushed herself away from the end of the dining table with surprising vigor and rolled over to me. "Welcome, Olivia," she said in accented English as she held out her hands. "I am so glad to meet you again after all these years. You look so similar to your mother."

I took her hands and held them lightly, afraid I'd break her bones if I grasped them. "I've never been able to see the resemblance."

I was excited. Someone who'd known my mother, who would talk about her. My father wouldn't. This journey could be valuable to me in ways that had nothing to do with Britain's war effort.

"Oh, perhaps not in photographs, but it's there when I see you in person. We've just sat down to luncheon. Won't you join us?"

"We'd love to. Thank you, Mrs. Jørgensen."

Two places sat unclaimed on the table, one next to my hostess who sat at the end of the table, and she indicated I was to sit there. The other open seat was at the far end by the man I recognized from Mike's folder as Olaf Jørgensen, who warmly greeted Christiansen as "Mikkel."

Mrs. Jørgensen pointed out the various dishes to me. A platter of smørrebrød, thin slices of dark bread with various meats, fish, and cheeses on top, was alongside bowls of frikadeller, fried meatballs served with boiled new potatoes, and rødbeder, which I discovered when I tried it was pickled beets with horseradish. Most of those at the table were drinking lager with their meal, but I asked for tea. The trip had made me thirsty.

Mrs. Jørgensen ate little, but along with the rest of the group, I had a large meal. Of course, that was relative, as the young men all ate twice as much as I could. "Would you like me to pass you anything?" I asked my hostess.

"No. I don't keep active, so I don't work up an appetite. But you, please enjoy."

"I am," I told her truthfully. Now that I was over the effects of the flight, I was famished. "Do all of these people work for your husband?"

"This is just a few of them. Beck and Nilsen are home with their wives for this meal. They live just nearby on the grounds of the institute," she added with a wave of her hand. "The dark-haired man is Porteur, he's French, poor man, and his accent is so thick I can't understand his Danish. Across from your friend Christiansen is Andersen. I'd hoped Katrine would like him. He's Danish, you know."

"She has no interest in him?"

"I'm afraid not. She likes that pirate with a patch over one eye sitting next to her. Friedrich Braun. He's," she whispered as if sharing a dirty secret, "German."

I was surprised Mrs. Jørgensen was expressing her views so openly where anyone could overhear us, even though we spoke in English. "Do these three men live here at the institute?"

"Yes. They're single and don't mind living in quarters in the institute building. It's much cheaper for them. Mikkel Christiansen will be staying with them until you head back to England."

"And me? Will I stay there?"

"Good heavens, no. Your mother would never forgive me for not looking out for you. You'll stay here at the house."

"I don't want to put you out."

"Not at all." She waved one hand with a small graceful movement. "I can't do anything. That's why we have domestic staff."

"Is that your daughter Katrine?" I asked, nodding down the table where a young woman sat. Seen up close, she was lovely, prettier than her photograph, with fair hair and dark blue eyes. She was leaning toward the chemist with the eyepatch. The German chemist.

The German was sitting upright, not leaning or turned toward Katrine. He was blond with handsome features, an attractive man despite the patch.

"Yes, that's my daughter," Mrs. Jørgensen said. "And next to her is Friedrich Braun. Katrine considers herself engaged to Braun, although he's not asked her father for her hand in marriage, and I've seen no sign of a ring or other pledge." Her eyes narrowed as she looked in his direction.

"Do they consider that old-fashioned?" I asked.

"Possibly. I consider it rude." Ailsa Jørgensen sounded as if she were against her daughter's choice of men. That might explain why she wouldn't leave without her daughter. She wanted her daughter safely in Britain and away from the German. And the Germans.

Mr. Jørgensen said in German from his end of the table, "You men grab any more coffee that you want. Quickly, quickly. If you ladies will excuse us, I need to see how Andersen's experiment is going, and Mikkel wants to see what we are working on these days." He glanced at me and switched to English. "We all speak German because it is the language of science. Do you have any interest in chemistry, Mrs. Redmond?"

The four young men went to stand around the coffee urn on its wheeled cart. They poured themselves more coffee and quickly passed the milk or sugar to drink another cup before going back to the lab. They surrounded it so closely that they seemed to be some eight-armed, four-mouthed creature that lived on coffee.

Jørgensen handed one of the arms his cup, and it reappeared, refilled, a moment later.

"I'm afraid chemistry is a subject I know little about," I told him, still fascinated by all the coffee being rapidly prepared and consumed.

"Then I'm sure Ailsa and Katrine will enjoy your

company. I will see you ladies at dinner." He gave us a hint of a bow after tossing off his own coffee. The men followed after gulping their coffee and setting the cups on the table.

I noticed Braun give a smile to Katrine that made his features even more handsome but didn't warm them. He was broad-shouldered and on the tall side, although not as tall as Christiansen. More interesting was the end of a scar that appeared through his eyebrow and disappeared into his eye patch.

I wondered what had happened to cause him to lose his sight in that eye.

Andersen could have been Christiansen's clean-shaven double in terms of blond coloring, slender build, and height. They were both Danish. I wondered if they were related somehow. Porteur was the shortest of the men and the darkest. In this country of tall, fair-skinned people, he stood out.

We ladies left the dining room last. I pushed Mrs. Jørgensen's wheeled chair while I studied it. The chair was made of interconnected metal tubes for its frame with two large wheels and two small ones. The seat itself appeared to be well padded with thick cushions covered in patterned upholstery fabric. The metal tubes were bent at the top of the back and covered with grips so I could take hold of the chair to push Mrs. Jørgensen. With a bit of whimsy, there was even a diagonal support across the back that was decorated at the top end with a rounded dragon's head.

Following her directions, I wheeled her down the hall to the music room, which was dominated by a grand piano.

"The three men who were here for luncheon are all single, the same as Mr. Christiansen, and live at the institute?" I asked. Always good to be certain of your facts. And since Christiansen was better looking than the German, had as cold and stuffy a manner, and was also single, I thought I'd mention him to see how determined Katrine was to remain loyal to the German. After all, her country was about to be invaded by his.

"Why? Are you interested in one of them, Mrs. Redmond?" Katrine said as she moved to a seat at the piano and began to play.

Her mother wheeled herself over to a small bookshelf by using the metal rims attached to the wheels and pulled out a photograph album, opening it on her lap.

"Just wondering who might be interested in leaving before the invasion," I told her.

"Fritz is staying here. As am I." She looked at me defiantly.

"Katrine," her mother said. "That would not be proper. You need a chaperone until you are married."

"Well, then, I'll get married."

Ailsa Jørgensen pressed her hand over her chest. "Katrine. You will kill me."

"Nonsense, Mother. You're as healthy as a horse."

"You will not get married without your father and me giving our blessing."

"Married or not, I'm staying here. What is there for me in England?" Katrine began to work on a complicated piece of music with talented fingering.

"Freedom?" I suggested. "I've been to Nazi Germany and Nazi-controlled Austria. Starting on Tuesday, the Danes are going to learn just how awful it is to be under Nazi rule and have no freedom."

"Olivia, look. This is a favorite photograph of your mother and me. Such happy times." Ailsa held up an enlarged photograph of two young women in wide-brimmed hats and old-fashioned dresses grinning cheekily at the camera. The young Ailsa looked as thin in the photo then as she did in person now. My mother was a little plumper. A little curvier.

I stared at the photo. "My mother looks so happy there." She looked surprisingly similar to me in that shot.

"She was. That was taken at a garden party in Copenhagen when we were both young and free." I heard Ailsa sigh. She was standing in the photograph. "You can't see it here, but her hair was the same auburn shade as yours. Oh, she was a lovely girl."

"It's a wonderful photograph," I said. "She looks the way I remember her. Happy."

"She was always happy. She loved life. It's too bad…" Ailsa's voice trailed off as she ran a hand over the photo.

"This brings back memories of my parents from when

I was very small," I told her.

"Nazi rule can't be worse than my parents," Katrine muttered, drawing our attention to her. Her attention was focused on the sheet music.

"How did Herr Braun lose the sight in that eye?" I asked her, choosing to ignore her comment.

"Someone attacked him with a knife while he was at university."

"Why?"

Katrine shrugged, which told me nothing.

I applauded as Katrine finished the piece she was playing.

"You don't need to be polite," she told me.

"I'm not. I'm being honest. You play very well."

"Do you play, Olivia?" Mrs. Jørgensen asked. "Your mother did. Quite well."

"I took lessons, but I never developed any skill." That was putting it mildly. My father, the Victorian that he was, thought it was a needed talent for any young woman to develop. I was more interested in attending university and studying modern languages and sketching. Wars have been fought over less.

"Oh, well. Not everyone can do many things well," Katrine said in German.

"That's very true," I replied in German.

"You speak German?" Katrine asked, sounding surprised that an ignorant Englishwoman could speak German.

"Yes."

"Good. It saves everyone from having to speak English for the weekend," she said with a labored sigh.

"I take it speaking different languages is not one of your skills," I said.

Her eyes blazed when she looked at me. "I don't bother with unnecessary skills."

"Katrine," her mother said. "Where are your manners?"

"It's all right," I said with a smile. "English is complicated, more complicated than German, and can be difficult to learn. And so, the English are patient people and are willing to overlook the mistakes of people struggling with our language. You won't be made to feel unwelcome if your command of English isn't as good as you'd want it to be."

"I don't intend to find out. I'm staying here," Katrine said and stalked out of the room, throwing over her shoulder, "with Fritz."

"I can't leave her here alone. If she won't go with us, I'll have to stay," Mrs. Jørgensen said. "And that will mean Olaf stays here too. I'm sorry you came all this way for nothing."

As silence fell on the music room, its green flocked walls matching its green silk-covered chairs, Mrs. Jørgensen looked at me. "I do not think you will change her mind," she said in English.

"Then can you find a chaperone for Katrine?"

She shook her head, looking downcast.

"I have the impression your husband wants to leave and have you travel with him."

"You are right. And I want to do what my husband wants of me. I am traditional in that regard. But the thought of leaving our little girl, our only surviving child..."

Only surviving child? "You've lost a child? I'm sorry."

"Our son, Vilhelm, died at ten of a fever. He's buried in the village churchyard." She gave me a sad smile. "Another child I do not want to leave."

"You wouldn't be leaving them forever. Only for a short time until war or diplomacy sorts everything out, including the fate of Denmark." I hoped that sounded balanced between "It will only be for a short time," and "Things will be bad here for a while."

"I have a wasting disease, brought on by the fever that took Vilhelm. I doubt I'll live long enough to return." Mrs. Jørgensen shook her head. "This weakness of mine complicates things."

Chapter Four

"I suppose there is no one you would trust to be a chaperone for Katrine," I said.

"My sister, except she likes Braun. She always was a silly woman. She would let Katrine do whatever she wants. Not a good characteristic in a chaperone," Mrs. Jørgensen said.

It appeared to me that Katrine was doing exactly what she wanted now, and her parents were following her orders. I decided that would not be a good thing to point out if I wanted the Jørgensens to come to England with us. "But it would be a way for you to go to England with your husband and have a chaperone you know and like here for Katrine."

"Perhaps." She didn't sound as if she found that a positive idea. "I'm going to lie down. Have one of the servants show you to your room upstairs." Ailsa Jørgensen gave a sigh, put the album away, and wheeled herself off, leaving me alone in a country where I did not speak the language.

This was the problem with the first maid I spoke to. She looked at me blankly and then walked off. I stood in the hallway, wondering what I should do next when the maid returned with another woman. "I am Mrs. Ulriksen, the housekeeper. May I help you?" she asked in thickly accented English.

"Where would I find Dr. Jørgensen and the other men? I hope to see something of the institute," I added unnecessarily.

She gave me directions and added, "Your case has been put in one of the guest rooms on the first floor. When you go up the stairs, it will be the third door on the left."

"Thank you." She handed me my coat and I walked along a path bordered by flower beds and bushes to a side entrance to the institute that faced the house. It was a plain, single door with only one step up needed to reach the level of the interior, and I found the door unlocked.

I walked inside and discovered myself in a long, wide, tiled hallway. I could hear men's voices at a distance so I followed the sound, realizing as I grew closer that they were arguing in German.

"You're not being fair to her, Fritz." The voice seemed to be coming from a door on the right-hand side of the hallway that had been left ajar.

"It's none of your business, Henrik," a second man said.

"You are welcome to Katrine," the first voice said. "I have no interest in coming between you. But I think you should be honest with her. And with Olaf."

I stood still in the hallway, listening. "Olaf" would be Dr. Jørgensen. "Fritz" was a diminutive for "Friedrich," that Katrine had used to refer to the German doctoral assistant she wanted to marry. What secret was he keeping from Dr. Jørgensen and his daughter? And who was Henrik?

It wasn't polite for me to remain and listen, but with only a short time to convince the Jørgensens to leave Denmark, I'd use anything I could uncover.

Working for Sir Malcolm had a terrible effect on my manners.

Wanting to get home before the Germans invaded had an even worse effect.

"Keep your nose out of my business, Henrik," the second voice said.

"You have to tell her, Fritz. It's not as if you can marry her."

"And if I don't?" Fritz's voice was full of menace.

"Then I'll tell her. I'll tell them all."

"Think they'll believe you? Think that will get Katrine to think of you as her savior? She won't. They'll all be mad at you for ruining Katrine's day, if she even bothers to listen to you."

"She has a right to know."

"I'll make certain you don't tell her." Those ominous words were followed by a crash.

I remained frozen in the hallway near the door, wondering what else I'd hear.

The door swung farther open and a Danish man who looked very similar to Mike Christiansen from behind burst into the hallway and hurried away in the other direction. I was glad he didn't look back to where I stood.

I followed him until I came to the main staircase. I hesitated for a moment, but Mrs. Ulriksen had said Dr. Jørgensen's laboratory and office were on the first floor, so I went up the stairs and looked in both directions. In one direction, there was a hall with several doors leading out. In the other, the hall stopped at a wall with only one door, with a sign on it that read "Privat." I recognized the word in German, but had no idea how it was spelled in Danish.

A man came out of a doorway in the long hallway. Until he came close, I thought it might be Andersen, but then I realized there was only a vague resemblance in this man's looks. "May I help you?" he asked in German.

"I'm Olivia Redmond, spending the weekend with the Jørgensens."

He nodded seriously. "You came to Copenhagen with Mikkel. I'm Peder Nilsen. Are you looking for Olaf?"

"Yes." At a distance, Nilsen could easily be mistaken for Christiansen or Andersen, except his hair was several shades darker, more of a brown. And he couldn't have been the one speaking German to Braun because he said his first name was Peder, and the man in the argument had been Henrik. Andersen must have been the other speaker in the argument with Fritz Braun.

"He's this way." Nilsen escorted me down the hall and knocked on a door.

A voice said something muffled in what I guessed was

Danish.

Nilsen opened the door and I walked in.

"Ah, Mrs. Redmond," Dr. Jørgensen said in English. "You have come to see my laboratory?"

"Yes. I was hoping to get a tour."

Nilsen nodded to me and left.

That was all that was needed to get a tour of Dr. Jørgensen's lab, which covered several rooms. I knew little about chemistry, but even I could understand how his work on rubber polymers and the effect of pressure on explosives could be useful to Britain.

"Rubber from seaweed and fruit pits? It seems fantastic," I said when he explained the sequence of beakers and hoses along a table against one long wall of the laboratory in a few words.

"It's a long process, and we have no idea yet if it will be successful on a large scale. The preliminary experiments have been exciting," Dr. Jørgensen told me. "I am very hopeful we'll be able to take naturally growing materials, such as seaweed and pits from fruits, and create something necessary such as rubber."

"I can understand why His Majesty's government wants to protect your research from the Germans."

"I didn't do this to have it used to kill people," he grumbled.

"Nevertheless, it might be, but rubber has many civilian uses, too. And explosives are similar to fertilizer, are they not? Do you want your work to be used by the

Germans or the British?"

"Neither. That is why I live in a neutral country."

"Until next Tuesday. Then it's no longer neutral and your research is no longer under your control." I was standing close to him now, staring up into his pale blue eyes.

"That is just a threat. Hot air from the Germans." He waved his hands and walked away.

I followed him across the lab, dismayed that he didn't seem as eager to leave as I had expected. I spoke simply and emphatically, hoping to get through to Dr. Jørgensen that the situation was dangerous. "They are massing at the border. You are in their way as they move to invade Norway. The German government has warned your government. They will be here Tuesday. You can count on that. Either you leave with us Sunday night, able to live in Britain, or America, which is neutral, or somewhere else, or you will live under the Germans doing research for them to help their war machine. It is your choice."

"Yes, it is." He kept his back turned as he studied the contents of a glass tube.

Before he threw me out, I wanted to ask, "Do all of the chemists here speak German?"

"German is the language of science. Everyone here, even the staff, even the cleaners, have to be fluent in it to communicate with their fellow workers."

"Do you know if Mr. Christiansen speaks German?"

"Yes. I seem to remember he does. Why?"

"I also speak German. If we have trouble communicating in English, I shall use German because Danish is beyond me." It was the truth, just not why I asked the question.

He smiled at that. "Few non-Danes speak Danish. Where would they use it outside of Denmark?"

I had to ask something simply to ease my curiosity. "Did my mother learn Danish while she lived here?"

"She did learn Danish. Very well. By the time she left, she sounded as if she'd grown up here."

"Thank you." I turned to leave the laboratory.

"Mrs. Redmond."

I stopped at the door and looked at him.

"Don't think for a moment that I favor the Germans. My desire to stay here is because of my wife's determination to stay with our daughter and my love of my homeland. I've known many Germans that I like, but I do not like these Nazis."

"I believe you and your wife will be safer and freer in Britain, at least until this war ends, but you must decide for yourself. The offer is there until Sunday evening. You don't have much time to make up your mind."

"Don't rush me, Mrs. Redmond." Annoyance was clear in his tone.

"I'm not the one rushing you. Speak to the German military if you feel pressured to make a decision." I left, walking down the hall and opening the doors to peek inside in search of Christiansen. The Jørgensens were fellow countrymen. What was he doing to convince them to travel to Britain with us?

The labs all seemed to be empty. Where had everyone gone?

With no luck on the first floor, I decided to go down to the ground floor. I heard men speaking in a language I didn't understand. Standing at the bottom of the stairs, I realized their voices were coming from the opposite direction of the side door facing the house. I followed the sound and opened a door to find Mike Christiansen and three other Nordic-looking men, all wearing lab coats, studying the contents of some beakers.

Mike glanced over and saw me. "Livvy Redmond, I don't think you've been introduced to these men. Peder Nilsen and Bjorn Beck weren't at lunch because they went home to their wives, but you met Henrik Andersen already at the house," Mike said, speaking German. I guessed what I overheard in the hall was Danish.

"Hello. I'm Livvy Redmond."

Peder Nilsen and Henrik Andersen had the same height and lean build as Mike Christiansen, while Bjorn Beck was a little shorter and a good deal stockier. Peder, who I recognized from our encounter in the hall, had brown hair where the others were blond, but they all had blue eyes. Mike was the only one with a beard. I hoped I'd keep them straight. At least they all spoke German.

We talked for a minute or two before Mike asked, "Have you seen Dr. Jørgensen?"

"Yes. He gave me a tour of the lab and explained his process for turning seaweed and fruit pits into rubber."

"Did you understand it?" Peder asked with a smile.

"Practically nothing," I admitted.

"You know fruit pits are the source of cyanide, don't you?" Mike asked, also smiling.

"Yes. That sounds dangerous." I shuddered.

"As long as you don't eat it or get it on your hands, you'll be fine," Bjorn Beck said. "There's not much that can be done for you if you ingest it."

I tried to remember if I touched anything in Dr. Jørgensen's laboratory. I didn't think I had.

"Don't worry," Henrik said, guessing the puzzled look that must have been on my face meant I was worried. "Dr. Jørgensen wouldn't let you accidentally poison yourself. He's very careful about safety. You have to be as a chemist."

I admit I felt relieved.

"But the important thing," Peder Nilsen said, "is that Dr. Jørgensen is finding a way to make synthetic rubber that doesn't require petroleum."

"Petroleum is nearly as scarce as rubber," Bjorn Beck told me in a lecturing tone, "while fruit pits and seaweed? We can grow more quite easily."

"If they can work the problems out, this will be a breakthrough for whichever side has the formula," Mike told me. "A game changer. A deciding factor in whoever wins this war. If Dr. Jørgensen can perfect the process."

No wonder Sir Malcolm wanted Dr. Jørgensen and his work in Britain.

After I expressed my admiration for their work, Mike offered to give me a tour of the village and translate for me, as he removed his lab coat.

We left the lab, only to run into two men in the hallway. Mike knew the short, middle-aged, portly man as Berde, who was a cleaner for the institute, and the two greeted each other warmly in Danish. Then Berde switched to German to introduce the man scarcely out of his teens who was standing beside him.

"This is Aleksy Klimek. He's you for this year, Mikkel. He's a chemistry student from Cracow University studying under Dr. Jørgensen," Berde said. "However, you can tell Aleksy is a chemist, because he doesn't have all this facial hair to catch fire." The man laughed. "How long have you been growing that beard? It's quite short and neat."

The two men teased each other for a minute before Mike introduced me, and I asked Aleksy, "Will you be able to go home after your study here is finished?"

"I have no home to go back to, and after Tuesday, I won't be able to stay here. I'm sure the Nazis will throw me out." He sounded bitter, and I'm sure he had every right to be angry.

"And you, Berde?" Mike asked.

The older man shrugged. "One job is the same as another. One boss is the same as another. Keep your head down and don't annoy whoever is in charge. I will be fine."

Mike patted him on the shoulder. "Good to see you again after all these years. I'll be around this weekend. We'll catch up."

We left the building and headed toward the gates. Ahead of us I could see Braun, the black strap to his eye patch visible against his fair hair. At first, I thought the woman with him was Katrine, but then I realized she wasn't tall enough or blonde enough.

He walked arm in arm with her. Was his sight so limited that he needed to be guided along the road?

Chapter Five

"Who is that with Fritz Braun?" I asked Mike.

"I don't know. Not Katrine," he told me, his eyes narrowing as he watched the couple some distance in front of us.

"What is going on here? Mrs. Jørgensen seems to want to travel to Britain with her husband, but she feels she can't because that would leave Katrine here without a chaperone. Mrs. Jørgensen's sister could chaperone, but Mrs. Jørgensen feels she'd be too lenient. Meanwhile, Katrine appears to run the house."

"She was just a child when I was here for my year in Dr. Jørgensen's lab, but she ran the house then, too."

"Was this when her brother was still alive?"

"Yes. Vilhelm was obviously the favorite of both the Jørgensens, but Katrine bossed him around. I think there was some jealousy there. Understandably. Oh, and Mrs. Jørgensen was still healthy and walking around unaided. I guess it was a long time ago," he added with a shake of his head.

Since I didn't have to carry my luggage this trip, the walk down the lane to the village was short and pretty, with green shoots in flower beds and a haze of green on tree branches. The buildings, mostly brick, contained houses and shops, a pub, a school, and a doctor's surgery, with more stretching along the lane past the train station.

When we reached the pub, which Fritz had already entered with the woman, Mike suggested we stop in too.

I followed him into the dark interior of the ancient building to find a cheery fire burning in the hearth. Once we saw Fritz had already fetched their drinks, I chose a table where I could feel the heat from the fire while Mike got us ours.

A hint of smoke and yeast filled the air, giving the room a cozy feel. Rather than one big room, there were wide stone pillars rising to the support beams in the ceiling, almost wide enough to divide the area into separate spaces.

From where I sat, I could hear a man and a woman speaking in Danish, but I couldn't see them around a couple of the pillars. I was certain it was Fritz and the unknown woman. It was frustrating not to be able to understand what they said.

Mike brought me a half pint of lager and sat down across from me. I tilted my head in the direction of the voices. He sipped his pint and listened, neither of us saying a word. I heard a feminine giggle and could imagine what was going on out of sight of most of the pub and the bar, hidden behind a pillar.

Then the man said something and Mike's eyebrows went up.

"What?" I whispered in English.

"They're planning a tryst in the attics of the Jørgensens' house tonight."

Imagine if Katrine found out was my first thought.

"The attics are where the servants sleep. She must be one of the maids," he told me.

"Dr. and Mrs. Jørgensen can't approve of that. Not with Fritz and Katrine more or less engaged," I whispered.

"Worse, he already has a wife."

I choked on my beer, and Mike smacked my back twice. I grabbed a handkerchief out of my bag and mopped my face as I drew in a breath.

When I finally could speak, I said, "How do you know?"

"The chemists told me. It's common knowledge among them. He keeps her in a flat in central Copenhagen, well away from the Jørgensens."

"That's terrible." Fritz couldn't marry Katrine or anyone else if he was already married.

"Not necessarily. Not if we can use it to our advantage."

"How do you plan to do that?"

He smiled. "We'll keep silent about this for the moment, until we can find a way to use it to move the Jørgensens to England."

Apparently, Mike didn't have a plan yet, but I knew how these plots were often created as events unfolded. "Don't you think they should know? It's a pretty important detail, having a wife." I was angry on behalf of the

Jørgensens.

"We can't prove it's true yet. Let's just keep this to ourselves. Who knows? We might not even have to use it."

"It's reprehensible."

"They also believe he's a member of the Nazi party, so yeah, reprehensible sounds about right." Mike listened with me as Fritz and the young woman left the pub. "Drink up. I want to follow them."

I pushed my still half-full glass aside. "Let's go."

He downed the last of his beer and we headed back out into the sunlight in time to see Fritz and the woman, walking arm in arm, enter a nearby shop.

When we drew level with it from the opposite side of the street, I could see it was a village shop sort of place. Newspapers could be seen through the window along with tobacco, candy, and other small, inexpensive items.

"I've seen enough of the village. Shall we go back?" Mike asked in a light tone as if we had been out for a stroll in England, not in Denmark on a mission for Sir Malcolm.

We walked back, enjoying the sunshine and the view. Once we returned to the institute grounds, Mike said, "I'm going back to the labs to see what I can learn. See what you can discover at the house."

Out of curiosity, I followed the path past the front door. I thought it might take me to the servants' entrance, but instead, it wound beyond the main house to three cottages on the grounds. At the first one, I saw a young woman taking down laundry on the line behind the house.

I walked in her direction, calling out, "Hello."

She replied with something that sounded similar to "Hi."

"I'm sorry. I don't speak Danish," I said in German. "Do you speak German or French or English?"

"German and French," she answered in German. "I'm Thyra Nilsen. Who are you?" She continued taking laundry off the line as she talked.

"Livvy Redmond. I'm a guest of the Jørgensens this weekend."

"I heard they had guests. Are you a friend of Katrine's?"

"I never met her before today. My mother and Mrs. Jørgensen were good friends before my mother's death many years ago. She wanted to meet me."

"Anything to do with the invasion?" She studied my face.

"You've heard about that?"

"It's not common knowledge, but everyone here at the institute knows. So, is it true you're here to take the Jørgensens to England?"

"Perhaps. That depends on what the Jørgensens want to do in the face of the invasion. What do you plan to do?"

"Oh, we're just beginning to talk about that." She picked up the laundry basket and walked toward the house. "Peder told me what he'd heard at lunchtime today."

"That was the first you had heard?" I took a few steps

toward her.

"Well, the government only received word last night, and we are out in the countryside." She gave me a brief smile. "Nice meeting you." Then she walked into the house and shut the door behind her.

There was no one else around. Nothing learned here. I walked back to the Jørgensens' mansion.

When I rang the bell, Mrs. Ulriksen opened the door. She told me Mrs. Jørgensen was in the drawing room and pointed out the way.

I opened the door to the drawing room, hit my foot on the raised threshold, and tripped my way into the room.

"Don't you have them in England?" Mrs. Jørgensen asked. "They keep out the drafts in winter when the doors are shut. Keeps the room we're in warmer."

"I've always lived in the south of England. Maybe farther north they have wood across the bottom of doorways. It sounds very practical, but it takes some thought getting my feet accustomed to it." I gave her a smile, still feeling embarrassed I hadn't noticed it before. Or at least avoided tripping.

"So where have you been?"

"All over. I went to the institute and met people there, and then Mike took me to see the village, and then I walked to the cottages and met Mrs. Nilsen."

"My, you have had a full afternoon."

It was a lot fuller with the discovery of Fritz Braun with

another woman and then hearing he had a wife. Things Mike didn't want me to mention. And for the moment, I thought he was right. We couldn't be certain any of this wasn't idle gossip. "It's a lovely area." That seemed to be a safe comment.

"We've always liked it here. Quiet. Private." The conversation dragged. Then she said, "Did you bring anything to wear to dress for dinner? We prefer to keep that custom."

"I brought one gown," I assured her. "You may grow tired of it by the second evening."

"Oh, we're not snobbish about fashion. I'm sure it's a lovely gown."

"I like it." I'd brought the strappy shoes and the paste jewels I wore with the blue gown in my hard-sided case, along with fresh blouses, unmentionables, and stockings for daytime to wear with my gray suit.

We exchanged distant, proper smiles before I said, "I'd better unpack."

"Olivia, that was already taken care of by one of the maids."

"Thank you. I'm not used to having maids, or servants of any sort. I just have a small flat."

"I couldn't get anything done without them. Michelle, that's my ladies' maid—she's French, you know—has to do practically everything for me. Then the housemaids do the rest. And the cook is in charge of the kitchen. Fortunately. Otherwise, I can't imagine how our meals would be." Mrs. Jørgensen smiled as if she'd made some sort of silly confession.

"It's hard to be a good cook. I'm shockingly bad," I admitted.

"Not you. I remember your mother was a good baker."

"I don't remember that. Of course, I was very young at the time."

"Oh, yes. She was a good baker and good at embroidery. She played the piano exquisitely. And she was so much fun to be around. Always a clever idea. Always a new adventure." She gave a contented sigh, bathed in her memories.

"Thank you for telling me. I don't remember any of this." My image of my mother, still blurry, had a few more details drawn in. I wondered what other facts I would learn that weekend.

"Your father didn't tell you?" Mrs. Jørgensen sounded shocked.

"He doesn't talk about her." Or about much of anything else with me, I didn't add.

"That is a shame. Your mother shouldn't be forgotten."

"I don't think he's forgotten her. I think he finds her loss too painful to talk about." After the words came out of my mouth, I realized it was very true. I'd never realized that before. Perhaps being married to Adam made me understand how hard it would be to lose someone you really loved.

I hadn't seen my father in nearly two weeks. If I had seen him more recently, I probably wouldn't have been so understanding. My father's criticisms tended to stick with me for days afterward.

Katrine came into the room. "Are you still here?" she asked, glaring at me.

Her mother said, "Olivia is our guest."

"Why? We're not going to leave with you, so you might as well go back to England. Now."

"I hope you don't mind, but I'm enjoying getting to know your mother and hearing more about mine. Surely you can put up with me for a weekend," I said with a smile in my voice.

She gave a groan and stalked across the room to drop into a well-padded floral print chair.

"Katrine," her mother said. "Stop being such a child."

"Maybe if you treated me as if I were an adult, I would act as if I were one."

"Perhaps if you made better decisions, we could treat you as an adult."

"You just don't like Fritz because you decided I should marry Henrik."

"No. I don't trust Fritz. I know I can trust Henrik. He would treat you as if you were the queen."

Katrine answered this with a stream of shouted Danish. I decided the best choice would be to quietly excuse myself and flee the room.

I went upstairs and found my room, only to be surprised when I walked in to find a young woman in a maid's uniform holding my jewels up against her and examining her reflection in the mirror. "They're fake," I said in German.

She jumped before she turned around, a big smile on her face. "They are very pretty." She was younger than I thought at first, no more than eighteen, with light brown hair and blue eyes.

I recognized her immediately as the woman I'd seen with Fritz Braun. "You understand and speak German?"

She quickly put the jewelry down on the dressing table and stepped back. "I have been practicing my German. For when they come." Then she thought and the smile slipped from her face. "I unpacked for you."

"Thank you. What is your name?"

"Greta. Is there anything else I may do for you?"

"You could tell me what you were doing in the pub with Fritz Braun."

"You saw us?" came out in a whisper.

"Yes."

"Please do not tell. I slipped away when I should have been working. But he is so handsome. So exciting. I cannot resist."

She was very young and not too bright or honest, I decided. "I thought he was engaged to Katrine."

"She insists, but he says no. He says he will not marry her. He loves me."

If Fritz turned out to be already married, at least half his words would be proven true.

Chapter Six

"You had better be cautious, or you will find yourself out of a job and without a boyfriend." I thought I'd better warn the young maid.

"I will be fine. I have nothing to worry about. And Tuesday, Fritz's friends come with the German army and then he will be in charge. Then he will get me pretty jewels the same as you have."

"Greta!" sounded from down the hallway.

"Mrs. Ulriksen," Greta whispered. "I will go now. Don't tell anyone. Please." Then she rushed out of the room and called out something in Danish.

I sat down at the dressing table and put my fake sapphires back in their case, wondering what type of craziness I had fallen into.

* * *

I went down to dinner in my blue gown that was cut on the bias to improve the drape. My fake sapphire jewelry looked terrific with my gown and could pass for real.

We were a good-sized group, with the Jørgensens, the three single chemists who lived in the institute building, Mike, and me. Since there were only three women, Dr. Jørgensen had Mike and Fritz on either side of him.

Otherwise, we alternated between men and women.

The soup course passed without friction, as we all kept to neutral topics. Food, the weather, and Mrs. Jørgensen's choice, my mother.

I heard about some garden parties my mother had attended, but nothing that sketched more detail into my mental image of my mother.

The main course, a fish deliciously prepared and served with potatoes and early greens, kept us quiet for a few minutes. Then Porteur said, "Have you seen anything of the village?"

"Yes, we walked down there for a short time this afternoon," I said.

Immediately, Mike added, "We stopped in at the pub and ran into Fritz."

The German's eyes turned dark as he glared at Mike.

"What were you doing down there?" Katrine asked, frowning a little as she glanced at her fiancé.

"Nothing. I just wanted to get away for a little while. Alone."

When he said the last word, my eyes widened at his untruth. Katrine saw my reaction and immediately jumped on it. "Why did you look as if Fritz told a lie?" she snapped at me.

"Did I?" I hoped she'd drop the subject or someone would knock over their wine and cause a diversion.

No such luck. Katrine looked at me with fury in her expression. "You did."

I looked at Fritz in silence, seeing out of the corner of my eye that Ailsa Jørgensen was watching both Braun and her daughter carefully.

Henrik Andersen never looked up. He studied his plate, his shoulders rounded as if he expected a blow.

Fritz set down his fork and replied in Danish and Mike translated it in English for me as, "'I won't be called a liar. And I won't have my every move scrutinized.'"

"That's hardly an answer," Porteur said in French at the same moment as Mike's translation.

Exactly what I was thinking, I thought as I gave him a smile.

"What did you say?" Fritz said in German, giving Porteur a ferocious glare.

"Don't you speak French?" Porteur said. "The language of diplomats."

"Why would I speak the language of a second-rate power?" Fritz said.

"You are. You're speaking German," Mike said.

Fritz turned an unhealthy red. "You'll see how second-rate we are on Tuesday. No, I guess you won't. You'll run off to England and wait for us to invade there."

"England hasn't been successfully invaded in nearly nine hundred years, and Germany will never break our streak," I told him. "Particularly a country of people who can't tell a believable untruth."

"Fritz?" Katrine asked, looking at him closely. "Who were you with?"

He swallowed the contents of his wine glass, rose, threw down his serviette, and stormed from the room.

Katrine started to rise when her father said in English, "Stay. He needs time to deal with his embarrassment. Let him settle down first, then you two can talk calmly."

She sat, sulking, while the rest of us finished eating and discussed the good fishing areas around Denmark and different types of fish.

To finish, we had an apricot pastry with a flaky, buttery crust that made me want to take the baker of this wonderful treat back to London with me. When I said so, Mrs. Jørgensen laughed. "This is very good, isn't it? I think the trick is she makes it from her own preserves and doesn't stint on the butter."

"Something else the English don't do well, besides showing good manners," Katrine muttered.

We all ignored her, but her sulking put a damper on our conversation and our mood.

As soon as we finished eating, Katrine left the table. The Jørgensens exchanged glances, and then her father said, "Looking for Braun, I imagine."

"Now," Ailsa Jørgensen said, "who did you see Fritz in the pub with?" Her stare was focused on Mike.

"Shouldn't you ask him that?" Mike asked.

"He had plenty of opportunities to explain himself. Who did you see him with?" Then she focused on me. There was no escaping her gaze.

I didn't mind telling her if it would help get everyone

moving toward England in time. "The maid. Greta," I told her.

"I didn't tell you," Henrik said immediately, hands in the air.

"There's no surprise," Porteur said, staring at Henrik.

"We both knew he was untrustworthy," Dr. Jørgensen said to his wife.

"Yes, but Katrine will be so disappointed," she replied.

"Why don't you young people go down to the pub? This afternoon, Nilsen and his wife were talking about going there tonight," Dr. Jørgensen suggested.

I suspected the Jørgensens wanted to talk privately. "That sounds as if it could be fun. Shall we go?" I said. "Gentlemen?"

We gathered up our heavy outerwear and went out into the cold, dark night together. Without a moon to guide us, we relied on the torch Porteur brought along to follow the road toward the village.

When we reached the pub, the men went to the bar to order beers while I took a seat next to the woman I'd seen taking down her laundry that day.

"Hello again. Thyra, right?" I said in German loud enough to be heard over the din of voices and laughter.

"Yes. Livvy? This is my husband, Peder."

"We met at the institute." I nodded to him across Thyra.

Porteur came over and told the Nilsens about the scene at dinner. By the time he finished, Mike had returned with our beers and then Henrik joined us.

"I can't believe they are so ignorant that they don't see through dear Fritz," Thyra said. From her tone, I could tell she didn't like him.

"It's Katrine who can't see through him. The Jørgensens know what he is," Henrik said in a bitter tone.

"Henrik," Peder said, "even if she saw through Fritz, she still wouldn't fall in love with you. No matter how much you adore her."

"Maybe." Henrik downed most of his beer.

"There are plenty of other girls out there. There are plenty right here. You don't need to waste your time on her," Thyra told him.

With a dark look, Henrik finished his beer and left the pub.

"One of these days, my encouragement will get through to him," Thyra said, adding, "I hope."

"The two of them had quite a shouting match today," Peder said.

"About Katrine?" Thyra asked her husband.

"No. It was Katrine and Henrik. They argued about the Jørgensens, the invasion, everything," Peder said.

"Good. It's about time Henrik decided to speak up," Porteur said.

"Henrik will never be happy until he can stand up to Katrine," Thyra told me.

"Until he gets over Katrine," her husband added.

"You knew about his girlfriend? The maid, Greta," I

asked.

"We all knew there was someone. Including the Jørgensens," Thyra said.

"You're certain about the Jørgensens?" Mike asked.

"They can't be completely blind," Porteur said.

"Katrine is," Thyra said. "Preferring that half-blind little thug to Henrik."

"How did he lose his eye?"

"I'd tell you what he said, but he was bragging and I don't think I believe him. I don't want to believe him, the little Hitler," Porteur said.

"It was complimentary to him?" I asked.

"Just the opposite. He is a terrible bully," Thyra said.

Porteur drained his glass. "I'd better get back and make sure those two haven't killed each other." He left the pub, leaving Mike and me with the Nilsens.

"How long has Mrs. Jørgensen been ill?" I asked.

"Longer than we've known her," Thyra said. "We've been here less than two years."

We stayed another half hour before the four of us walked back to the institute. "Do you want me to come in and help you break up any fights?" Peder asked Mike.

"No, I'll be fine." Then Mike turned to me. "I'll tell you in the morning if I learn anything."

Mrs. Ulriksen let me in the front door of the house and told me everyone had retired for the night. Now that I was in, she could finally go to bed. I felt chastised. I tiptoed upstairs to my room, listening for any footsteps or voices. Nothing.

I readied for bed and then sat looking out the window into the blackness. Where was Adam? Was he in England? Scotland? Overseas? I missed him so much, made worse by worrying about where he was and what kind of danger he was facing. Was he seeing the same stars I was? Was he sleeping soundly in a warm bed?

I didn't know and couldn't know until I saw him again or the war ended. Soon, please God, I prayed.

I was wondering what my mother would have thought of Adam when a flash of light under my window caught my attention. It took me a moment to realize it was a torch. Someone was walking around the grounds of the institute. Was it a night watchman? Someone who couldn't sleep? Or someone with mischief on their mind?

The torchlight wandered away from the house, finally stopping at and disappearing into what must have been the side of the institute.

* * *

I woke up, surprisingly rested after a short night's sleep, and washed and dressed to hurry downstairs to discover who rose early in this place and whether breakfast was as good as dinner had been. I wore the skirt from my gray suit with a different blouse and a warm cardigan in a muted red.

Dr. Jørgensen was the only one in the dining room, and he greeted me with a smile and a wave of his hand toward the server, where covered dishes gave off heavenly smells. I helped myself to eggs, porridge, toast, and bacon with its wonderful aroma and then poured myself a cup of coffee.

I was on my first bite when Mrs. Ulriksen came in. She came up to Dr. Jørgensen and spoke in a low voice in Danish. After a short conversation, he rose from the table. In English, he said, "If anyone comes looking for us, Mrs. Ulriksen and I will be up in the servants' quarters. It seems we've had a death in the staff."

"Oh, no. How awful. Who?"

"Greta," he said as he left the room.

Was it murder? I had suspected she was a thief and Mike had overheard that she had planned a tryst with Fritz for the night before. The sort of foolish girl who might get murdered. Grabbing another bite, I rose and hurried after my host.

We climbed up two flights of stairs, the second steeper and uncarpeted. It opened onto an undecorated hallway with closed doors on either side. I followed them to the one that stood open.

Greta lay sprawled on her back on the thin carpet in her room, blood smeared on her left temple. She wore a scarlet negligee that I could tell immediately was imitation silk. Nowhere did I see a weapon that could have been used to strike the maid.

"Oh, dear," Dr. Jørgensen said, standing just inside the doorway.

"She is cold. She has been dead a long while," Mrs.

Ulriksen said, standing by Greta's feet.

Greta had a small stack of magazines on her table. I didn't read Danish, but I recognized the Hollywood actors on the covers. That and the negligee made me think the young woman had been a dreamer with big plans.

"When did you last see her?" I asked Mrs. Ulriksen.

"When she finished her chores after dinner. Before nine."

"Did she have a boyfriend in the house or in the area?"

"Not to my knowledge," the housekeeper told me. Nothing was mentioned of Fritz Braun.

"We must notify the police," Dr. Jørgensen said, staring down at the dead girl. "Please lock the door and let us all go downstairs and be about our business until the politi want to speak to us."

I led the way back downstairs. By then, my breakfast and my coffee were room temperature, but after seeing that pitiful young woman, hardly more than a child, lying dead, struck down in her attic room, I wouldn't have been hungry under any circumstances.

Hoping the cold fresh air would settle my stomach, I went outside. Down the path to my right, I heard a woman's voice say in German, "Why not get married today? Then my parents will leave us alone."

A male voice said, "There is much to do to get ready for Tuesday. It'll be a couple of weeks before I'll have time to get married."

Their footsteps seemed to be coming closer. Not wanting to be caught listening, I hurried inside and returned to the dining room. I sat at my place at the table and stared at my plate without seeing it.

Mike came in, helped himself from the serving dishes and sat next to me. "What's wrong?"

"Greta, the maid with Braun yesterday, has been murdered. In her room. Upstairs."

He was speechless for a minute. "Wow. Have the politi been called?"

"Yes."

He picked up his fork and took a bite, finishing it before he said, "This is going to keep us from getting back to England before the invasion if we're not careful."

I gaped at him in a rising panic. "I want to go home." The last thing I wanted was to be trapped behind enemy lines in the middle of a war. By not speaking the language, I'd stick out in a crowd.

And I knew enough about the Nazis to know I didn't want to stand out in front of them.

Chapter Seven

I waited with Mike while he ate his breakfast and I toyed with mine. Henrik, Porteur, and Katrine arrived for breakfast one at a time and we sat silently, listening to the police stomp up and down the stairs.

I was surprised Braun didn't come to breakfast with Katrine. I wondered what she was thinking and feeling about being rebuffed. The argument I had heard outside had to be between the two of them.

Eventually, I was called by a policeman to speak to the detectives. As I left the room, Katrine wondered aloud in English, "Why do they want to talk to *her*?"

I was taken to the library, where two detectives sat at a desk across from the chair they pointed at to tell me to sit. They introduced themselves as Vicepolitiinspektor Larsen and Politikommissar Behr.

Then Larsen spoke in Danish and looked at me for a response.

I shook my head. "English?"

Larsen replied with something I couldn't understand.

I shook my head.

Politikommissar Behr shut his eyes for a moment while Larsen raised his eyebrows. Then the vicepolitiinspektor said, "Do you speak German?" in that language.

"Ja."

He looked relieved, knowing we could communicate.

"What are you doing here?" he asked.

"My mother was a friend of Mrs. Jørgensen. She died many years ago, and Mrs. Jørgensen wanted to meet me to find out how I turned out."

"But you don't speak Danish. How did you find your way out here? We're not in the center of Copenhagen."

"I flew Danish Airlines to Kastrup Airport, and a former student of Dr. Jørgensen was on the flight. He guided me out here."

"Who is this former student?"

"Mike Christiansen. He's staying here this weekend, too."

"Had you met him in England?"

"We met at the airport. The Jørgensens arranged it." That was pretty close to the truth. Well, close enough.

"Had you met the young woman who was murdered?"

"She unpacked my suitcase and closely examined my jewelry." I raised my eyebrows.

"Had you invited her to do so?"

"No. I walked in and found her admiring herself with it in the mirror."

"What did she say?"

"It was very pretty."

The two policemen exchanged glances. "What

happened this morning?"

"I had just fixed my breakfast when Mrs. Ulriksen came in to tell Dr. Jørgensen that Greta was dead. We then rushed upstairs and found her on the floor with what appeared to be a nasty wound on her head."

"Did you touch her?"

"Mrs. Ulriksen said she was cold, and that meant she'd been dead some time. So, no, I didn't touch her."

"Why did you go upstairs?" The older of the two policemen stared at me through incredibly pale eyes as he spoke. I didn't think he believed anything I said.

"To see if I could help. I guess I didn't believe she was really dead and I hoped I could do something. Anything."

"Did you see Greta interacting with any of the residents here?"

"When I went into the village with Mr. Christiansen yesterday afternoon, we stopped by the pub. Greta was in there with Fritz Braun, one of the chemists. They seemed friendly."

"How friendly?"

I shrugged. "Friendly."

"When did you last see Greta?"

"When she was studying my jewelry after putting my clothes away. That was shortly before dinner."

"At no time after that?"

"No."

A uniformed policeman came in and spoke softly in what I guessed was Danish to the two detectives.

Vicepolitiinspektor Larsen said something in Danish in reply that included "Dr. Jørgensen" and then said to me in German, "Stay there."

Dr. Jørgensen arrived a few minutes later, and seeing me, immediately switched to German. "What can I do for you?"

Larsen said, "We've checked all the doors and windows. Either Greta's killer was already in the house, or someone let him in."

"Or she let him in," the doctor said. "Before you ask, she was that type of girl."

"I saw someone with a torch walking near the house last night after we'd all gone to bed," I told them.

They all turned to look at me. "Where was this?" Larsen asked.

"From my window. It faces the front of the house."

"What time?"

"After eleven. I wondered if the institute employs a night watchman."

"No. We don't. Nothing here the usual burglar would be interested in," Dr. Jørgensen said. "And we have a fence around the entire perimeter of the institute to keep anyone from just wandering in."

They excused me then and I went back to the dining room in search of a fresh cup of coffee. Ailsa Jørgensen was seated in her wheeled chair drinking coffee and talking to Mike. "My dear child. I hope the politi didn't upset you too much," she said in English.

"It's her death that's upsetting. She was so young."

"Eighteen. Still giddy and boy mad," Mrs. Jørgensen said.

"Do you think one of those boys she was mad about killed her?" Mike asked.

"Probably. She had the morals of a barn cat."

"And you kept her on in your house?" I asked. I was surprised Mrs. Jørgensen was that broadminded.

"Between Mrs. Ulriksen and me, we hoped to settle her down. We had curbed her petty thieving."

"Golly." Greta must have been a handful. I wondered if she'd planned to steal my jewelry. It was pretty, but it would have been petty thievery at best since it was glass.

I wondered if Greta could have told the difference between real gems and glass. Probably not.

I knew better than to ask if there was anything I could do. It would be bad manners, since I would be suggesting Mrs. Jørgensen and Mrs. Ulriksen couldn't manage the house without my help. "Was she close to the other maids?"

"She wasn't with Michelle, my maid, but Michelle is a few years older and more settled. She has a steady beau in Porteur without making any fuss about it." Mrs. Jørgensen thought a moment. "I don't know about the other maids. She might have been friendly with them."

"You rely on Michelle a great deal, don't you?" I said.

Ailsa Jørgensen leaned back in her wheeled chair and gave me an angry look. "Of course. I have to rely on her.

I'm limited in what I can manage on my own. I'm trapped here."

I quickly shook my head. I didn't want her annoyed with me. "I meant she finds out what is going on in the household for you. A second pair of eyes and ears. That's very useful."

"Yes. She is very handy for that." She sounded a little mollified by my explanation.

"How did Greta die?" Mike asked me.

"A blow to the head. She was facing the person who struck her," I told him.

"Probably a young man she had led on. I imagine they can be quite—violent when their blood is up. When they want..." Mrs. Jørgensen's voice trailed off.

"In that case, probably an accident. A spur of the moment thing," I said. "I hope it doesn't prevent us from leaving tomorrow night to go to England."

"I don't know if we'll be able to go with you. Katrine is still refusing to leave." She sounded sorry not to be able to escape.

"Because of her young man?" I asked. The one who had been cheating on her with a maid who was now dead.

"Her German young man," her mother said with a disgusted tone.

"You're against the friendship?" Mike asked.

"I don't trust him. Unfortunately, Katrine is too trusting."

"We'd prefer that you come with us. I know you're

worried about Katrine, but we'd enjoy taking all three of you, and Michelle, to Great Britain with us. You don't have to stay in England if you don't want. You can go to America. France. Wherever. But at least you'd be safe from the Nazis." I used a pleading tone, but I was desperate.

This wasn't the first time I'd tried to help people come to England who were reluctant to leave their homeland. Esther's Jewish grandmother hadn't wanted to leave Berlin since her husband was buried there, but her daughter and I convinced her in the end. I had some experience with this. I expected confusion, dithering. I didn't expect resistance.

"You think I'm foolish, don't you?" Mrs. Jørgensen sounded sad.

"No. I understand your reasons. But I've also seen life under Nazi rule," I told her.

Mike nodded. "So have I. Life in their areas isn't the way the Nazis paint it."

I glanced over at him, wondering what part of occupied Europe he had been in.

"Madame, it's time for your exercises," Michelle said in French from the doorway.

"Thank you," Mrs. Jørgensen said and wheeled herself out of the room with a smile to both of us.

"Where did you go?" I asked Mike in English.

"German North Sea ports as a Danish sailor. You?"

"Berlin. Vienna. As a newspaper reporter."

A look passed between us. We recognized similar talents.

"Shall we go for a walk while they get the room ready for lunch?" he asked me.

"Yes." I rose from my chair and looked at the maid standing by the server, ready to set the table. "What's your name?" I asked in German, not certain I'd get a response.

"Lise." She was Greta's age and height, but blonder.

"I imagine you miss Greta."

"Why? She was always skipping out on her share of the work." Her cold tone told me she wasn't trying to hide her sorrow.

We left the room and let Lise get on with her task.

Once we were out of hearing distance of anyone, I quickly filled Mike in on the explanation I'd given the police on how we came to be traveling together. Mike said in English, "We don't seem to be getting anywhere with convincing the Jørgensens to come with us."

"I don't imagine the police think I'm a suspect in Greta's death, but that doesn't mean they'll let me go, let alone the Jørgensens."

"This just gets better and better," he said through clenched teeth.

"Worse, the Jørgensens still seem to be of two minds about leaving with us tomorrow night. We don't have much time to convince them to go with us, provided we are allowed to go. Oh, what a mess." I took a deep breath.

"What do you think is the best way forward?"

Mike shook his head slowly. "I don't know. And when I told Dr. Jørgensen we'd need to take his papers on the train and ferry to England with him, he said he found my attitude disheartening and insulting."

"Really?"

"Those were his exact words. I told him we didn't want him working for the Nazis, although he'd be free to work in a neutral country such as the United States, and we didn't want his papers falling into German hands, either."

"That sounds reasonable to me. But he found it upsetting?" I didn't understand his attitude.

Mike made a face. "I must have pushed too hard."

"I have a feeling we'll have to push them to get them to move. They don't seem to be in a hurry." On the other hand, I was in a big hurry.

"When tomorrow night arrives," Mike said, "we'll have to get you on your way back to England, no matter what else happens."

"What about you? And what about the murder?" I was concerned about both problems.

"If I have to, I can blend in. I have family here I can call on. And I came in on my Danish passport."

"And you have friends in the maritime trades." He'd been to German seaports as a Danish sailor, so he must have contacts.

He nodded. "I know people. I'd rather not have to stay

and use them, but don't worry about me." He glanced toward the institute, where several men were leaving by the side door to walk toward the house. "It must be time for lunch."

We turned toward the front door of the house. "On Saturdays, Berde and Klimek join the chemists and the Jørgensens for lunch," Mike told me.

"And so are we," Peder Nilsen said in German. He had been walking behind us with his wife Thyra and Bjorn Beck.

"Where is your wife, Mr. Beck?" I asked. Someone had told me her name was Inge, but we had not yet met.

"She does not feel well, so she stayed home." Beck's German was heavily accented.

"I'm sorry to hear that. I look forward to meeting her."

He gave me a weak smile.

We entered the house and went to the dining room, where Beck gave his wife's regrets to Mrs. Jørgensen.

"She's so shy you never notice her when she is here," Katrine said quietly to no one in particular.

We took our seats as directed, the chemists at one end with Dr. Jørgensen, the two lab workers in the middle, and the women at the other end. Katrine managed to follow the pattern and still sit next to Fritz Braun. They'd obviously practiced this maneuver.

There was a soup course first, this time a potato chowder. We all complimented the delicious thick, rich broth, asked after Mrs. Jørgensen's health, and otherwise kept quiet.

Mrs. Ulriksen and Lise cleared away the soup bowls and brought out platters of smørrebrød with fish and pickled onion and beet on top. Again, we complimented the food, which really was tasty if salty, but otherwise we kept conversation to a minimum.

"I'm sorry your wife didn't join us," Fritz Braun said to Beck. "Please tell her I look forward to seeing her again soon."

Beck glared at him but kept chewing his smørrebrød so he couldn't speak.

"What? Cat got your tongue?" Braun asked. There was an uncomfortable air to the room. I didn't understand it, but I had the feeling Braun was pushing his advantage of being German just before the invasion. And somehow, Mrs. Beck was at the center of it.

Ailsa Jørgensen was watching Braun with an expression of distaste. No wonder she wanted to get her daughter away from him, if her face was showing her true feelings about Braun.

It was Berde who rose from the table first. "Excuse me, Frau, but Klimek and I need to get back to start our afternoon's work."

"Surely you want some coffee. Did you get enough to eat?"

"Yes, Frau, we did, and we'll get coffee at the institute when we get a chance. Thank you so much for inviting us for this wonderful meal." Berde shot Klimek a sharp look, which made him rise while palming a smørrebrød, thank Mrs. Jørgensen, and hurry out after the older man.

Mrs. Jørgensen, trying to hide her smile, said to her husband, "I don't think we feed Klimek enough. He is a growing boy."

"He's a pig," Braun said.

"You don't speak that way of anyone at my table," Mrs. Jørgensen admonished him in a quiet tone.

For once, it appeared Fritz Braun remembered he was a guest at this dining table and he supposedly wanted the woman chiding him to be his mother-in-law. After an instant when I thought he would bark something rude, he kept silent.

Chapter Eight

Mrs. Ulriksen came in to collect the plates and Lise wheeled in the coffee cart, dissipating any lingering tension. Cups and saucers ringed the large coffee urn with its flanking sugar bowl and cream pitcher.

"Men, hurry and get your coffee and finish it quickly. I have something amazing to show you at the institute," Dr. Jørgensen said.

"What is it?" Nilsen asked.

"You have to wait until we go over there and I can show you."

The chemists started to pepper him with guesses, but he only laughed and said, "You have to wait."

As soon as one man rose, all five chemists as well as Mike rushed to the coffeepot. It was miraculous that no one was burned with hot coffee as they all shifted positions and reached and leaned in to fill their cups and add sugar or cream. Braun used his shoulder to shove Andersen a little to the side out of his way, and Christiansen slipped in sideways between them to get his cup filled. Porteur nudged Beck aside to reach the sugar. Nilsen wiggled in to force Porteur out of his way.

No one could have kept track of all the hands around the urn or the cups, but they continued to work as quickly as possible to fill their cups and get back to their seats to drink their coffee.

Mrs. Ulriksen dodged the young men to put slices of strudel at each place to go with the coffee or tea.

Mrs. Jørgensen nodded to Braun and put her hand on his sleeve as he passed by her wheeled chair at the end of the table. He set his cup down and looked her in the eye. She said, "I'm sorry I spoke harshly to you, Fritz, but he's only a boy. I'm sure you had a huge appetite when you were his age."

She gave him a smile and he returned it. "You have a point."

Mrs. Jørgensen released her grip and patted his sleeve and Braun went back to his seat next to Katrine, drinking his coffee as quickly as the other men.

Lise brought cups of tea to Mrs. Jørgensen, to Thyra Nilsen, and to me. I noticed Mrs. Ulriksen take cups of coffee to Katrine and to Dr. Jørgensen, but he waved the housekeeper away. "None for me. I'm more excited about my finding than they are."

"Just give me one more minute," Mike said, trying to gulp his coffee and widening his eyes as he burned his mouth.

"You're such a weakling," Braun said, gulping down his coffee.

"I've had enough," Beck said, setting down his cup and rising. I wondered if he meant of the coffee or of Braun.

Dr. Jørgensen jumped up with the energy I would expect from a younger man and left the room. With thanks to Mrs. Jørgensen, the chemists rose as they got down another gulp of coffee and hurried away, Mike last of all.

"Ah, now we can drink our tea in peace." Mrs. Jørgensen continued speaking in German as she leaned back in her wheeled chair and sipped with her eyes closed. "I think this is a lovely flavor of tea," she said as she opened her eyes. "What do you think, Thyra?"

"It is very good."

I finished my tea in a few minutes and said, "I want to go over to the institute and hear about this discovery. Anyone want to go along?"

Thyra and Katrine both shook their heads. I told Mrs. Jørgensen how lovely the luncheon was and rushed out to get my coat and follow the men over to the institute.

When I entered the building by the side door, I could hear men's raised voices. "Is that all you can think of? Your own pleasure? Your own advancement?" the first voice said in German with a Nordic accent. "Is there anyone else you think of?"

"I think that is my business," the second voice, I thought Fritz, replied in German.

"Business. That's all it is to you," the first voice scoffed.

"Of course. Applied chemistry is all about business." I felt certain that was Fritz Braun.

"What about loyalty? What about integrity?"

"I am loyal. To those that matter. To Olaf. To Germany."

"Hardly. You are only loyal to your ego and your wallet."

I heard a metallic crash, and then a tall blond man wearing a lab coat stormed out of a doorway ahead of me, slammed the door, and stalked off in the other direction and up the stairs. I couldn't tell from the back if it was Henrik Andersen or Mike Christiansen, and I couldn't see if he had a beard.

I wondered if Dr. Jørgensen had shown his big discovery yet. I was curious and hurried upstairs to see what the excitement was in his laboratory.

When I knocked and opened the door, I found Jørgensen talking to Mike in English. "You just saw an example of Braun's behavior, threatening Porteur with a prison camp. What sort of father would I be if I left her alone in this country with Braun and his brownshirt friends while I escaped to England?"

"I suspect he'll call off the engagement and any further dealings with you or her after Tuesday. And by then, it will be too late for you to leave. That's all he's interested in," Mike said.

"I fear you are right. Oh, yes, I fear it. But I am powerless against his tricks when it is my little girl involved." Then Dr. Jørgensen looked at me. "You wanted to know what the discovery is?"

"Yes."

I would like to say that it was brilliant. I would like to say I understood his finding. Unfortunately, I had no idea about the first and the second was not true. After a minute, Mike left, trying not to laugh at the puzzled expression on my face.

Dr. Jørgensen only spent a couple of minutes trying to explain his chemical breakthrough, but in the end, he gave up and politely told me he had to get back to work and I was welcome to watch. I thanked him for his generous offer, but I thought I'd go and find Mike.

I checked all the other laboratories on the first floor and found no one in any of them before I headed down to the ground floor. I opened two doors before I opened the one where one of the Danes, either Mike or Henrik, had exited earlier. It took me a moment to understand what I was seeing.

Five men stood or knelt around someone on the floor who seemed to have collapsed. I couldn't see who the man was, only that he wore a lab coat with brown trousers. Otherwise, the other men blocked my view.

Christiansen saw me staring into the room and came over to quickly pull me back into the hall.

"What...?" I was nearly speechless.

"It's Braun. Looks as if it's cyanide."

"Oh, no. Dr. Jørgensen said they use cyanide in their experiments to make a rubber substitute. Was he careless?" I knew in Britain it was used in some industrial processes.

"Didn't Olaf tell you? He's very strict about proper procedures and careful handling of chemicals in the lab."

"With the cyanide?" I hadn't been interested in my science classes in school, and they were increasingly a long time ago. This was beyond anything I could comprehend.

Christiansen nodded. "Of course with the cyanide. Look, this isn't very pretty. Why don't you go up and tell Olaf what's going on? The police are on their way." For once, his voice was gentle.

I nodded and retraced my steps, being careful not to look into the laboratory where the men were congregated. Then I ran the rest of the way, arriving in Dr. Jørgensen's laboratory out of breath. The doctor was still working in his lab when I reached him.

"Braun has ingested cyanide," I gasped out. "In his lab."

For a moment, he looked as if I'd hit him with a brick. Then he turned off the burner under a beaker, slipped past me, and dashed down the stairs. I raced behind him.

When we reached the doorway, the five living men were all standing still looking at the prone figure on the tile floor. Again, all I could see were his shoes and trouser legs.

Dr. Jørgensen rushed into the middle of the group. "Have you called for an ambulance? How did this happen? It wasn't even his day to work on the rubber experiments." He knelt and the others stepped back while he felt for a pulse on Braun's neck.

Andersen said something in Danish, and Jørgensen leaped up. He shouted something in Danish, clearly berating the man as he leaned toward him. Without knowing a word of what was said, I could tell Dr. Jørgensen was hysterical, angry, out of control.

The men began arguing, partially in Danish, partially in German. I could make out phrases such as, "It was Nilsen's turn today," and "You can't get poisoned if you follow protocols for using the cyanide."

"Do we have a poisoner among us? Porteur, political assassination would be right up your line," Beck said, his finger pointed at the swarthy Frenchman.

"No one wanted him dead more than you did, Beck," Porteur said as he shoved him, before the other men pulled them apart.

"Stop it," Dr. Jørgensen snapped in German. "This must have been an accident. But how?"

Mute headshaking was the only response.

"Is anyone else ill?"

The men glanced at each other before Nilsen said in German, "I don't see any cyanide containers in this lab."

"Who was the last person to use the cyanide?"

"I'll get the logbook," Beck replied. I got out of his way as he hurried past to walk inside a doorway at the far end of the ground-floor corridor.

"That's the storeroom," Christiansen said, suddenly appearing at my side. "The logbooks are kept there. And the cyanide."

"Are there other poisons kept there?"

"Yes, and non-poisons as well."

"Who found him this way?" Jørgensen asked in German, his gaze falling on everyone.

"I did," Andersen said. "He was already dead, I think. I felt for a pulse. Nothing. I called out and the others arrived one at a time in the next few moments."

The main front door echoed as it banged open. Four men, all in Danish police uniforms, walked over to us. One of them I had met. "Vicepolitiinspektor Larsen," he introduced himself to the others. The rest of what he said was in Danish. I looked at Christiansen.

"He's the police inspector in charge of the investigation," he told me as one of the other policemen checked for a pulse and sniffed above the dead man's face.

"He is also in charge of the investigation into Greta's murder," I told him in English, surprised he hadn't been questioned. Of course, he wasn't living in the house and hadn't run upstairs to see the body as I had.

In hindsight, that was not one of my more brilliant moves.

"Terrific. Now he has two murders here. He thinks at least one of us if not all of us are homicidal maniacs," Mike translated and winked.

Oh, dear. It would be funny if it weren't so serious.

Larsen, another policeman, and Jørgensen carried on a rapid conversation, pausing only when the logbook arrived. Meanwhile, the other two policemen stood behind us, blocking anyone from leaving the area.

I heard "Braun" but nothing else that made sense as they spoke rapid Danish.

"Braun worked on the rubber experiments yesterday and he signed out some cyanide. No one signed out any today," Mike translated.

"Maybe it was some sort of freak accident," I said.

Mike shook his head. "I've worked with Jørgensen and his protocols before. There's no way there could have been an accident. This had to be murder."

"Again," I said.

Chapter Nine

I glanced at the two policemen standing behind us. From their lack of expression, I guessed they didn't speak English and didn't recognize the word "murder." But I did. And I recognized this could mean we would be stuck here until after the German invasion if the police couldn't solve these killings and didn't let us leave.

Once the Germans arrived, we'd be stuck here for the duration of the war. I'd hoped to spend the war in England, not Denmark. While I wanted to learn more about my mother, spending the war in jail, or worse, was too high a price to pay.

This was a nightmare. Friedrich Braun alive was a complication to our plans to get the Jørgensens out of Denmark. Dead, Braun was a roadblock. Murdered, Braun was a catastrophe.

The police inspector Larsen and Dr. Jørgensen were speaking again in rapid-fire Danish with occasional comments by the policeman squatting by the body. Christiansen listened and then said, "The police suggested suicide, but Jørgensen said it was impossible. Braun was German, looking forward to the Germans' arrival, and he was engaged to be married to Katrine."

"I'd like it better if he thought it was possible." Much

better.

"A tidy conclusion. Yes, I like that better, too," Christiansen said. The smile he gave me was more of a grimace. Apparently, he recognized the same problem I saw looming.

The inspector and the famous chemist seemed to argue and then they both walked out of the lab, forcing Christiansen and me to step back into the hall. The four remaining chemists followed and then Christiansen took my arm and led me behind them. The two other staff members that I recognized from lunch lingered in the hallway, and they received a command that caused them to fall into step in our procession.

We went up, past the first-floor landing and up to the top of the staircase on the second floor. There the hallway was shorter and we entered the doorway to one side that led to a large drawing room or waiting room. The windows were in little dormers, the furniture seemed to be castaways, and the carpet and the wooden floor had only been given a cursory sweep. On a table between two dormer windows was a hot plate with a coffeepot, several mugs and cups, and a sugar bowl with a crack in it.

"We're under the eaves on this floor," Mike murmured in English.

The police inspector was already at the coffeepot, asking questions as he lifted the coffee mugs and studied them. He asked for something, because Jørgensen must have told one of the chemistry assistants to take care of it.

Berde left the room, and the police inspector checked the sugar bowl and the coffeepot. Jørgensen said something and then two of the chemists spoke at once. Inspector Larsen gestured to the chairs and the men began to sit. I took a wooden chair since I wasn't too sure of the cleanliness and insect-free state of the sagging stuffed sofa and chairs. Christiansen sat next to me on another wooden chair.

The assistant returned carrying a box, which a policeman took from him and walked to the table. All the mugs, the coffeepot, and the sugar bowl were loaded inside while Larsen continued to speak in Danish.

When he finished, Christiansen said in English, "They're taking all the coffee supplies to be tested at the police lab, since this is the only place in the institute where anything can be consumed. Then they're going to question us one at a time and take the fingerprints of the regulars here, to match the cups to the owners."

"I know from this morning that they speak German. I wonder if one of them speaks English?" I asked.

"We'll find out."

Oh, goody. Questioned by the police in German again. Just before the nation was flooded with Germans. The room, not warm before, all of a sudden felt very cold.

Jørgensen left with three of the policemen, including Larsen and the one who was carrying the box with the coffee supplies. The last policemen was left to stand by the door, I guessed to listen to us.

Or to make certain we didn't escape.

The men in the room must have thought the same thing, since everyone kept quiet. Finally, Beck shifted his stocky frame on the sofa, ran a hand through his fair hair, and said in German, "Who found him?"

"I did," Andersen said, also in German.

From the puzzled look on his face, the policeman didn't speak German. I could have cheered, because I did speak German and finally, I could understand what was being said.

"Do you think it was suicide?" Nilsen asked.

"The chief said absolutely not," Beck said.

"Not since his buddies will be pouring over the border in a few days. He was looking forward to showing us how important he was," Porteur said. Even if the policeman couldn't understand German, he would have been able to tell by his sneer and his tone that Porteur didn't like someone.

"Does this make their job easier or harder?" Andersen asked, glancing at us.

"If you mean us, harder. Definitely harder," Christiansen said.

"I don't understand why the chief wants to leave," Nilsen said.

"Do you want to work for our enemies?" Porteur asked.

"Surely they'd allow us to continue with our pure research," Nilsen replied.

Everyone sitting silently in the room stared at him as one.

His gaze traveled the room. "Well, wouldn't they? We are neutral."

"You'll soon find out what that's worth," Klimek, the laboratory assistant, said. He was young, dark-haired, and stocky, but taller than Porteur.

"You're just angry because they walked over your country, Klimek," Nilsen said.

"As they'll soon do to yours," Klimek replied, his voice rising.

"No, not the same as yours," Nilsen said.

Klimek appeared ready to jump up and pound on Nilsen. I hoped to calm the charged atmosphere and said the first thing that came to mind, thanks to my boarding school education. "Excuse me, Mr. Klimek, but I don't think anyone told me. Will you be graduating from school this year or next at Krakow University?"

He turned to me and took a couple of calming breaths before he said, "I don't know if the university is still functioning or if I'll ever be able to graduate. Who knows when anyone will be able to sit for exams or defend theses? The most useful thing I am able to do now is to work as a cleaner and beaker washer when they need someone to do it."

A couple of the researchers chuckled, but it was without malice.

I looked into the young man's eyes. He couldn't have

been more than twenty. "Knowing what they did to your homeland, I imagine you don't want to see them coming here now."

"This doesn't solve how Braun ingested the cyanide," Andersen said, "and learning that is the only way we can get out of here before the hordes arrive at the gates."

"You sound as if you're in more of a hurry to leave now that Braun is dead," Nilsen said.

I noticed no one was saying the names of countries or anything else easily translated by the policeman.

"He'd just had a full meal. Would that slow down the action of the poison?" I asked.

A few of the men nodded or said "Yes."

"Would it have a noticeable taste?"

"It's bitter," Nilsen told me. "Supposedly."

"So the coffee would hide the taste," I said. I was beginning to get a picture of what could have happened.

"That must be why the police inspector took the coffeepot and all the cups," Beck said.

"And the sugar bowl," Christiansen added.

"Does anyone know if he came up here after you returned from lunch?" We had just had a full meal with coffee and strudel at the end of it.

All the men shook their heads or shrugged.

I didn't envy the police their task of solving this suspicious death.

One by one, the men were called out of the room, but none returned. When it was only Christiansen and me, he said in English, "I wouldn't mention Sir Malcolm if I were you. Might raise awkward questions."

"And how do I know you?" I prompted.

"We were both coming over this weekend, so they suggested I travel with you since I speak the language."

"Very kind of them." If I didn't get out of here before Tuesday, Sir Malcolm would have a great deal to answer for when I was finally able to catch up with him.

And that raised another question. Was Braun murdered to stop Jørgensen from escaping before the invasion? "Is anyone else here German or a German sympathizer?"

Before he could answer, Christiansen was called out of the room by a policeman. I was alone with my thoughts and one puzzled young policeman.

I would have loved to use the time to figure out the solution to the murder, but I was too busy worrying about my position as a foreigner who didn't speak the language. That would put me in an uncomfortable position after Tuesday. If I were stuck here after Tuesday, I would need a place to live. And a job. And a way to avoid the Nazis.

The more I considered my untenable position, the colder I felt. I began to shiver. Then as I thought about how guilty that would make me look, I trembled more.

I wondered if I could beg for mercy and leave this country now. Would the police inspector let me do that?

Then the door opened. I turned and found a second policeman staring at me. Wordlessly, I rose, following him, and walked into the hall. I was led to a doorway across the hall, which the policeman opened for me.

I walked in to find a smaller room with only one dormer window. I could see it was still light outside, but in here only one bulb hanging from the rafters lit the center of the room, leaving the corners in shadow. Across the table from me sat two men in police uniforms. "Vicepolitiinspektor Larsen. Politikommissar Behr," Larsen said, reminding me of their names, with gestures pointing to himself and then the younger man. Once we again worked out a common language, German, they began.

"Frau Redmond, why are you at the institute this afternoon?" Larsen's German was serviceable, but mine was more fluent.

"Frau Jørgensen was a good friend of my mother. She had invited me, and I came."

"Without speaking a word of Danish?"

"The Jørgensens speak excellent English. It was suggested I travel with Herr Christiansen, who speaks both English and Danish and was coming to visit his former chemistry professor, Dr. Jørgensen, this weekend."

Larsen gave me a suspicious look. "Dr. Jørgensen was here at the institute this afternoon, but Frau Jørgensen wasn't."

"Dr. Jørgensen said he made a promising discovery. I came over to hear what it is."

"And what did you learn?"

I opened my eyes a little wider and looked at the

police inspector innocently. "It was all in chemistry."

"How much do you know about chemistry?"

"Very little."

"And yet," Larsen said, "I understand you are a graduate of Cambridge University in your country." He gave me a smile that seemed to indicate my imminent incarceration. He'd been checking up on me. Who knew what he had found?

Chapter Ten

"I had a few sessions in biology and math, but my field of study was modern languages. I speak both German and French. And by the way," I added, "as a female student, I cannot graduate from Cambridge, although I can take their examinations."

Larsen and Behr, who'd been taking notes, glanced at each other. "Had you ever met Friedrich Braun?"

"Before yesterday? No. And I'm not really certain I'd met him then, either."

"Did you kill him?"

"Good grief, no." They'd never find Friedrich's or Greta's murderer at this rate.

"Do you know who did?"

"I have no idea."

"We have been called to two murders here at the institute in the past six hours and you have been present at both. How can you account for your presence both times?"

"Bad luck?"

"Frau Redmond, it is more than just bad luck."

"Terrible luck?" I suggested.

He gave me a skeptical look. "How well do you know Herr Christiansen?"

The police were wasting their time considering Christiansen or me for this poisoning. "He traveled with me as a favor to the Jørgensens. I'd never met him before this trip."

"The cyanide had to have been stolen from the store cupboard. Do you know anything about this?"

"Nothing." I wish I did. "Are you certain the poison was meant for Herr Braun?"

"All of the coffee cups in the lounge across the hall are of different designs and different patterns. If someone put the cyanide in one of the cups, they knew who would be using it." Larsen sounded very certain.

"Did anyone have any coffee after they returned here from lunch? They all had coffee at the Jørgensen home right before coming over here," I told them. "That was only a short time before Braun died."

"We'll have to see if traces of the poison are found in anything from the lounge." Larsen sounded as if he could already count on this.

There was one thing that was at the forefront of my mind. "I'm supposed to return to England on the Monday morning ferry. Will there be any problem with my returning?"

"That depends on whether we find our killer before then. Otherwise, you'll be staying here along with everyone else."

"But the Germans are invading Tuesday morning, and I'm not Danish. I'm British. An enemy of theirs."

"They might be invading. It makes no difference."

It made a great difference to me. "They are invading. And I have either never met these people before or haven't seen them since I was two years old."

Larsen leaned across the table. "I have two murders to solve, and you are a suspect. You are staying here until we find the killer."

Oh, great. "Has anyone spoken to Frau Jørgensen or Katrine?" I asked, still in German. Katrine in particular would be upset when she heard.

"I don't know. Perhaps Professor Jørgensen has gone back to the house and told them the bad news," Vicepolitiinspektor Larsen replied. "Now, do you know or have you seen anything that might help us investigate this murder?"

I shook my head. "No." I was regretting coming on this mission for Sir Malcolm. I hadn't decided to help someone escape the Nazis so much as I wanted to meet someone who could tell me more about my mother. My father was reticent when it came to talking about her, and I barely remembered her.

But if I didn't get on that ferry Monday morning, my curiosity might mean my death.

"You are excused. You may go back to the residence, but make yourself available for more questioning." Larsen and Behr both rose.

I had no choice but to stand and walk out of the small room. I looked in the larger room across the hall, but no one was there. Walking down one flight of stairs, I gazed around the first-floor hallway and wondered what I should do next.

The laboratory cleaner, Berde, stepped out into the hall, saw me, and walked over. His face was deeply lined and he was dressed in a lab coat that showed some inexpertly removed stains. "You are staying at the professor's?" he asked in hesitant German.

"Yes."

"They have all gone over there."

"Thank you, Herr Berde. The police didn't give you a difficult time, did they?"

"No. I'm not important enough." He gave me a smile and walked away.

I went downstairs and walked back to the Jørgensens' large residence. A maid took my coat in the front hallway and pointed toward a wide door to the right.

Following her direction, I opened the door and walked into a large drawing room done in blues and greens with touches of gold. Ailsa Jørgensen sat, red-eyed, in her wheeled chair, a handkerchief clenched in one hand. Katrine sat huddled up in an overstuffed chair, her hands over her eyes, shouting at anyone who dared speak to her.

Beck said something in a low voice to Dr. Jørgensen in what I guessed was Danish, and Katrine gave what sounded as if it were a dramatic speech in Danish, ending with her collapsing and issuing noisy cries.

Dr. Jørgensen responded, equally low voiced, and

Beck and Nilsen nodded to Mrs. Jørgensen before fleeing from the room.

"They asked to go home because there wouldn't be any more work done today at the institute since the police are calling it a crime scene, and Jørgensen said yes," Christiansen said in English as he stepped close to me. I hadn't seen him in the corner.

"And Katrine?" I whispered.

"Oh, where to begin?" He shook his head.

She cared about a man who'd just been brutally murdered. I felt she had a right to be upset. Then she threw out her hands and screamed, drawing everyone's attention. I noticed then her eyes were dry.

Before I could reply, Mrs. Jørgensen wheeled herself over to us and said in English, "It would be a shame if you didn't get to see anything of Copenhagen before you leave. Why don't you take the opportunity to go into the center of town and look around for what's left of the afternoon? Dinner won't be until eight."

"Thank you." I gave her a smile, wondering if she wanted us out of the way while she tried to calm her daughter.

This was, after all, a family tragedy.

Christiansen and I left the house and walked toward the gate. Several policemen were searching the flower beds and under the bushes as we walked past. One of them picked something up and shouted for his sergeant. I wondered what he'd found.

When we reached the train station, we only waited a couple of minutes before the next train in our direction arrived. Once we arrived at the Central Station, Mike led me outside and across a busy street and then around a corner to enter the gates to Tivoli Gardens.

Lights were strung from trees just beginning to bud, creating a fairyland feeling. People strolled along the paths between flower beds showing still-tiny plants, children and adults rode the amusement rides, and I could glimpse inside windows to see that the cafes were busy. Easter had been two weeks before, and everyone wanted to enjoy spring, no matter how early in the year this was.

I tried to lighten my mood to match those around us. "Are there any local foods I should try while I'm here?"

"Beer, sausages, pastries. We had smørrebrød and one type of a meatball dish at lunch yesterday." He gave me a smile. "I could do with a beer after listening to Katrine for a few minutes. I don't know how her parents stand it."

I wasn't certain why I asked, but I said, "Did she sound sincere?"

He studied me as if considering. "Katrine? I don't know. Why?"

"It might be because she's so young, but she appeared to be more hysterical than...oh, I don't know. She seemed angry rather than sad."

"As if she were a child who has been told 'No.'" He looked at me, and we both nodded.

"Did you notice her eyes?"

"No."

"They were dry." I raised my eyebrows.

"Oh." Mike nodded. "Interesting."

"This is supposed to be a good restaurant," he said, pointing, after we'd walked a little farther.

"Before we go in, what is a politikommissar? It sounds important."

"Behr is a police sergeant. Larsen is his boss."

"Oh." I'd thought the silent policeman was some higher-ranking official.

I didn't understand Danish at all. Danish might be a Germanic language, but everyone spoke it so fast that my ears hadn't caught up with their speech yet. Given a few months, I'd probably be able to understand simple conversations, but that was months I didn't have and didn't want to have in an occupied country.

"Come on. What do you want to eat?" he asked as he held the door open for me.

"Pastries always sound good. Particularly with tea." It was more or less teatime and I was British.

"Not so much with beer," he said and smiled. "I'll get sausage, called polse, and we can split it so you can say you've tasted the best sausage in the world."

We were seated at a table near a window and Christiansen ordered for both of us in Danish. If I was going to spend any more time in Copenhagen, I would need to learn the rudiments of the language.

When the food came, the tea was ordinary, but the pastries and the sausages were delicious. Christiansen said his beer was excellent. The foam got on his mustache and beard, and he grabbed a napkin to wipe it away.

"I imagine you loved coming here as a child," I said.

"We came in the summer when visiting my grandparents. They lived on the north side of Copenhagen. With them, every day was an adventure."

"You sound as if you miss them," I told him. I could hear it in his voice.

"I do." He cleared his throat. "Who do you think killed Fritz? Excuse me, Friedrich Braun."

"I don't know. I only met him yesterday. I think we can rule out Mrs. Jørgensen acting on her own. It would have been too difficult for her to get the poison. The other researchers, the lab assistants, Dr. Jørgensen, even Katrine. None of the others are out of the running." I really wished I could narrow it down. It might help get us out of here in time.

"Braun wasn't popular," Christiansen told me. "Especially since the Germans made their announcement. He's been rubbing everyone's faces in the fact he'd be in charge. He told Katrine she'd be a fool to leave with her parents when she could stay here with the new head of the institute."

"Provided Dr. Jørgensen left," I added.

"No. No matter what, Braun said he'd be in charge as Jørgensen's boss."

"Good grief. Was he that good a chemist?"

"No, not at all." Mike looked surprised that I would ask that.

"Would Braun be in trouble with the Nazis if he didn't deliver Dr. Jørgensen to work at the institute and invent substitute products for them?"

"Probably," Mike said, "but that wouldn't explain Braun getting murdered before the Germans arrive. Oh, and Braun told Katrine she'd be the new lady of the house, replacing her mother."

"He sounds as if he were a very nice man," I said in a dry tone.

"Oh, yes. Typical Nazi. Beck plans to pack up his wife and leave for Sweden on Monday. Porteur wants to go to England with us. Nilsen and Andersen are Danish so they'll stay here, I think."

"And the assistants and the servants? What about them?"

He shrugged. "I'll leave the servants to you to interview. There are only two assistants currently, so I'll-"

"Wait a minute. I don't speak Danish. How can I talk to the servants?" I might not be the only one who saw the benefit in questioning the servants, but we had a very large barrier.

Chapter Eleven

"Have Mrs. Jørgensen help you," Mike suggested. "As far as the assistants are concerned, Klimek is the only one of any interest. He and Braun clashed any number of times and Klimek admits he was passionately anti-German even before Poland was invaded. Berde, on the other hand, will keep cleaning the institute as long as someone pays him. He appears to have no interest in politics, and very little interest in who is actually running the institute."

He gave me a fleeting smile. "He treats working at the institute as a job very much the same as working at Carlsberg Brewery. You do your job, you collect your pay, you go home. Idiot bosses come and go."

"Is that how you feel about Sir Malcolm?" I couldn't resist asking. I knew next to nothing about Mike Christiansen, and I'd have to work closely with him if we were to succeed in moving the Jørgensens to England.

"I don't think he's going anywhere. Not that it isn't a pleasant thought."

I felt the same way. "Do you work for him full time?"

"Yes, but ordinarily in London. This has only been my third trip back here since war was declared. And you?"

"I'm one of his part-timers. I started working for him in 1938. This is the first time I've traveled outside of

England for him." Then I decided to be forthcoming. "I traveled to Germany, Austria, and Czechoslovakia before the war for my real boss. I work for the *Daily Premier.*"

He took a sip of his beer. "Sounds like an interesting job."

"It is." Then I remembered I should be generous. "Do you want a bite of my pastries before I finish them?"

"No. Help yourself. Are you enjoying them?"

"They're heavenly." I wondered how long it would be before I'd taste anything as rich and buttery again.

"What would you enjoy seeing while we're here?"

"Besides a quick solution to the murder and Katrine willing to travel with us so her parents will come along?" I gave him a smile. "I don't know much of anything about the city. I put myself into your hands completely."

"That sounds dangerous." His smile was fiendish.

"Before you come up with anything too wild, I'd like to see a little more of this park. It's unique, at least to a Londoner."

"It's the only one of its type in Denmark, too, I am certain." Then he added, "You should see it in full summer. Flowers everywhere. Children everywhere. The days are long and warm and the evenings linger, making everyone reluctant to go inside and miss a second of this magical time."

"I think I'd like to experience that."

"Unfortunately, it seems that will be impossible for either of us this year." He sounded bitter as he stared into his beer.

I sipped my cooling tea and then nibbled on a pastry. The pastry was delicious, but the tea was not up to the standards of even the French. If the blockade on British shipping tightened, English tea might not be up to our usual standards, either.

When Christiansen remained silent, I asked him, "Where are your parents?"

"My mother is in Scotland, knitting for the RAF. My father died last year. Here, in Denmark. My parents split up when I was young. I have half-siblings in both Scotland and on the north side of Copenhagen."

"Don't you want to go see them instead of showing me the sights?" I instantly felt guilty keeping him away from his family. Family he wouldn't see again until the war ended.

"I've been ordered not to. Too many things to explain about me being here and why only for a weekend."

"You can't tell them…?"

"No." There was finality in that one word. Then he unbent. "The government knows, and the police, and the institute since we've told everyone there. But the country as a whole hasn't been informed yet. It's still a rumor. A rapidly spreading rumor, but a rumor nonetheless. I think it's because the government hasn't agreed on their response."

That has to be difficult, when he has a last chance to see his siblings. "My only relative is my father. And of course, my husband now that I'm married. He doesn't have many relatives, either."

He grinned at me. "I thought I didn't have many relatives, but after listening to you, it feels as if I have dozens."

We finished our food, Christiansen paid, and we headed for the exit by another route so I could see more of the park. Then we walked in the direction away from the station and toward the center of town. It was beginning to get dark, early compared to what I was used to because we were so far north and it was still early in the year. Fortunately, all the street lamps blazed the way they couldn't in London. The lights gave the city a fairytale glow.

As the sunset brought new shades to the sky, the lights seemed to become brighter. As accustomed as I'd become to the blackout in England, all this light in the evening made me nervous.

Christiansen, who'd been identifying some of the large, stately buildings to me, said, "Relax. This is a neutral country."

"For how much longer?"

He replied with a grumbling sound as he glanced around us. I had already judged people were too far away to hear my comment, even in the unlikely event they spoke English.

Christiansen slowed down as we reached what he apparently wanted to show me. "That's the Borsen. The stock exchange. Can you see the tower? It is built of four dragons with their tails entwined. Having a dragon on a building is supposed to make it fireproof."

"Does having four work even better?"

"Yes. It's never burned." He grinned. "I suppose it's as symbolic of Copenhagen as any building here."

I stopped and looked up at it. "It's certainly impressive standing here overlooking the canal. There seems to be water everywhere."

"It comes from being on a series of islands. And being so close to sea level." Mike steered me in another direction. "I want you to see the Christiansborg Slot from over here. Slot is the Danish word for palace. It's the seat of government and an impressive set of buildings."

As we walked down a street, I could see some magnificent pale stone buildings ahead of us. As we reached a cross street, I could see the road went over a bridge above another canal. The road led from the town into what Christiansen pointed out was Christiansborg Slot.

It was one of the figures walking toward us from the government buildings of the palace that caught my attention and slowed my feet.

Christiansen turned back to look at me and murmur in English, "What's wrong?"

I shook my head slightly and laid my hand on the shoulder of his jacket. "Wait here. I'll explain later."

Then I changed course so I could block the path of one

of the men headed our way on the opposite side of the street. Dressed in civilian clothes, I noted. I stopped under a street lamp at the corner a few yards ahead of him and waited until he saw me.

When he glanced at me, I smiled and said, "Herr Bernhard."

I saw him hold up a hand to detain the younger man he was with. Then he walked up to me and said in German, "Frau Denis. What a pleasant surprise." The smile on his face appeared genuine.

I wondered if he'd been assuring himself that the Danes wouldn't fight his troops since he was coming from the direction of what Mike told me was the parliament building. I'd known Oberst Wilhelm Bernhard of the German army since he was posted to the German embassy in London three years before.

Since he'd left London, wherever I'd met him, German troops had already taken over or would soon invade.

"It's Frau Redmond now. I remarried last summer," I told Oberst Bernhard in German.

"Herr Redmond is a fortunate man." He guided me along the road and down the bridge a short way so we were in shadow and no longer under a street lamp. "Sorry. Old habit, not to stand in the light making a good target."

"It's *Captain* Redmond, British army. Another reason why I wish this madness would stop."

"I hope you'll be going back to see him soon." Oberst Bernhard appeared nervous even as he smiled at me. I had never seen him look so uneasy. "It's not good to leave a newly married man to his own devices. He may burn down your kitchen."

"Is that the voice of experience speaking?" I asked. We were talking around what we really wanted to say. *What are you doing here? How long until you take Copenhagen and block my escape route?*

From across the road, Christiansen watched us in silence, as did the man who'd been walking along with Oberst, as I always thought of him. This unknown man now lingered twenty feet away toward an archway leading toward Christiansborg Slot.

"I'm afraid I should never be allowed in a kitchen," he told me.

That made me think of his son and daughter, who'd lost their mother and rarely saw their father. "How are your children?"

"Hardly children any more. They are almost grown. I'm proud of how they have turned out." He smiled, and I knew that smile, thinking of his children, was genuine.

I smiled in return. "I hope they stay safe."

"I've done my best to assure that."

I couldn't avoid a change of tone when I said, "Are you here at the behest of Canaris?"

"In a manner of speaking."

That told me everything. "So it's true."

"Doing some shopping?" Oberst asked, which was no answer at all.

"Just seeing the sights."

"I fear this time we will not be able to go to dinner together."

I'd had some lovely meals with him in Germany, when I knew I could safely call him "Oberst." "Will you be staying here long?" I asked.

"Longer than you, I imagine." His voice was as quiet as the evening breeze.

At least that was honest. I dropped my voice to match his. "Do I need to leave by Monday?"

"Yes."

A chill ran across my shoulders. "I hope I can. The police—"

Oberst raised his eyebrows.

"—won't let us leave until they find the murderer of a German research chemist at the Institute of Applied and Theoretical Chemistry and a maid there." Then I had a thought. "Had you heard about the death of your countryman?"

"Yes," came out in a grumble. "How many suspects?" At least he didn't ask if I did it.

"It's a closed place. A dozen at most. Perhaps six good possibilities." I included Christiansen in that number, but not Dr. Jørgensen. I could well have been wrong.

He frowned. "Can you clear it up before Monday?" He was showing great faith in me.

"I don't know."

He must have seen fear in my eyes, because he

studied the darkening sky for a moment before he said, "I can't help you. Before the war began, perhaps, but now? Especially involving the death of a German chemist." He shrugged. "It would endanger us both. And my children. I won't endanger my children. You are on your own."

That didn't sound like Oberst. "Are you in trouble?" I whispered.

Chapter Twelve

He nodded once. I could see fear and resignation in his expression. Perhaps being a nonpolitical officer wasn't a safe option in the army of Nazi Germany. Then he wheeled at the sound of footsteps behind him and said, "Frau, this is my colleague, Herr Schultz."

I saw fear in Oberst Bernhard's gaze as he turned back to me. His position as a high-ranking military officer must have grown precarious for him to tell me he could not lift a finger to help if I were trapped behind enemy lines. Or maybe Braun was more valuable to the Germans than I'd realized.

Schultz did a small bow over my hand as he held it. I wondered what the rank of this rat-faced man was.

A cold breeze swept over us. "If you'll excuse me, I'm sure my guide to this lovely city wants to go home. Farewell, Herr Bernhard."

He bowed over my hand almost low enough to kiss the back of my glove. "Farewell, Frau. I wish you a speedy return." He didn't say to where.

I hurried across the roadway to Christiansen and said, "Shall we go?"

We turned and headed back to the train station. "Do you want to tell me what that was about?" he murmured in English.

"Not until we can get someplace where we won't be overheard." I needed to consider how much I should tell Christiansen.

* * *

By the time we returned to the institute, I'd told my colleague that the advance party of Germans was in the country and ready to go on Tuesday morning. We had to leave on the ferry Monday morning, which meant the murder had to be solved by Sunday night. There was no respite from that deadline.

We decided I would get Mrs. Jørgensen's help in questioning the staff to find out if they'd seen anything earlier that day, and Christiansen would talk to the chemists to find out what they had noticed.

But when we arrived at the house, it was time for us to quickly dress for dinner and get down to the dining room. We were the last to arrive, following the rest of the party to the table. Without Friedrich Braun, or Fritz as Katrine called him, and the lab assistants and the two married researchers, we were a party of seven.

Katrine wore a dramatic low-cut black gown, possibly to symbolize mourning, although it didn't make me think of sadness. Quite the contrary. Her mother's gown was black also, but with sparkly threads in the fabric.

Definitely not mourning.

We kept up a light conversation for the soup course, using Danish, English, and German. When the fish was brought out, Dr. Jørgensen said, "How was your tour of our city? Did you see any sign that we're about to be invaded?"

"Surely, there won't be an invasion," Andersen said.

"The Poles didn't call it a friendly merger," Porteur grumbled into his fillet.

"Perhaps they'll change their minds," Mrs. Jørgensen said.

"I recognized one of the advance party for the German army. He's in the city with colleagues. He let me know we need to solve the murders and be on the ferry on Monday morning," I told them.

There were gasps and cries of "What?" in different languages.

Katrine silently gave me an appraising gaze.

"You spoke to him?" Mrs. Jørgensen asked.

"How do you know all this?" Andersen asked.

"I spoke to him. I've known him for over two years now, since he was posted to the German embassy in London. That is his assignment, to do advance reconnaissance. That's why he was in Vienna when I was, among other places."

"How do you know he is telling the truth?" Andersen said.

"He doesn't lie to me." Of that I was very sure.

"Every man lies," Katrine said. Her eyes could be said to look red and puffy, if anyone studied them closely for signs of crying. At a glance, she looked annoyed.

"Yes, but he doesn't lie to me. He's never felt the need to."

"I think this German must be sweet on you," Mrs. Jørgensen said with a smile.

"I think it's more a case of my never putting any pressure on him about his work or his beliefs. That and I speak to him as one human being to another, not something one often sees between an Englishman and a German these days."

"So we know our deadline," Christiansen said. "Anyone who's going to leave has to be on the ferry on Monday."

"Not without finding Fritz's killer," Katrine said.

"Agreed," I said. "Will you help me, Katrine? We may have different reasons, but our goal is the same."

"What do you want?" She sounded intrigued.

"For you to translate for me so I can question the servants. They may have seen something. Something they may not think is important."

She ate a bite of fish, frowning, and then a second. Finally, she said, "Why not? I'll help you. I want you to find his killer. I want to see his murderer suffer."

Dr. Jørgensen said, "Katrine, that's not very nice."

"Neither is murder, Father. Or did you kill him? You didn't like him."

Before he could answer, the servants entered to trade the fish course for a poultry and vegetable course. Katrine stared at him the entire time.

"Well?" she said when they left with the dirty dishes.

"Don't be silly, Katrine. I would not kill Braun," her father said.

"But you didn't like him."

"True, but there's a long distance between dislike and murder."

Silence fell around the table as we ate the tasty chicken flavored with herbs, egg noodles dripping with butter, and spring peas, all served with a side of root vegetables. I noticed the three young men enjoyed their meals. The rest of us picked at ours. I didn't know about anyone else, but the atmosphere, both at the table and in the country, was wearing on my nerves.

We finished the meal with cheese and coffee. As soon as we were halfway done, Katrine said to me, "Shall we question the servants?"

When we rose, the men all rose with us and then sat back to finish their coffee in peace. I hoped Christiansen would use this opportunity to ask pointed questions.

Katrine and I went into the kitchen, where the staff had finished their meals. The scullery maid ignored us as she went to work on the dishes, not a problem since I was certain she wouldn't know anything, and I faced the housekeeper.

"Mrs. Ulriksen, we have permission from your employers to ask all of you some questions about what happened here earlier today," I told her.

"But Mr. Braun died at the institute."

"It's possible someone slipped the poison to him here during lunch. Before they went back to the institute."

Mrs. Ulriksen said something in Danish to a tall, beefy woman with muscular arms while Katrine smirked. The woman came over and, without saying a word I could understand, made clear she was cursing me.

Katrine laughed aloud.

"Is she the cook?" I asked.

"Yes," Mrs. Ulriksen said.

"Tell her if anything had been wrong with her cooking, we'd all be dead. I suspect someone added something to Braun's coffee cup at the end of the meal."

The message was translated for her. She barked something at me and walked off. I doubted it was an apology.

"Is the way I saw today the way the coffee is always served at lunchtime?" I asked.

"Whoever comes over from the institute serves themselves from the big urn. I wheel it in from the kitchen. The cups and saucers are set out on the cart at the same time as the table is laid for lunch," Mrs. Ulriksen told me.

"Did you notice anyone fixing anyone else's coffee?"

"I fixed Dr. Jørgensen's and Katrine's coffee, but they are still alive. You, Mrs. Nilsen, and Mrs. Jørgensen had tea, which was brought to you. I didn't notice anyone else. I left."

I glanced around the room. There were two men, gardeners, I suspected, and six women including Mrs.

Ulriksen, the cook, and the scullery maid. The two men said something to Mrs. Ulriksen and walked out of the kitchen.

"They are outdoor staff. They wouldn't have seen anything," she told me.

"Did they see anyone drop anything between here and the institute? Perhaps in a flower bed? And did they see anyone outside arguing in the last day or so?"

"I will ask them at breakfast," she assured me.

"How about you ladies? Did you see anyone fixing anyone else's coffee?" I asked the maids standing and staring at me the entire time I spoke with Mrs. Ulriksen.

The housekeeper translated, and all three shook their heads.

"Did they overhear any arguments in the last day or so?" I asked.

Again, the question was translated. While they all shook their heads, one of them, a pretty brunette, gazed at me with frightened eyes. I'd have to try to speak to her when Katrine and Mrs. Ulriksen weren't able to hear what she had to say.

Who could I use as a translator? Ailsa Jørgensen? Mike Christiansen?

"How did Greta get along with Braun?"

"The way she got along with all men. Too well," Mrs. Ulriksen said. She sounded disgusted. Oddly, much more so than Mrs. Jørgensen. Was that because Mrs. Jørgensen had hoped Greta would break up the romance between

Braun and Katrine?

"Do any of you speak English?" I asked and received blank stares.

I asked in German, and a chunky blonde answered me. A few questions in that language told me that the maid, Anna, could get by but wasn't fluent in German.

Katrine left the kitchen, shaking her head and muttering something in Danish that I guessed was *What a waste of time.*

Then I tried French. The dark-haired girl, Michelle, answered me in fluent and rapid speech. "I'm Mme. Jørgensen's maid. She wanted a French maid, but it needed to be someone who could help an invalid. I've had some hospital training in moving patients and massage. A nursing assistant, if you like."

"Why a French maid?" I asked.

"She wanted to practice the language."

"Couldn't she practice with Porteur? He's French, isn't he?"

Michelle laughed. "He has a terrible accent. His parents, and maybe he, are from Poland. Porteur is fluent, though, so he must have been young when he arrived in France."

The others, bored with words they didn't understand, left or went about their duties.

"Do you speak French with him often?"

"He is supposed to stay at the institute except at mealtime, well, all the chemists are, and I am to take care of Madame. We seldom see each other."

I had to smile at that. Her protests were too insistent. "Unless you make plans to see one another."

She blushed, bringing a rosy color to her cheeks and making her even prettier despite her drab dress.

"What did you really want to tell me?" I asked, continuing in French.

"Mademoiselle and her beau had a blazing row this morning after breakfast, and it wasn't the first one I've heard in the past few days. This morning she said she was going to leave with her parents and he could have his rank and honors for all the good it would do him."

Chapter Thirteen

"That must have been something to hear. What language did they fight in?" I asked Michelle, Mrs. Jørgensen's lady's maid.

"German. I don't admit to knowing it, but I do understand it."

"The argument was this morning?" That would have been when I heard a part of a fight between Katrine and Braun about getting married. "What started it?"

"Katrine wanted to get married today. Immediately. Braun refused. He said he'd be busy because of the invasion and she'd have to wait. Little Miss Delightful doesn't like to wait for anything she wants. It went downhill from there."

"She mentioned his rank? Do you know what she meant?" I suspected Braun would receive an army rank when the Germans came across the border, and Katrine somehow found out.

Perhaps he bragged about it. Perhaps that would be his reward for keeping a Nobel Prize winning chemist at home in Denmark during the invasion.

"I don't know, but I know Porteur has his suspicions," the maid continued in French.

"You discussed this with him?"

"Of course. He needs to get out of here before we are invaded. Porteur is Jewish." Michelle's eyes widened and a pleading tone came into her voice.

"Does he want to go back to France? Do you?"

"He wants to go to Great Britain and continue the work on synthetic rubber. I want to go as Madame's maid and assistant."

"How does Monsieur Jørgensen feel about having Porteur as his assistant?" I asked.

"I don't know. I know little about what happens at the institute."

"So you don't know if Friedrich Braun and Porteur had any disagreements lately?" And would she admit it if she knew?

"Friedrich had disagreements with everyone, especially after we learned the Germans announced they would be arriving on Tuesday. He was difficult enough before, afterward he was terrible. He even…" Michelle stopped, blushing.

"What happened?"

"What do you think?" She shuddered, rubbing her hands up and down her arms. "Monsieur caught him twice, once with me, and told him off."

"How did Braun react to being scolded by his boss?"

"He told Monsieur that after Tuesday he would no longer be in charge. And then the swine just walked off." She shook her head. "I want to leave here. Get away from these people."

"Did Mademoiselle know?" And did this knowledge lead to Katrine's fight with Braun?

"I don't know. I wouldn't dare tell her."

"Would his bad behavior lead to someone killing him? Either the girl or her beau?" I gave her a wide-eyed stare, thinking of her and Porteur.

Michelle turned her dark eyes to stare at me. "Or his fiancée or her father?"

"Would it?" I pressed.

She gave me a Gallic shrug. "I don't know. I certainly didn't. Neither did Porteur."

"So Porteur is your beau." I had confirmation now.

"He is a friend." She gave me a look that said she found me slow-witted. "The only Frenchman in this village."

"Any other arguments with the deceased?"

"Not that I know of, but that German seemed ready to fight with anyone. You'll have to ask someone who moves around more. I am almost always with Madame." She gave me a smile and walked off.

I found I was alone in the kitchen. With a sigh, I wandered back to the main hall, and then heard voices coming through a closed door. I knocked and walked in.

The room was cozy with a fire burning. Overstuffed chairs were covered in a fabric with large pink flowers next to a massive sofa in deep green. Bookshelves lined the walls in dark paneling filled with leather-bound tomes. A thick carpet lay on the floor with a pink and green pattern over dark brown. And the air was thick with tension.

Mike Christiansen sat in one of the chairs, leaning forward, making his point with a hand gesture frozen in midair. Dr. Jørgensen sat across from him, leaning back, pale and frowning. Andersen also leaned forward from his position on the sofa, appearing ready to leap into the conversation as soon as Christiansen stopped talking.

They all turned and looked at me, slightly rising from their seats as all well-bred men would do.

"Please, sit," I said in German, giving the well-bred reply I had been taught to this chivalrous action. I sat on a spare chair and asked, "Are we any further forward in finding Braun's killer?"

All three shook their heads.

"Andersen, were you the one I heard arguing with Braun shortly after lunch yesterday? And if you were, what is the secret he was keeping from Dr. Jørgensen and Katrine?" I asked.

He jerked backward. "I don't think so, but I can imagine what the secret was. We all knew. Or suspected." He leaned back on the sofa and crossed his arms over his chest, glancing once at Jørgensen before looking away.

"Andersen, what is it?" Dr. Jørgensen asked.

"Braun had been in the employ of the Germans for quite some time. How do you think he was paying for the flat he keeps in Copenhagen? Or the jewelry he was buying for someone who is not your daughter?"

"He has a kept woman?" Dr. Jørgensen, who'd always

seemed so calm before, now thundered.

Andersen shrank back, but then took a deep breath and straightened his shoulders. "The rest of us compared notes from time to time. Then one weekend in January, Porteur followed Braun into Copenhagen on the train and then directly to his flat. Apparently, it wasn't hard. He waited outside, and soon Friedrich Braun came out with a buxom blonde in a fur and expensive bracelets."

"You've been jealous of Braun since he stole Katrine away from you," Jørgensen said.

"I wasn't the one who followed him. Ask Porteur if you want to know the truth. If you want all the sordid details." Andersen sounded disgusted.

"That doesn't mean he bought them for her or that he was paying for the flat. She could be a relative. She could be anyone." Dr. Jørgensen scowled at Andersen.

The younger man sighed and shifted uncomfortably in his seat. "Porteur was thorough. After they left, he went to the concierge and asked which flat was Herr Braun's. She replied that Herr and Frau Braun live in 3B."

"Do you know the street address?" I asked.

"Of course. We all learned it from Porteur." Andersen recited an address.

"That's in central Copenhagen not far from Tivoli and the central train station," Christiansen told me. "It's a nice neighborhood."

"We need to tell the police," I said.

"Absolutely not," Christiansen said. "They will find it a

reason for Dr. Jørgensen or Katrine to have killed Braun and then we won't be able to get them, or us, out of here."

"I wonder how much of this Katrine knows?" I asked.

"You will not distress my daughter any further." Jørgensen was definitely giving us orders.

That I couldn't allow. "Dr. Jørgensen, Katrine was heard this morning after breakfast arguing with Friedrich Braun. She said she would leave with you and Mrs. Jørgensen and he could keep his rank and honors."

I watched the scientist scowl as I spoke before he looked surprised. Then he smiled. "She said she is going with us?"

"This morning, yes."

"So all we need to do is find the murderer. Good." Dr. Jørgensen smiled and rose from his chair. "I will leave that task with you young people. Good night."

We rose when he did and waited until he left the room before dropping back into our seats.

"All we have to do," Christiansen said and gave me a grim smile.

"I think we should visit Mrs. Braun in the morning. At least we can learn the truth about her relationship with Braun and maybe where he found the money to pay for the flat." I looked at Christiansen.

"You want me to go along?" he asked.

"In case all she speaks is Danish." I was the only one with that handicap. "It was you, wasn't it, Andersen, who had the argument with Friedrich Braun? Dr. Jørgensen isn't here now. Please tell me the truth."

"Yes, I had an argument with Fritz Braun shortly after lunch both yesterday and today, but today I wasn't the only one. I practically had to stand in line."

"Who else did he fight with?"

"First there was Porteur, and Fritz started it. We'd just returned to the institute when Nilsen said, 'The Germans aren't really invading, are they? We're neutral.'"

Andersen rose and began to pace. "Fritz passed Porteur in the hall as he said, 'You'd better be gone before Wednesday, Jew.' Porteur jumped Fritz. Nilsen and I pulled him off."

"Was that the end of it?" Christiansen said.

"Braun went into his lab whistling, and Beck followed him in. Beck tried to give him a lecture on how we are all scientists and politics has no room in the pursuit of science. Before he was anywhere near finished, Fritz was already laughing in his face." Andersen shook his head at the memory and continued to pace about the room.

"And then?"

"Beck does not believe in violence. He stormed out of the lab, cursing. And then I went in."

"What was the first thing you said to him?" I asked.

"I told him we all knew about Mrs. Braun in flat 3B, and why didn't he let Katrine go with her parents. Her mother was desperate for her to go with them."

"And what was his reaction?" I asked.

"Fritz was always Fritz. He laughed. I admit at that

moment I wanted to kill him, but I didn't." Andersen clenched and unclenched his fists.

"What was Braun's plan?" I asked.

"Oh, I got the full Fritz explanation. He, as a representative of the master race, would ensure that Jørgensen stayed to do German research while Fritz, with an army rank, would be in charge of the facility. And all he had to do to keep Jørgensen here was to keep his daughter, keep Katrine, attached to him until Tuesday."

"He was using her," Christiansen said.

"He was a monster. I wish I had killed him. Fortunately, somebody beat me to it," Andersen replied, curling his hands into fists.

"How long did all this take? From the time you returned to the institute through Braun's arguments with Porteur, Beck, and you?"

"Not long. The fight with Porteur took maybe thirty seconds. The argument with Beck maybe two minutes, and then another two or three with me. Why?"

"Cyanide works very quickly," I told him. "You know that. Unless its absorption is slowed by digestion. What was the last thing Braun said or did before you left his lab?"

"He was so angry he kicked over a metal stool. I think he was trying to frighten me," Andersen said. He looked down at his fists and opened them.

"That may have been his initial reaction to the poison," Mike said. "What did he do next?"

"I don't know. I left. I fled. I didn't want to hear any more."

"You're still in love with Katrine," I told Andersen.

Andersen and Christiansen both glared at me.

"Even if this had been the beginning of his fatal attack, though, this doesn't tell us who killed Braun," Christiansen said, ignoring my comment. "Everyone had access to the poison."

"Everyone had coffee after lunch today," I said. "Except those of us who had tea."

"I thought the poison was in one of the cups in the attic coffee room," Andersen said, looking from one of us to the other.

"The police should know by morning, but I bet Braun was poisoned here, in the dining room, at the end of lunch. Where he sat next to Katrine for the entire meal," Christiansen said and shook his head. "And Katrine knows where everything is in the storeroom at the institute."

Wonderful. If the police detained Katrine, we'd never get any of the Jørgensens out of Denmark.

Chapter Fourteen

"Do you think when he kicked over the metal stool is when Braun started showing symptoms of poisoning?" I asked Mike.

"I think he was all right when I left, and that was maybe five or six minutes, certainly no more, after we left the Jørgensens," Andersen answered. He dropped into a chair. "I calmed down enough to return about ten or fifteen minutes later to ask him about the formula for pressure on explosives, and he was lying on the floor. I tried to find a pulse or whether he was breathing and then I shouted for help."

"Kicking the stool could well have been the first signs of poisoning, but it would have already been too late," Mike said. "Who came first when you called for help?"

"Beck or Porteur. I'm not sure which. Klimek next, but he ran out to call for an ambulance. Then you came in with Nilsen, followed by Berde. Then Mrs. Redmond. After that, there seemed to be people rushing in and out."

"If you were to guess, who do you think killed Braun?" Christiansen asked.

"I have no idea. I know I seem to be your favorite suspect, but I didn't kill him."

"You were the last one we know of who was with the

victim before he died, and you were the first one to find the body," I said.

"I didn't kill him." Andersen raised his voice as if that would make me more likely to believe him. Then he sank into the chair more as he said, "He didn't trust me. He wouldn't have taken anything laced with cyanide from me."

"And I don't see how or why you would have killed Greta, and I think the same person murdered them both," I told him.

"It doesn't make sense that we'd have two killers loose at the institute at the same time," Mike said.

"I'm not sorry he's dead, but..." After his initial display of relief, Andersen shook his head. "It wasn't me. I didn't have the nerve, if you want me to be honest. If it were anyone else as victim, my bet would be on Fritz Braun as the killer."

"He was the only one to have, what, the determination?" I asked.

"It was more than that. Fritz was not only wild enough, but conceited enough, to try anything. He believed he was the only person whose feelings mattered."

I heard a telephone ring somewhere, and a moment later, the maid Lise came in and said Mr. Nilsen wanted to talk to Mr. Christiansen. Mike, or Mikkel as I had learned he was called in Denmark, went out to take the call and I sat waiting with Henrik Andersen.

Christiansen came in a few minutes later and said, "We've been invited to the Nilsens' cottage tonight. I didn't mention you, Andersen. But if you'd like to come along...?"

"No. If you're going to do your job, you don't need me in your way all the time." Andersen rose and the three of us left together, bundled up in coats and hats and gloves. Andersen went to his quarters in the institute and Christiansen and I followed the smaller path to the side of the main house.

I studied the Nilsens' cottage more closely than I had the day before when Thyra was hanging laundry. The brick building was definitely a cottage, a small building with perhaps four small rooms on the ground floor and another two under the eaves on the first floor judging by the light from various windows.

When we entered, I saw the furniture in the drawing room was well stuffed but sagging. We took seats on the sofa and Mrs. Nilsen brought out some small smørrebrød, some slices of cake, and plates while Mr. Nilsen handed us glasses of beer.

Mrs. Nilsen said to call her Thyra. She and I discussed food and cottages until Mr. Nilsen said, "It seems important you learn from everyone where we were and how we got on with Braun. What do you want to know?" Fortunately, they both spoke excellent German.

"Everything," Christiansen said.

"I was at the luncheon yesterday with Thyra. You

know that. I went to the institute with everyone else. I didn't notice that Braun was ill at that time. I went into Dr. Jorgensen's laboratory with you and then we left there for my own laboratory until we heard shouting about Braun. We hurried out and followed the voices," Peder Nilsen said.

"Did Braun go to Dr. Jørgensen's laboratory with you?" I asked. No one had mentioned him there.

"I didn't see him," Nilsen said. "You?"

"No," Mike said. "We were only in there a few minutes. Could he have already been dead?" We looked at each other, and I suspected he wondered the same thing I was thinking. *Had the politi realized this?*

"Are you friends with Katrine Jørgensen?" I asked Thyra.

"We're both Danish, university educated, and about the same age. That said, we have nothing in common. Katrine is still a child. Of course, I think it is her parents who keep her childlike."

"Did she really love Braun?"

"Who knows?" Thyra replied with a shrug.

"Thyra," Nilsen said. "She must have loved him. You make her sound so shallow."

"Well, I think she is." Thyra gave me a smile aimed at making me a part of the "Katrine is a child" clique.

I wasn't certain I agreed, but I decided to keep my own counsel for the moment.

"Katrine wasn't the only woman Braun was

romancing," Thyra told me.

"Thyra." Her husband growled out her name.

"There were two or three others I suspected," his wife said. "Besides his wife."

"How did Braun find the time to woo all these ladies?" I asked.

"Rather than being a dedicated scientist, Braun believed in working a standard work day and then leaving to carry out his own pursuits. If he hadn't been killed, he would have left mid-afternoon today to spend time with his, ah, wife until Sunday night or early Monday morning," Nilsen said.

"And somehow he always talked Andersen into doing all his Sunday experiment readings for him," Mrs. Nilsen said over the rim of her beer glass.

"Henrik's a nice guy. I imagine he never learned how to say 'No.'" Her husband's blue eyes narrowed as he looked at her. The same look I'd seen when my father tried to warn me without words to keep quiet.

"Oh, Peder, don't be silly. How many times did he leave Andersen to do his work on Wednesday evenings while he picked up a trinket for that slut at the house and afterward while he took her to some hidden place at the institute for an hour of fun?"

"Well…" Peder Nilsen looked uncomfortable. Then he brightened. "At least he only used Beck a couple of times to cover for him when he and Inge…" Realizing where this conversation was heading, he reddened and fell silent.

My eyes and mouth must have been round with shock. Even I knew Inge was Mrs. Beck.

Thyra Nilsen seethed with righteous fury. "Braun used the husband to take care of his experiments while he seduced the wife? How awful." Then she turned her attention from her husband to me. "Oh, Livvy, even I never suspected things were that bad."

Christiansen looked at Nilsen. "Things weren't nearly this exciting when I lived here as a student."

I shot a quelling look at Mike. "How did Mrs. Beck feel about Braun?" I asked.

"She's terrified of him," Thyra and Nilsen answered in unison.

"Then why...?"

"Because he could. And because Inge was too frightened to say anything to her husband. Apparently, Braun told her if Beck tried to do anything about it, he, Braun, would get Beck fired," Thyra told me.

"What a horrible person." It would be hard to find Braun's killer because there were too many good candidates.

"I thought Andersen was a good friend of Katrine's," Mike said.

"He was and is."

"Then why would Andersen make it easier for Braun to cheat on his good friend?" If Mike hadn't asked, I would have.

"Maybe he hoped Katrine would find out and pay

attention to him when she dropped Braun," Thyra Nilsen said.

"But Andersen was making it easier for Braun so he wouldn't get caught. If he slipped out and didn't do his work, wouldn't Dr. Jørgensen want to know why? Especially since it seemed to have happened frequently," I said. There was something very wrong here, with so many people bullied and abused by Braun under the nose of Dr. Jørgensen.

And Katrine.

"Jørgensen would definitely want to know why someone wasn't taking care of their experiments or writing up their results. That's the reason we're here," Nilsen said.

"And with Braun, sneaking out was at least a weekly occurrence," Mrs. Nilsen said, her lips thinned in disapproval. "In fact, it was almost daily."

"Dr. Jørgensen never caught on?"

"Henrik Andersen made sure he didn't," Nilsen said.

"Why would he do that?" I asked.

"You'll have to ask him. And that's all I'm going to say on the matter. Thyra, may I have another piece of your wonderful cake?" Nilsen said, closing down the conversation on Braun's misdeeds.

There was a knock on the door and Nilsen went to answer it. "It will be the Becks. I hope you don't mind, but they may be able to help solve this mystery so we can all get away from the Nazis in time," Thyra said. "Of course, when I invited them I didn't know..."

I had met Beck before, but I had never seen his wife. She was breathtakingly beautiful in the Midnight Sun, pale blonde style, trim, with wide blue eyes, and, when she took off her coat, a magnificent figure. I thought Christiansen would fall out of his chair before he came to his feet.

"This is my wife, Inge," Beck said.

Inge murmured her greetings. Within five minutes, it was obvious the Swedish woman was shy, spoke little German or Danish, and was terribly frightened.

What was she frightened of? That we knew her terrible secret with Braun?

"Beck," I asked, "did you think Braun would marry Katrine or would he continue to play the field after the German invasion?"

"They really are coming?"

Christiansen and I both nodded.

Beck said something to his wife, who reached out and grabbed his hand. The others seemed to understand what he said, and then Christiansen mouthed "Swedish" to me.

"Oh, I think Braun would have done both if he could. I believed Porteur when he said Braun was married already, and you saw it didn't stop Braun from promising to marry Katrine. He would do anything." Beck's face reddened as his tone turned bitter.

"You hated him," I asked quietly. *And you knew. You must have.*

"Yes." Then he looked around the room. "I didn't kill him." Then he switched from German to what must have been Swedish and faced his wife. I guessed he again denied killing Braun or maybe he admitted hating him.

Inge burst into tears, murmuring something. Then she jumped up from where she sat, pulled on her coat, and dashed out the door, her husband putting an arm through a sleeve of his coat as he ran out after her.

Nilsen shut the door after them and returned to the drawing room, staring at his wife.

"Oh, my," Thyra said.

"I'm sorry," I told her. "I seem to have upset them and ruined your party."

"I hadn't suspected Braun had used Beck to make it possible to terrorize Inge," Thyra said. "How awful."

"You have to find out who killed Braun if we're all to get out of here before Tuesday," Nilsen said. "The politi don't show any sign of finding the murderer."

We kept up another quarter hour of small talk, posing questions and theories, but the Becks didn't return and the Nilsens didn't say anything else that would help us.

At the end, we gave up and said good night. Outside, I asked Christiansen, "What did Inge say before she ran out of the house?"

"That she was sorry. That it was her fault."

"Was she saying she killed Braun?" She seemed so innocent. So frightened. So devastated.

In the faint light along the path, I saw Mike shake his

head. "No, she was apologizing to her husband for her actions. She wasn't talking about murder."

Once we reached the house, Christiansen went off to the institute to go to his quarters. Mrs. Ulriksen let me in, telling me how glad she was that she could finally lock up for the night and go to bed, and I came inside and then went upstairs through the cold hallways.

I got a shock when I walked into my room and found Katrine sitting on my bed. The bedside table lamp was on and a cheery fire burned, warming the room.

She stared at me, looking pale, but her eyes were dry. Fortunately, she spoke in English. "My father tells me I had a close escape with Friedrich dying. That I should be relieved to go to England with him and Mother. And that you will find out who killed Friedrich."

Kicking off my shoes, I said, "I'm certainly going to try to find the killer. I have no desire to be trapped under Nazi rule. We are at war with them, and I want to go home."

"It must be difficult, not speaking our language or having any family here." Katrine spoke softly as she watched me.

"Yes. Being trapped here with no money, no job, and no home for the duration of the war is not appealing." I smiled and admitted, "I like to eat."

She smiled in return. "Will your government take good care of my parents?"

"Of course." I had to ask. "How long has your mother been ill?"

"It started when my little brother came down with a terrible case of influenza. It was 1934. He was ten. I was sixteen."

I waited, hoping she'd say more without my having to prompt her.

After a minute, she continued. "When he died, my mother lay down on her bed and said she couldn't rise again. She went to his funeral in a wheeled chair and she's been in one ever since. The doctors can't explain it. They come up with new theories every year, but nothing that gives us any hope or a new treatment that works." Katrine looked at me and sighed. "Do you know how hard it is not to know? To live without hope?"

"She must rely on you a great deal," I answered.

"I wish she didn't. I want a life that doesn't revolve around my mother and her needs. That's what made Fritz so appealing. Running off with him meant not being there to answer my mother's shouts and demands."

"Is she completely paralyzed?"

Katrine gave a small snort. "I bet she's not. I bet she's not really paralyzed at all. She just wants everyone to be at her call, waiting on her day and night. Paying attention to her, as if she's a queen or something. Therefore, the wheeled chair."

She sounded so bitter. "Your parents will be going to Cambridge. There are plenty of opportunities for you to work or to study and to have a life of your own there without being in conflict with your parents," I suggested. I wanted to give her a measure of hope.

"I've tried. Whenever I have anything important, well, important to me to do, my mother has something only I can do for her. I'm told I shouldn't be selfish. Me, selfish. She should look in the mirror." She sounded glum.

"What about Michelle?"

"Suddenly, something can't be done by Michelle and must be done by me and me alone. She is apologetic, she is all charm and sweetness, but it means I can't carry on with my plans." Her shoulders slumped as if they held the weight of drudgery.

"How about a position at your embassy? War work? Charity work? Something in London. I have no idea what you're interested in."

"Art."

"Of course. Why not?" I was trying to make England sound inviting. Why did I get the feeling I was failing?

She hung her head. "My father calls it a waste of time. He says I'm not dedicated enough, while my mother calls me ungrateful."

"From what little I've seen, you seem to be able to convince your parents to go along with anything you want."

"Ha. My father seemed quite cheerful just now. He told me everything was fine, and for me not to worry about the future." She stared at me. "He's taken to patting my head as if I were a child. I'm not a child, Olivia. I want the truth, no matter how unpleasant. Will you tell me everything you find out about Friedrich and his life and why he was killed?"

"Wouldn't you rather keep your memories intact?"

Her stare turned hard. "I want the truth. I don't want to be left wondering. No one else will treat me as if I were an adult."

"I don't know the truth yet, but I hope to get confirmation tomorrow morning. Will you still want to hear the truth then?" I suspected how painful that knowledge would be.

"Yes."

And once I told her, she'd probably blame me.

Chapter Fifteen

The next morning, Mike Christiansen must have come over for breakfast before I was bathed, dressed, and downstairs. He was plowing through eggs, toast, coffee, and an apple when I entered the dining room, while Porteur, an empty plate and cup in front of him, was just rising.

"Good morning," Porteur said in German. "I am off to the laboratory. It's my day to watch all the experiments."

"Do you each take a day?" I asked.

"Not every day, but we each take a Sunday in turn. Today is mine." He nodded and walked off.

Christiansen gestured to the sideboard. "Help yourself."

I did and then sat down to enjoy my breakfast. "When will we be able to get the first train into the city?"

"Before you were ready to catch it. It's already left," he added unnecessarily.

"I wish you'd have told me when they start running on a Sunday morning."

"I didn't realize you'd sleep all morning." He glared at me over his coffee cup.

"How was I to know what you expected of me?" I said. "I can't do anything about missing the first train, but we have to work together if we're going to get back to England safely."

"Don't be so sensitive. You obviously don't realize what a tight schedule we're on and how very important this is. Sleeping in is all right for you, but I wish Sir Malcolm would have chosen someone else," Mike growled in a disgusted tone. "Someone who understands chemistry and speaks Danish."

"I wish he had, too. Certainly someone who can speak the language and wouldn't need to rely on your translations. Or sending me off to rely on the translations of the housekeeper." I was as unhappy with him as he was with me. The strain of not knowing if we could leave that evening for England and relative safety was wearing on us. Now we were taking it out on each other.

His glare deepened with fury. "I haven't said anything that wasn't the correct translation. And what are you doing with a contact in the Abwehr?"

He must have meant Oberst Bernhard. "I don't…" I heard footsteps and fell silent.

Dr. Jørgensen walked into the room and gave us a smile. "Have you seen Porteur?" he asked in German, I imagined to include me.

"He's gone to the institute," Christiansen said in a flat voice.

"Good. Then I can stop for breakfast." He fixed himself a heaping plate and sat down to join us. "Any plans for this morning?"

Christiansen and I exchanged frosty glances.

"We'll head off once Mrs. Redmond is finally ready." He rose and left the room.

"Well, I'd better hurry." I gobbled down the last of my eggs and toast and gulped my still-hot coffee. "If you'll excuse me."

Jørgensen half rose from his chair as I hurried away. It took me two minutes to get my coat, hat, gloves, and bag and then to reach the front door. Looking out, I saw a policeman pick something out of the flower beds to the left of the door.

"What do you have there?" I asked in German when I reached him.

He hesitated for a moment before showing me what was in his gloved hand. It was a folded piece of paper with traces of colorless crystals stuck to the inside. There was no writing on it and the paper was still crisp. It couldn't have been sitting out all night, since it hadn't become limp from the dew.

"You found it just here?" I had to assume it was cyanide.

He nodded.

"I wonder why the killer waited so long to dispose of that." When the policeman looked at me blankly, I said, "It shows the poisoning was done here at the house during luncheon."

His response in Danish was undecipherable, except for "Politikommissar." The constable walked off toward another uniformed policeman that I guessed was his sergeant to show him his find.

Christiansen came up behind me. "Shall we go?"

We rode the train to the Central Station and then walked, Christiansen leading us to where we were going in silence. The building turned out to be five stories built of a gray stone with large windows to let in whatever light was available in this northern city.

The door to the main hallway was unlocked and we walked in. In front of us were the stairs with the concierge's flat to our left. Whoever the concierge was, they didn't check to see who had entered the building, so we climbed the stairs to 3B.

The woman who answered the door was chubby, rosy-cheeked, and blonde. She couldn't have been more than in her early twenties. She looked at us warily, as if wondering what we were selling.

"Mrs. Braun?" Christiansen asked in Danish. I could make out that much.

She nodded.

"Mrs. Friedrich Braun?"

Again, she nodded.

Christiansen said the wrong thing, because after a few words of Danish, she began to beat on his chest with her fists.

"Frau Braun," I said in German, "haven't the police notified you of your husband's death?"

She shook her head as she bent over, sobbing. I put

an arm around her and led her inside to the drawing room. It was small but cozy and well-furnished with high ceilings. Most of the newspapers and magazines on the end table were in German.

I sat both of us on the sofa, and Christiansen sat on a chair across from us, out of range of her fists. "How long have you been married?" I began.

"Six months. We married the last time Fritz was home and then I came back here with him." She told us this between sobs and wiping of her eyes and nose.

"Why didn't he tell the institute formally that he'd married?"

"He didn't want to lose his position at the institute, and he only has a few more months before his experiments will be completed." She paused as if she had something more to add, but then she clamped her mouth shut.

"Did he think he would be let go if he married?" I asked.

"Of course. The rule was, only single men worked there."

As she wiped her tears again, Christiansen and I exchanged glances. I gave him a brief shake of my head to warn him not to tell her that wasn't true.

"You need to get in touch with the Copenhagen police. They don't know about you, and I know they'll want to talk to you," I said.

"How did you find me?" she asked, her eyes

narrowing.

"Mr. Braun confided in his colleagues."

"Did he get into trouble? Is that what killed him?" She burst into a new volley of sobs.

"No, they were discreet until after he died." She looked so innocent I had to ask, "Do you have any family around here?"

"No. They're all home in Germany. In Munich."

Christiansen rose and said in English, "I'll call the police from the concierge's flat." He left, shutting the door behind him.

For lack of anything better to ask, I said, "Would you like a cup of tea?"

She shook her head. "There's some coffee in the kitchen. It'll need to be reheated."

"Of course. Why don't we do that?"

There was a small table and two chairs in the small kitchen, squeezed in by a glass-fronted cupboard and not far from the stove. I began to reheat the coffee while Mrs. Braun sank into a chair.

"What's your name?" I asked.

"Mrs. Braun." She looked at me as if I'd lost my mind.

"No." I smiled. "Your Christian name."

She smiled in return. "Annemarie."

"I'm Olivia. Cups?" I asked, looking at the large cupboard.

She pointed. "Are you married?"

"Yes." I decided on telling her because maybe I could

give her a little hope for the future. "Second time. My first husband was murdered when I was twenty-six."

"Good grief."

Fortunately, no one had mentioned murder in her husband's case. That shock was yet to come. "Where did you meet him?" I asked.

"My family and his have always been friendly. I guess I've known him all my life. And when I found out I was..." She lowered her head.

I poured the coffee and brought both cups to the table. She put sugar in hers. "Where is the baby?"

"I lost it a month after the wedding."

Friedrich had to marry her. Would he have stayed with her once he took over the institute, or would he have sent her back to Germany and married Katrine? Either way, someone would have been hurt, and it wouldn't have been Friedrich Braun.

"Tell me about your husband."

"He was brilliant. He'd always received the top marks in school and then in university. Once he had his doctorate, he had offers to go to several institutes and companies. I'd hoped he'd stay in Germany, but someone decided he should come here."

"Who decided? His family? His professors?"

"The Party. They had plans for him to take over the institute here." Her face beamed with pride.

"When?"

"Soon." She looked startled, then fumbled for an

answer. "I guess. Perhaps when he finished his two years here."

"We know the German army will attack on Tuesday," I told her.

"You do?" She sounded astonished.

Did Braun tell her nothing? "Admiral Canaris told both the Danish and Norwegian governments last Thursday that they are invading on Tuesday. Since Fritz is dead, will you return home or stay here?"

Her face crumpled. "I don't know. I don't know what to do."

"You don't have to make up your mind immediately. That's the nice thing about being suddenly widowed. People are kind." I had found them to be that way. Except my father.

But he was always the exception.

I heard the door to the flat open and several sets of footsteps enter. "Mrs. Braun," I heard Christiansen's voice call out in German.

Then another voice called out in Danish. "Politi."

"We're in here," I called out in German.

Christiansen crowded into the small kitchen followed by Inspector Larsen and Sergeant Behr taking up the rest of the space.

"It's true, then?" Annemarie Braun said in German. "Friedrich is dead?"

Larsen frowned at me before he told the young widow she needed to show them her wedding license. She rose from the table and trudged into the bedroom, returning a minute later with the paper marking Annemarie Bernberg's marriage to Friedrich Braun, dated the preceding September.

Larsen then said something in Danish, which Christiansen translated for me as "Go back to the institute and wait for me there."

I wished Annemarie good luck in whatever she decided to do and then left with Christiansen. On the way back to the Central Station, I looked around, knowing if our plans worked out, this was the last I'd see of Copenhagen for a long time.

But to leave Copenhagen, we'd have to find a killer, and I still had no idea who had caused Braun's death.

There was no one sitting nearby on the train, so I asked Christiansen in English if he had any idea who we were looking for.

"I was hoping you learned something useful from the widow."

"I learned Braun had his choice of places to go after he was awarded his doctorate, and it was the Nazi Party that decided where he would go. Annemarie had hoped for somewhere inside Germany."

"It makes sense if the Nazis told him which job to take, then they would be paying him. What I don't understand is why he married the girl if he was making a big play for Katrine?"

"Their families had known each other forever, and she

was with child. He told her he had to be single to work at the institute, so they kept the marriage a secret although he brought her to Copenhagen."

"And the baby?"

"Lost it." Poor girl, alone in a strange country. Trapped in Denmark, I understood her feelings of isolation.

"I'd be less surprised if the wife, or rather, the widow, was the one murdered. Then Fritz Braun would have been free to marry Katrine," Christiansen said.

"Maybe he had no intention of marrying Katrine," I said with my eyebrows raised. "The Nazis had promised him the directorship without any need to marry her. And if her parents weren't here…"

A shake of the carriage as the train hit a bump in the rails punctuated my words.

Christiansen nodded. "He'd already found a compliant bride. He didn't tell anyone about her, and she stayed dutifully quiet."

"Katrine would never be docile," I said, remembering the times I'd seen her complaining in full voice. "I wonder if she knew about Mrs. Braun."

"A good reason for murder, but I think if she'd known, we'd all have heard the result. Screams and explosions. She'd probably have used an axe." Christiansen tried to hide his smile.

"You're right. Poison is not her style." But whose style was it, I wondered. "If this is about Braun being married, Beck and Nilsen wouldn't care. They are already married, plus Beck is Swedish. He could just take his family home if the Germans take over."

"Porteur has no interest in Katrine, but Andersen has been giving her puppy-dog eyes. This is his third year here, and the other men think he stayed an extra year so he can remain close to Katrine," Christiansen said, "even though he doesn't stand a chance."

"Katrine and her parents are the ones most affected by Braun being married. While Katrine would have been furious, her parents would have rejoiced. And would have told Katrine immediately." I shook my head. "I don't see them as our killers. What else have you learned?"

"Porteur, because of his background, and Klimek would kill Braun as an act of war if they knew he was being paid by the Nazis. They're both angry about German occupation of their Polish homeland."

I stared at Christiansen. "So it all depends on who knew what. Dr. Jørgensen, Katrine, and Andersen might poison Braun because of his marriage and his shoddy treatment of Katrine, Beck might murder Braun for terrorizing his wife, and Porteur and Klimek might kill Braun because of their Polish background if they knew he was on the payroll of the Nazis." I looked out the window as we drew into the familiar institute stop. "And we're no closer to leaving here tonight than we were before."

"That would be no great loss," Christiansen said in a low voice, but I heard him, "if only we could keep Jørgensen's work from falling into Nazi hands."

"You speak the language and have family here. You have the advantage over me," I told him. "I need to leave here. Before Tuesday."

Chapter Sixteen

Mike gave me a hand up as the train came to a halt. "If it's only you who can leave, I'll get you on a flight back to England at Kastrup airport tomorrow morning. Don't worry."

"Thank you." I appreciated the offer. Mike Christiansen was being kind and so far I hadn't seen that side of him often.

When we entered the gates to the institute, I looked at the massive trees, the immaculate flower beds, the wide lawns, and sighed, imagining what terrible use the Nazis would make of this place. Mike Christiansen didn't spare me a glance as he headed directly to the institute. I walked on to the main house.

The housekeeper, Mrs. Ulriksen, sent me into the small drawing room off to the left as she took my coat and hat. I walked in to find Ailsa Jørgensen talking to a woman of her age or perhaps a little older. There was a great deal of gray in her dark hair and a cool considering expression in her dark eyes. She wore a fashionable hat, a fur stole, and expensive-looking jewelry.

I couldn't imagine why I was asked to come in to join them unless this woman had known my mother, too.

"Ah, Olivia. Sit down. I want you to meet Mrs.

Rothberg. Ruth, you remember Phyllida Harper. Do you see the resemblance in her daughter, Olivia?" Mrs. Jørgensen spoke in German.

"Yes, I do." She held out a well-manicured hand and I shook it. "Is it Miss Harper?"

I took a seat on one of the yellow upholstered chairs. "Olivia Redmond. My husband's a British army officer."

"Any children?"

"Not yet. We've been married less than a year." This woman sounded the same as my father, who was looking forward to a grandson, since I had, regrettably to him, been born a girl.

"Your mother was a good friend of Ailsa's, which is how I first met her. She was a very well-educated woman, very well read, and quite clever. She knew her own mind. I really liked her. I was sorry when Ailsa told me she died during the flu epidemic," Mrs. Rothberg said.

"I'm glad you have such good memories of her," I replied.

"I'm sorry I didn't stay in touch with your father after your mother died, but it would have been difficult. You were just a little girl. Ailsa and I have stayed in touch all these years, in part because my daughter Anne and Katrine were friends and schoolmates. They are a few years younger than you."

She smiled. "It was very nice of you to come visit Ailsa and I'm glad to have the chance to see you all grown up, but you may have chosen the wrong weekend to come here." I could hear the irony in her tone.

"I'd be on the ferry back to England tomorrow morning if the politi weren't holding me here, holding all of us actually, while they investigate the murders of the maid, Greta, and the German chemist, Herr Braun."

"Ah, yes. The pirate." After a slight pause, Mrs. Rothberg added, "I understand Ailsa will be traveling with you."

She was working toward something. I just wasn't certain what. "Yes," I replied. "I hope the seas aren't too rough. Otherwise, we should have a jolly journey."

"If I give Ailsa a package to deliver to my daughter who lives in London, will you help her deliver it?" she asked.

"Of course. All we have to do is figure out who killed Greta and Herr Braun and we'll be able to leave." I tried to make it sound less daunting than it was.

"If you're as clever as your mother, I'm sure you'll figure it out in no time," Mrs. Rothberg said.

"This package wouldn't be dangerous if found by the Nazis, would it?" I asked.

"No. They'd simply steal it." Mrs. Rothberg gave me a rueful smile. "We're speaking of heirloom jewelry that will rightfully go to my daughter someday. With the Nazis invading, there's no way of knowing what our position will be. We're Jewish, you see."

"Do you want to leave the country?" I asked.

"No. We get along well with our neighbors. If we have

to, we'll simply travel to Sweden for an extended stay. But this package is my daughter's legacy. It is valuable enough to tempt the Nazis, and I do not want that."

She rose. "I don't want to keep you from your investigation, and I must pack everything in a traveling case. I'll return late this afternoon. In the meantime, put on your thinking cap, Ailsa. You know these young men. You must have some idea who is most likely to be the killer."

She bent over Ailsa Jørgensen, kissed her cheek, and left, pulling on her gloves. She left the door to the drawing room ajar.

Mrs. Jørgensen looked at me with her eyebrows raised. "You've learned something, Olivia. What is it?"

"This is going to come as a shock."

"I doubt it," she said with a hint of a smile.

"Friedrich Braun was married. His wife lives in a flat in Copenhagen."

I turned to look behind me when I heard a gasp. Katrine stood in the doorway, one hand pressed against the gray and yellow wallpaper. "She was lying. Fritz told me about some girl from his hometown who followed him here. She had a terrible crush on him."

"I'm sorry. I've seen the marriage certificate," I told her.

"And she just told you, 'Hello, I'm Fritz's wife'?"

"At least some of the other chemists knew about her. They told me. I just confirmed their story."

Katrine strode into the room and faced me, her cheeks a vivid red. "Well, why didn't anyone see her here the same as we do Mrs. Nilsen or Mrs. Beck? They live here."

"Braun told her none of the chemists were allowed to be married while working here, so he had to keep their marriage a secret." I didn't add, *So no one would stop him from romancing you.*

Katrine let fly a burst of rapid Danish. If what she said matched her facial expression, it was a curse.

This was the woman who wanted to be treated as an adult and told whatever I learned. I had been right when I guessed that if I told her something she didn't like, it would be all my fault.

A baritone answered her in Danish. Inspector Larsen entered the room and barked what I guessed were orders as Sergeant Behr pulled out some papers. Katrine walked over and slammed herself into an overstuffed chair, and Ailsa Jørgensen appeared to graciously invite the policemen into her home.

I sat and waited to find out if I was needed, in a language I could understand. After a minute or two of Danish spoken loudly while Katrine looked through the proffered papers and then threw them on the rug in an expression of disgust, Larsen turned to me.

"You should have allowed me to tell Miss Jørgensen about Braun's wife," he said in German.

"I told Mrs. Jørgensen. Katrine came in behind me and

overheard what we'd learned."

"Any other surprises planned for us, Mrs. Redmond?" Larsen's tone was even more ironic than Mrs. Rothberg's.

"No. Any idea who the killer is, Inspector?"

"We'll find their murderer. Don't worry."

"If you don't find him in the next few hours and let us go, I have to face the army of a country at war with mine. They'll put me in a prison camp or shoot me by firing squad as an enemy of the Third Reich. I hope you don't want that on your conscience, Inspector Larsen."

"If it comes to that, I'll get you into Sweden myself, Mrs. Redmond. Now, I want to speak to your friend, Mr. Christiansen."

But what I want to do is go home. "He's at the institute. I'll get him."

I rose and walked away, heading out of the house without my coat into the bright, chilly spring air. The cold speeded my steps.

I found Christiansen talking in German to Beck in one of the labs. "He's the only one I was certain had a real hatred of Fritz," Beck was saying in German.

"Why?" I asked as I came in.

"Braun threatened Porteur with incarceration in a prison camp as soon as his friends arrived just because Porteur is Jewish."

"Would any of the rest of you turn Porteur in to the Germans?" Christiansen asked.

"Good grief, no."

"And Klimek?" I asked. "He's very angry about what happened, and is happening, to his country. Braun was outspoken about German superiority. I had the feeling Klimek hated Braun."

"That's been going on since last autumn. Why wait until now to kill him?" Beck replied.

"And perhaps if Braun had three women in love with him, he might have had a fourth. Have you heard anything about that?" I asked.

"No!" Beck slammed a metal clamp down on the workbench, took a deep breath, and said, "No. I've not heard anything about that. Now, if you don't mind, I need to concentrate on my experiments."

Christiansen and I left the laboratory before I told him the police wanted to speak to him.

"Again?" Mike Christiansen strode off, grumbling.

I was about to follow him when Henrik Andersen came out of another door while removing his laboratory coat. "Hello," I greeted him in German with a smile. "What are you working on?"

"I've wrapped up my work for the day, so I'm going to go over to see Dr. Jørgensen."

"And Katrine?"

"Well, uh…"

"Then be prepared. I told Mrs. Jørgensen about the existence of Braun's wife, whom I met this morning. Katrine overheard me."

Andersen closed his eyes and shook his head at my

last words. When he opened his very blue eyes and focused on me, he said, "Mrs. Beck and Mrs. Nilsen are having lunch today at the Jørgensens. This could be a painful lunch for everyone."

"It could. So, who hated Braun enough to kill him?"

"Hated him, many people. But enough to kill him? Most unlikely," Andersen replied.

"Someone did. What about Beck?" His reaction to my asking about a fourth woman in Braun's life had been strong and bitter.

"He didn't like Fritz flirting with his wife, Inge," Andersen said.

"'Flirting'?" I asked.

"Visiting Inge for an hour or two when Beck wasn't home," Andersen said, eyebrows raised. "It's time someone talked some sense into that girl."

"Inge? Or Katrine?"

Andersen glowered at me without answering.

He hung up his laboratory coat on a coat-tree in another room as I asked him, "Why did you cover for Braun so the Jørgensens wouldn't find out when he was seeing his wife or his girlfriends?"

His answer was to hurry downstairs with me rushing after him. He reached the Jørgensens' home in record time. Andersen snapped something in Danish at the maid, who said something in reply.

By the time I caught up to him, Andersen had entered the music room and stood facing Katrine. Whatever he'd said to her, she looked past him at me and said in German, "Oh, Henrik. Don't go passing on dirty gossip."

"It's about time you saw Braun for what he was," Andersen said.

"And what exactly is that?" Katrine demanded. I think she'd already forgotten I was there.

"Handsome, daring, smooth-talking, egotistical, vindictive, cruel. He really believed he was part of the master race. I know he hated me," Andersen replied.

"Why?" I asked. I probably shouldn't have broken into their conversation, but I really wanted to know.

"Because he knew I still love Katrine. If she found out what the rest of us knew, he'd lose her every bit as much as I have."

"I told you, Henrik, we're friends." Katrine lay a hand on Andersen's shoulder as if he were something more.

"Ah, friends. The kiss of death." Andersen busied his hands by pulling at his shirt cuffs.

Katrine gave a deep sigh and strolled to the door. Once there, she turned and said, "Just don't try to tell me what to do or what to think. There are enough people doing that already. Oh, and be on time for luncheon. Mother's orders."

"I was planning to be on time," Andersen grumbled. "I'm here, aren't I?"

"Luncheon will be set up the same as yesterday?" I asked.

"Just the same as yesterday," Katrine said and walked

into the hall, shutting the door.

"Was Braun afraid you'd tell Katrine about his wife and his other women?" I asked Andersen.

"Probably. I threatened to on Friday."

"Why?"

"We got into an argument. I didn't think he was treating Katrine fairly. He told me I was a bigger fool than Beck. Beck married a very beautiful woman, and Braun was focused on seducing her. Once he did, I suspect he was the one to call off the affair. His actions nearly broke both of the Becks' hearts. Everyone could see it but Katrine. Sometimes..."

He stood with his fists pressed on the back of a chair, staring at us. "I lost my temper and told him I'd tell Katrine everything. His wife, his affairs, his threats. He grabbed me by the lapels and told me he'd kill me. I think he meant it too. I avoided him the rest of the day, until his temper cooled off."

"Did his temper cool off quickly?"

"I think so. It doesn't make much sense to carry a grudge."

But was Braun a man who had sense? "And when it grew late? There were only the five of you sleeping in the institute, even with Mike Christiansen and Klimek living there. How could you avoid him then?" I asked.

"I locked my door and placed a chair under the door handle." Andersen shrugged. "Braun might still have been angry enough to do something, maybe pour a bucket of water on me as I slept. I wanted to avoid that possibility."

"Did he go in for those sorts of tricks?" I asked, disgusted.

"Only as a last resort. Or when he was certain no one could pay him back."

"Were you afraid he'd carry out his threat to kill you?" I stared into his eyes, trying to see the truth of whatever answer he'd give me.

"Of course not."

I kept staring.

"Well," he admitted, "he might have. Braun was bold enough to do something that would endanger others. Endanger anyone who would cross him."

That sounded closer to the truth. I told him, "He sounds too awful for words."

I nearly walked into Michelle when I left Andersen in the music room and walked down the hall. Seeing that no one was nearby, I quickly asked in French, "How often did Friedrich Braun try anything on with you out of sight of the Jørgensens?"

"Just the one time a few days ago. I fought back and Dr. Jørgensen came. Braun realized he wouldn't get very far."

"Anyone else he tried it on?"

"Yes. Greta. She wasn't too particular about who she granted favors to, as long as she liked their presents."

I raised my eyebrows and Michelle smiled. "What kind of presents?" I asked.

"Scarves, gloves, cheap jewelry, perfume. Bits of finery that she couldn't afford to buy for herself."

"Too bad we can't get her to admit it now."

"Oh, she would have admitted it, because it's true, and she didn't care who knew."

"How many people were aware of their arrangement?" If it had anything to do with Braun's murder, someone must know.

"I'm not sure. If Mrs. Ulriksen or Mrs. Jørgensen knew, they haven't said anything about it. I heard Dr. Jørgensen say something about it to Braun, who told him it meant nothing and there was no reason to make Katrine unhappy."

"What did Dr. Jørgensen say?"

"He said, 'One day you'll go too far, Braun, and someone will put a stop to your selfishness permanently.'"

"You have a good memory. When was this?"

"It doesn't take a good memory. It was last week."

Chapter Seventeen

I decided Andersen could hold the key to the murder, since he seemed to be closer to the Jørgensens than the rest of the chemists. Leaving Michelle, I walked back to the music room. I found him sitting on a straight-backed wooden chair, doing nothing, his hands hanging by his sides, staring at the far wall. "Why did you do it?"

He glanced up at me. "Kill Braun? I didn't. I might have wanted to, but I would never kill him. And he knew it. He was much braver than me."

"It doesn't take bravery to kill someone. It's much more difficult to deal with someone as cruel as Braun without resorting to violence."

He gave a snort. "No. It only takes fear."

"What were you afraid of?"

He was silent for so long I thought he wouldn't answer. Finally, he said, "I made a mistake in a calculation in a series of experiments. The mistake, which I didn't catch, made the results look better than they were. In itself, the error makes no difference and the product was unimportant, but this was the paper that convinced Dr. Jørgensen to take me on. If he knew, he'd throw me out in disgrace."

"You're certain he doesn't know?"

"He would tell me if he knew."

"But Braun knew?"

"I don't know how. Only three or four people ever read that paper. But he came to me and pointed out the error. I went back and checked, and he was correct."

"So, you made a mistake. Why...?"

He turned around in the chair and faced me, his tone now strong and defiant. "I'll tell you why. Because Braun promised to make a big deal out of how shoddy work was part of the institute's legacy. How it would reflect badly on Jørgensen. How he'd have to throw me out to save his reputation.

"I begged him not to. He agreed, if I'd undertake certain tasks for him."

"So not only were you doing your experiments, you were doing his two or three days a week while he saw his wife and his girlfriend and Katrine. That had to hurt."

"It did. And then we received word of the invasion on Thursday. By Friday, I'd had it with Braun and his master race and his secrets and lies. And you and Mikkel came to help the Jørgensens escape. That's when I told him I'd tell Katrine and Jørgensen about his wife."

"You knew about our true purpose in coming here?" So much for that secret.

"Mrs. Jørgensen told me."

Why had she done that? "And that's when he threatened to kill you?"

He nodded, hanging his head.

"And the next day, he was dead."

He raised his head and looked straight into my eyes. "But I didn't kill him. I couldn't. I haven't the nerve. And you certainly don't think I killed Greta. I had no reason to. Plus I'd never break into the Jørgensens' home."

I hoped it was the truth. "Where did you get the courage to tell him you'd had enough and would tell the Jørgensens?"

"I decided to leave. To give up my position here and flee to Sweden or England before Tuesday." He looked around the room and added, "There's nothing for me here. Nothing to keep me."

"What about your family?"

"It's only my mother, but I have a brother and sister who live not too far from her. And I've asked Nilsen to look after her, too. She'll be all right whether the Germans invade or not."

He followed me into the hallway as Christiansen came toward us. They greeted each other in Danish and then Christiansen walked me back into the music room while Andersen went in the direction of the front door.

As we stepped toward the far side of the piano, I whispered in English, "Now we have another motive. Braun was blackmailing Andersen."

"Why?"

I didn't understand complex scientific papers but I managed to make the gist of the error clear. "And then on Friday, Andersen had enough of being at Braun's every whim, having to work his own job and Braun's too, and knowing the real reason why we were coming, threatened to tell the Jørgensens about Braun's wife."

Mike looked furious. "He knew? How?"

"Mrs. Jørgensen."

"Do you believe him?"

"I'd like to," I admitted. "I'm not certain. What we don't have is any reason for things to change so that Andersen would feel the need to poison Braun. Telling the Jørgensens about Braun's wife was more effective and completely legal."

"You'd think Braun would want to kill Andersen if he was threatened with exposure that would ruin his chances with Katrine, not the other way around," Christiansen told me. "And that only makes sense if the coffee cups were somehow switched."

Suddenly, I had a picture of the six young men crowded around the coffee urn, good naturedly shoving and reaching. "At the end of lunch yesterday, when you and the others were rushing to get your coffee before Jørgensen called all of you away to hear his new scientific breakthrough, could the coffee cups have been switched around?"

"Oh, I don't know. Sounds far-fetched." Christiansen thought a moment and then said, "I ended up with sugar in mine, although I didn't put sugar in. I never do. There were so many hands and so many cups in such a small space, and we were all rushing. When I was here before, we lingered over our coffee, discussing our morning's work. It's possible. In fact, you may have something there."

"You ended up with sugar, and Braun ended up with poison. It could have been two cups or more were switched around."

He gave me a considering gaze. "How do we prove it?"

"There will only be five instead of six, and I doubt there will be a big rush for cups of coffee after lunch today. That's a shame, because if you could drop salt in someone's coffee, anyone's coffee, it could prove our theory." I watched him to see if he agreed.

"It wouldn't prove anything."

"Except that the cyanide could have been introduced that way by anyone at the coffeepot. It wouldn't prove that Braun poisoned himself by accident. Are you willing to try?"

Mike frowned as he stared at the wall. "Braun poisoned himself? By accident? Killer as victim? That's different."

"It makes as much sense as anything else."

He smiled. "Why not? I'll talk to Jørgensen and perhaps we can create some type of rush on the coffee at the end of the meal. I heard the inspector is joining us for this meal. Do you trust me to try this out on my own?"

He must have been aware of how unsure I felt having to rely on his translations instead of knowing what people said. But I realized he was the only one in a position to carry out an experiment with the coffeepot and the cups, and because of his relationship with Dr. Jørgensen, he could get the cooperation needed to carry it off.

I gave him a smile. "Yes, I trust you. Good luck."

We walked toward the dining room and met Mrs. Ulriksen at the door. "Oh, good. Two more. And we have the inspector joining us."

"The Jørgensens like a party," I said.

"Is not a time for parties. We are to be invaded." Mrs. Ulriksen twisted her fingers together and hurried off.

"Yes. This seems more of a good idea all the time," Christiansen said with a faint smile. He walked off, leaving me standing alone in the hallway yet again.

Thyra Nilsen came in the front door and said in German, "Oh, we're going to have a big luncheon group." Then she stopped as her eyes widened. "And no Braun." A smile crossed her lips.

"I understand the inspector is taking his place."

She reached out and grabbed my arm. "Does that mean...?"

I held up my other hand. "All I know is the inspector is joining us for lunch. Why, Thyra? What do you know?"

"Nothing. It was just something Peder said."

"What?"

Thyra held onto my arm and walked me down the hallway to the door to the music room. No one was inside. "He said yesterday morning that Henrik Andersen made him promise to look after his mother. When Peder asked him why, was he going to England with Dr. Jørgensen, Henrik said he doubted he'd survive to go anywhere."

"Why did he say he wouldn't survive? Survive what?"

Thyra mutely shook her head.

"He must have indicated something." If he hadn't, we were no further ahead than we had been.

"No." Then she stepped closer and whispered. "Peder and I thought the same thing. Only Braun would kill someone. Was Henrik in danger?"

"I don't know, and Braun can't tell us now." I had barely met him, but from what I'd learned, I didn't like Braun. Still, there was a long distance between thinking a man was odious and thinking him a killer.

"No one else here was a warrior. How do you think he earned his scar and lost the sight in one eye?" Thyra was still whispering. No one had been willing to tell me the story before. I stood silently and waited for her to tell me.

"When he was a student, he was part of a mob that attacked some Jewish fellow students. They fought back. Two of the Jews were killed and the rest injured, but one of them had a knife and tried to defend himself. Braun lost the sight in one eye and another student needed several stitches. Braun claimed one night, while he was drinking with the other chemists here, that he later killed the student who dared take his eye."

"It could just be a boast."

She shook her head. "They didn't think so. And there's something else you don't know. Inge Beck? I've talked to her. She tried to resist Braun. Time and again. When Beck found out, he went looking for Braun. Andersen and Porteur separated them before anyone was seriously hurt, but Braun tried to get Beck fired for attacking him. The others went to Dr. Jørgensen and prevented Beck from being fired."

"Did they tell him what started the fight?"

Thyra shook her head. "Well, they said not. They might not have told him outright but I think they hinted around to Dr. Jørgensen. Peder admitted as much when I asked him today."

"Unfortunately, this just gives Beck a better motive to kill Braun, not the other way around." I sighed, wishing clues would point to one particular killer rather than practically everyone at the institute.

Thyra scowled at me. "Braun would never have killed himself. But I can imagine him murdering someone else to avenge some slight. But I certainly can't imagine Beck killing anyone, not even Braun."

"And yet, Braun was the one who died. Someone killed him." I hoped our experiment would clarify how the German might have killed himself.

Would Christiansen be able to carry off the test? Would Jørgensen go along with the plan? Would the inspector understand when we explained what had happened?

"And no one seems to have a motive to kill Greta," I added, still trying to puzzle out who'd killed the maid.

"Perhaps it was a jealous boyfriend. I don't know of anyone else who could possibly have wanted to kill her," Thyra said.

"The house wasn't broken into, so if she let in her killer, it was by prearrangement," I told her. From what Mike told me he'd overheard when we were in the pub, that prearrangement had been with Braun.

"It sounds typical of Greta." Thyra looked puzzled. "But very risky if Mrs. Ulriksen had caught her."

"Just wait and watch. Hopefully, some of our questions will be answered." And we could get safely back to England on time.

Thyra gave me a considering look before we went into the drawing room, where Mrs. Jørgensen was talking to Katrine. At least the young woman was no longer screaming at anyone or berating Andersen. She glared at me, winning her a whispered warning from her mother.

"We've invited the inspector to lunch today. Hopefully we'll be able to convince him that you and Mikkel, at the very least, couldn't have killed Greta or Braun and should be allowed to return to England," Ailsa Jørgensen said in English.

"That would be a great start," I said with a smile.

"Start?" Katrine asked, looking startled.

"I'm hoping you and your parents, at the very least, could accompany us."

"Haven't you done enough?" she snapped at me in a high-pitched shriek. "I can't imagine going anywhere with you."

"It isn't her fault Herr Braun died," Mrs. Jørgensen told her daughter. The doorbell chimed and she added, "That must be the inspector. Shall we all go into lunch?"

Chapter Eighteen

By the time we reached the dining room, with me pushing Ailsa Jørgensen's wheeled chair, the rest of the guests were already standing around the table. Inge Beck stood close to her husband and looked down, blushing, as Katrine walked into the room and glared at her.

After I wheeled Mrs. Jørgensen to her place at one end of the table with Dr. Jørgensen standing at the other end of the table, the rest of us took the five straight-backed chairs on each side. I went to stand next to Christiansen with Porteur on my other side and so deliberately chose a place across the table from where the coffee urn would sit later. I hoped Christiansen had convinced Dr. Jørgensen to let him hold our experiment.

The first course was a hot and delicious soup. Porteur leaned over to murmur in my ear in French, "When you leave, can you take me with you?"

"If Dr. Jørgensen will say he can use you in his laboratory, then yes, it should be easy," I whispered in return.

"What are you two whispering about?" Katrine snapped in German from across the table.

I smiled at her and said, "The hope that there is enough soup left to have some at dinner. It's excellent."

"You could have said that aloud," Katrine said.

"I just did," I told her.

Her response was to glare at me.

"It is excellent soup," the inspector said in his halting German. He apparently translated as he spoke, making it harder on himself. He was being polite to me since everyone else there spoke Danish.

"Are you a fan of smørrebrød?" I asked him.

"Yes. I like the variety. And you?"

"This weekend was the first I'd tried it, and I liked it very much." I had no idea how long we could carry on a discussion on food.

Neither, apparently, did Inspector Larsen, and he had no desire to try. "We believe only the people at this table had the ability to obtain the poison to kill Friedrich Braun, the proximity to deliver the poison, and the access to attack Greta upstairs in her room."

"What about the lab assistants?" Nilsen said, continuing the discussion in German.

"They could obtain the poison, true, but they could not have put it in the coffee here, since they left before the urn was brought in and they would have had trouble entering this house and going upstairs to kill the maid. They lacked access. The ladies would have had difficulty getting the poison or adding it to the coffee." The inspector nodded to Mrs. Jørgensen.

"What about the kitchen staff?" I asked.

"Others would have been ill if the poison had been in anything besides the coffee, and no one member of the staff could have assured that Braun received the one tainted cup."

"Are you saying Braun was not poisoned at the institute? How do you know that?" Mike asked.

Inspector Larsen scowled at him, but he kept his voice level as he said, "There was no trace of cyanide in any of the things we took from the institute to be tested. And we found a vial containing some cyanide in the flower beds along the path from here to the institute."

"So only one of six people could have killed Fritz," Katrine said.

"And his wife is not one of the six," Thyra Nilsen said, looking at Katrine as she emphasized the word "wife." Katrine reddened and turned away.

I wanted to point out the killer was actually one of seven, but I'd wait until Christiansen had a chance to prove it before I said anything.

Mrs. Ulriksen and Lise cleared the bowls and brought in the fish course served in a white sauce along with crusty bread. We ate in silence while Inspector Larsen openly watched all of us.

Andersen picked at his food, his normally robust appetite apparently gone. Porteur shoveled in his food mechanically with his shoulders hunched. Inge Beck appeared to be close to tears, not taking a single bite, while her husband kept giving her encouraging smiles.

Katrine looked angry. She had been in the dining room at the right time. Could she have entered the storeroom at the institute undetected and poisoned Braun's coffee cup when he brought it back to the table? I thought it possible. She would have had a very small window of opportunity, but we couldn't yet eliminate her from the suspicion that she'd poisoned her lover. And she definitely could have attacked the nearest rival she was aware of, Greta.

The servants removed the fish course and brought in the meat course, pork with dumplings and gravy, carrots, and sauerkraut. The same as everything else I'd eaten here, it was good.

The meal continued in silence except for the sound of silverware scraping china or being set down too quickly. We finished the meal in what I suspected was record time.

At a glance from Christiansen, who was toying with the salt shaker, Dr. Jørgensen said, "If you gentlemen will have your coffee quickly, I have had another breakthrough in my laboratory this morning that I am eager to share with you."

He was immediately flooded with questions. He shook his head and said only, "I'll have to show you the results. It's amazing. Now please, hurry with your coffee."

The four remaining chemists, Christiansen, and the inspector all crowded around the coffee urn that had been wheeled in with the cups and saucers, cream and sugar. There was a great deal of reaching, of bumping into each other, of "Pardon me," of "Oops."

The presence of the inspector seemed to have put

them all on their best behavior. There was no shoving as there had been the day before.

They came back to the table with their cups filled and took large swallows. Inspector Larsen set down his cup with a clunk and made a terrible face. I didn't understand his Danish, but I imagined it was somewhere between, "What is wrong with the coffee?" and "Are you trying to poison me?"

"Vicepolitiinspektor, my apologies," Christiansen said in German. "We developed a theory of how Braun was poisoned yesterday and wanted to try it out. We told Dr. Jørgensen, who approved the experiment as long as no one was hurt. I'll be glad to fix you another cup of coffee and we can discuss what this experiment shows."

He rose and went to the trolley. "Cream and sugar, sir?"

"Sugar."

Christiansen fixed the inspector's coffee and brought it to the table. "You didn't see anyone add anything to your coffee, did you, sir?"

Inspector Larsen shifted uneasily in his seat. "No. What was it?"

"Salt. Table salt."

"In the sugar."

Christiansen shook his head. "In my hand. You were the only one to get the salt. Just as Braun was the only one to be poisoned yesterday."

The inspector sat silently for a full minute before he

said, "How did this little experiment match what happened yesterday?"

"It was even more chaotic yesterday. Not only did Braun get poison in his coffee, I ended up with sugar in my coffee, and I didn't put sugar in my coffee."

"You ended up with someone else's cup?"

Christiansen said, "Apparently."

"Did anyone else end up with the wrong cup either yesterday or today?" the inspector asked.

"I ended up with too much sugar yesterday," Andersen said, "but I just thought I'd made the mistake myself and put sugar in twice."

"A great deal of sugar was being added. What about cream?"

Beck and Porteur, the only ones who took cream, shook their heads.

"What about you, Nilsen?" the detective asked.

"I take mine without cream or sugar, and mine was fine today and yesterday. Of course, I was at the opposite end of the coffee trolley from Braun."

"You remember that?"

Nilsen looked at the inspector. "Yes. I imagine we've all thought about where we sat at lunch or stood afterward in light of Braun's death."

"And have you come to any conclusions?" The inspector looked around the table.

"I'm glad I wasn't next to Braun," Nilsen said.

"Who was?"

"Christiansen and I," Andersen said.

"So all the mistakes happened where you were." There was an accusation in the inspector's tone.

Mistakes. I had an idea, but how would I prove it? How could I prove it in only a few hours? Maybe by casting doubt on the inspector's ideas. "If cups were mixed up, perhaps Braun wasn't the intended target."

"Do you really think so, Mrs. Redmond?" Inspector Larsen gave me a withering look.

"Yes. And that brings up another thought. If Braun wasn't the intended victim, then he could have been the killer. We have one more suspect than we had before."

There were gasps around the table as a few heads nodded and Katrine cried out, "No."

"How do you expect the police to prove that?" Inspector Larsen asked.

"I don't know. It is only one more possibility you need to consider as you carry out your investigation." And one Christiansen and I would be examining as we tried to clear up this mystery and get out before the Nazis threw us all in jail.

He gave me a smile that lacked warmth and friendship. "Yesterday, my men searched the grounds for anything the poison might have been carried in to bring it over here." He must have seen my nod because he said, "You see, Mrs. Redmond, we're not all fools."

"I didn't think you were." I felt I had to add, "And then this morning, I saw one of your men find a paper in the flowerbed outside the door that could have contained poison."

He ignored my comment. The vial he'd mentioned must have been picked up yesterday. What was the significance of the paper, then? "And since I'm not a fool, I know why the two of you came here this weekend."

I wondered who had told him as I said, "And that is?"

"The assistance of certain citizens who plan to take refuge in Britain."

I looked at him in silence. What could I say? And what words could aid us in getting home safely?

Christiansen answered something in Danish.

Larsen nodded, and I was left wishing once more that I spoke the language.

The maid Lise brought Mrs. Jørgensen, Inge Beck, Thyra Nilsen, and me cups of tea. Katrine rose, marched over to the coffee urn, and poured herself a cup, all the while ignoring the rest of us. I think she was angry I suggested Braun could have been the killer and not the target, and no one was disagreeing with me.

"Unfortunately, Mrs. Redmond, while there were fingerprints on the vial of poison, they didn't belong to anyone we took samples from yesterday."

"So you want to take the ladies' prints?" I asked.

"Yes."

"I doubt it will do you any good, Inspector, but you are welcome to do it here as soon as luncheon is finished," Mrs. Jørgensen said.

Things broke up quickly after that, with the men leaving for the institute and more questioning while two policemen came in with fingerprinting cards and ink. Inge Beck and Thyra Nilsen had their prints taken before they quickly thanked their hostess and left, wiping their fingers.

Mrs. Jørgensen had her prints taken next. I gestured to Katrine to go ahead of me, but she turned away, her arms crossed over her stomach.

I went next, allowing one of the policemen to maneuver my fingers one at a time through the inkpad and then onto the heavy white card. I wiped my fingers on a rag and waited while Katrine reluctantly came over. I rose so she could take my seat and go through the process.

When the policemen thanked us, packed up their equipment, and left, Mrs. Jørgensen pushed away from the table and suggested Katrine and I follow her to the music room. I pushed Mrs. Jørgensen's wheeled chair and Katrine went ahead. She was already seated at the piano looking through sheet music as we entered. Mrs. Jørgensen suggested Beethoven. Katrine began to play Tchaikovsky.

"My husband and I have been talking," Ailsa Jørgensen said in English. "We are leaning toward traveling back to England with you tomorrow."

"Oh, that's good news." I gave her a wide smile.

"I'm not going with you," Katrine also spoke in English, ceasing her playing.

"Why would you stay now that Braun…" her mother

drifted to a halt. Apparently, even she was afraid to risk Katrine's temper by talking about Braun.

"Why would I leave?"

"At least now you don't need a chaperone." Something hard and determined underlined Mrs. Jørgensen's voice. I hoped her determination would hold until we reached England.

"I'm glad we agree on something." Katrine began to play the piano again.

"I wonder how long the Germans will allow you to live here?" her mother said.

Katrine's playing stopped immediately. "What do you mean?"

"Your father and I will be gone. Beck and his wife are going to Sweden, the other researchers are coming with us or going elsewhere. It will cease to function as a chemical laboratory. This house, the entire institute, belongs to the nation. And the nation will belong to Germany. This place will no longer be your home."

"What will I do for money? Where will I live?" Katrine's voice started to trail upward into a wail.

"That's a good question. If you sail with us, we will of course look after you. We won't be able to do that if you stay here." Her mother stared at her, eyebrows raised.

Katrine turned on me. "This is all your fault."

"Your parents will be moving to Cambridge. It's a lovely university town. You are certainly welcome to come with them."

"Oh, you'd like that, wouldn't you?" she sneered at me. "Capture the great Dr. Jørgensen for Britain."

"It's an offer. One that expires in a few hours. Your parents think it's a good offer, allowing your father to continue his research in a safer environment."

"Until Germany invades."

"We don't have a land bridge directly to Germany such as Denmark has. And we haven't been successfully invaded in almost nine hundred years." I didn't hide the ringing pride in my voice.

"You are welcome to come with us, Katrine. Otherwise, you will stay here alone." Ailsa Jørgensen emphasized the last word before she turned and wheeled herself out of the room.

Katrine rose from the piano and moved to stand in front of me, blocking my path. "Don't think that is the final word on the subject. I am their daughter. Their only surviving child. You are an English nobody."

"I agree. You could make your parents very happy by going to England with them. Nothing I could do would accomplish that."

Katrine gave me a superior smile.

"Apparently your father and the other scientists have made up their minds, and your mother has decided to go with your father. Now it's your turn to make up your mind." Mentally, I crossed my fingers.

"We'll see what Inspector Larsen says about that." Katrine flounced out of the room.

Chapter Nineteen

I lingered for a moment, trying to decide what I should do, before making up my mind and leaving the house. I walked outside while pulling on my coat to see Katrine entering the institute by the side door. I followed her.

There was no one in sight on the ground floor, so I headed up the wide staircase. I could hear voices above me, coming from the second floor where the workers' sitting room and the small office where Inspector Larsen and Sergeant Behr had carried out their interviews were.

I followed the sounds to the second floor and stood in the hall, listening to Katrine's voice and the voices of various men arguing in Danish in the sitting room. I wished once again I could understand them.

There was no way I could find out what was going on without walking through the doorway. I knocked and opened the door to step inside.

Katrine gave a small shriek and walked off, her arms folded over her stomach.

Dr. Jørgensen started speaking in Danish and quickly changed to German to speak to me as well as the others. "My daughter accuses my wife of killing Braun because she didn't want our child to marry a German and stay here. She says Ailsa doesn't want her only child to leave her side and she could force Katrine to come with us by killing Braun."

"But Mrs. Jørgensen couldn't have obtained the poison or administered it," I replied, looking from Katrine to her father.

"My mother paid one of them." She pointed at the researchers sitting and standing a little distant from where Katrine, her father, and the inspector had apparently held an argument. All three had flushed faces and stood staring daggers at each other. "It could have been Mikkel Christiansen for all I know, but I think it was Andersen."

The inspector glanced at Christiansen, who gave his head a small shake.

Andersen started to protest, but the policeman held up a hand to silence him.

"I think the conversation between Katrine and her mother explains these charges," I said.

Katrine turned and screamed at me in Danish. I felt sure they weren't words of friendship.

"What was said?" the inspector asked, ignoring Katrine.

"Mrs. Jørgensen told Katrine she will join her husband in sailing to England. Katrine can come with them and expect to have a place to live and be supported, or she can stay here and earn her own living and find her own home."

"Ailsa said she is coming with me?" Dr. Jørgensen said, a big smile spreading across his face.

"So typical," Katrine shouted in German. "No one asks

what I want."

"Because you always tell us before we can ask," her father said.

Turning to the police inspector, Katrine said, "I still think she paid someone to poison Braun to force me to go to England with them. And I'm going to prove it." Then she stormed out.

I began to wonder if she had any other way of exiting a room.

"Mrs. Jørgensen will corroborate your version of the conversation?" the inspector asked me.

"Yes, although she's probably lying down at the moment and you may need to wait," I told him.

"Will we be able to leave tonight to catch the morning ferry?" Christiansen asked.

The inspector shrugged. "That depends on whether we can find Braun's killer. We've had no luck with Greta's killer, except to think she and Braun were killed by the same person for the same reason."

"And what is that reason?"

Larsen glared at me silently.

"Have you taken Braun's fingerprints?" I asked.

"And why do you think I should do that?" Inspector Larsen asked.

"Because he may have been the murderer."

He looked at me and shook his head. "Why would he kill himself?"

"I don't think he meant to. I think he was tripped up

by the confusion at the coffee urn and put the poison into his own coffee."

"It sounds awfully foolish."

"I think the victim was supposed to be Andersen, who had threatened to tell the Jørgensens about Frau Braun, and who was standing next to Braun at the coffee urn until Christiansen got in the way. Remember, Braun was blind in one eye. I think somehow the extra coffee cup in front of him at the wrong moment threw him off."

"I suppose you'll tell me that Braun took sugar in his coffee."

"Yes, he did," Nilsen told the policeman. "We all joked about it behind his back. The master race couldn't stand coffee if it wasn't sweetened. Not so tough, after all."

"Would that disguise the cyanide?" I asked.

"The taste, probably," Larsen admitted. "Not the smell."

"If he could smell it," Dr. Jørgensen said. "Not everyone can smell the bitter almond odor of cyanide."

"I'm going to see how they are faring with the new fingerprint samples," Larsen said as he headed for the door.

"Fingerprint Braun," I called out before he left.

The policeman glared at me and walked out.

"We might as well wrap up our work for the day and start packing for our voyage. I'm going to believe the inspector will allow us to go. But only take what you can carry," Jørgensen added, looking at Nilsen.

"I tend to travel with a great number of books," Nilsen told me with a sad smile. I suspected he had more than he could possibly take with him.

As we headed downstairs in the institute, I pulled Christiansen aside. "At least we know there are fingerprints on the vial."

He rubbed his hand along his beard and asked, "What if the killer wore gloves and the fingerprints belong to a person who touched it earlier?"

"Still, you'd think the killer would have destroyed the vial rather than just dump it into the flower beds."

Christiansen raised his eyebrows. "You mean, if the killer was still alive to do anything with it."

I nodded. "Would Braun have carelessly dumped the vial if he hadn't poisoned himself?"

He shrugged. "Did he know then he had poisoned himself, or did he expect to live to see his countrymen take over Denmark? Now all we can do is wait for the politi to return to make an arrest based on those fingerprints."

"I'm going to help Mrs. Jørgensen pack, if she wants my help." I left the institute and returned to the Jørgensens' huge manor of a house. The Germans would definitely take over any facility as grand as the institute by Wednesday at the latest.

I met Mrs. Rothberg at the front door. "Have you heard if you are allowed to leave?" she asked me.

"Not yet, but we have suggested who the killer is to the politi," I replied.

"Who?" she asked, definitely interested. A traveling case was in her hand. I suspected it held the jewelry she wanted taken to her daughter in England.

When I told her our theory about the mix-up in the coffee cups, she said, "Easy to understand, since he only had vision in one eye. The only time I met him, we were in a large group. I remember him moving his head around constantly, trying to figure out who was speaking and where his coffee cup was."

One of the maids, Lise, answered the door and Mrs. Rothberg walked in, speaking Danish. I followed, picturing what she had told me.

We were shown into the blue and green drawing room where Ailsa Jørgensen was directing the packing of some framed photographs. The two older women kissed cheeks and greeted each other warmly in Danish.

Then Mrs. Rothberg said in German, "Mrs. Redmond has been telling me how Braun's loss of an eye may have led to him killing himself."

"That's the theory some of us prefer," Mrs. Jørgensen said with a small smile.

"But will the politi accept it? Or had they already agreed to let you leave for England before the invasion?" Mrs. Rothberg asked.

"Not yet, but Mr. Christiansen, who traveled here with Mrs. Redmond, made a cunning demonstration of how the poison could have ended up in Braun's coffee cup. I know Olaf is talking to the vicepolitiinspektor and those over his head in the politi about letting all of us leave for the good of Denmark," Mrs. Jørgensen told her.

"Thank you for offering to take this to my daughter," Mrs. Rothberg said, setting the travel case down on an end table. "I wish you a safe journey, and I hope you can return here soon."

"Oh, Ruth, I doubt we'll see each other again in this life." The two women hugged, and I could see how thin Ailsa Jørgensen's arms were.

They began to chatter in Danish, and I slipped out of the room.

I readied my own suitcase, not wanting to be tardy if we received approval to leave Denmark. Having this task done would free me to help Mrs. Jørgensen and Katrine pack. I suspected neither of them could travel lightly. I had no idea who would move the mountains of luggage that I envisioned.

It took me hardly any time at all to repack my suitcase. I was determined to leave on the ferry tomorrow, or by air if I had to, whether anyone else came or not.

At that point, I didn't care if Sir Malcolm was unhappy with the results of our efforts. And I hadn't had a chance to learn much about my mother other than that she had been well liked.

I went to help Ailsa Jørgensen pack, but she was taking a nap. I walked down to the village and back, enjoying the weather and the exercise. I wouldn't see any of this again until the war was over, I hoped, and I wanted to remember the view.

When I returned, I met Mike by the gate to the institute grounds. "Come on. The politi are here and they've found the murderer. Things are working out."

"Not for someone," I said. "Unless the killer is Braun."

"Why would he kill the maid?"

"If Greta threatened to tell Katrine about their affair, he might have killed her in a rage. Braun didn't want anything to come between him and control of the institute."

We went into the house and found everyone in the large drawing room, focused on the inspector. He finished speaking in Danish and then said in German for my benefit, "We have proof of the identity of the killer in the form of fingerprints. You are free to leave the country, Mrs. Redmond."

"What do you mean, you have fingerprint evidence of the identity of the killer?" I asked Inspector Larsen. "Is this from the vial or the folded paper? Can you get fingerprints off of paper?"

"Paper?" He looked at me as if I were simple. "That must have been a piece of trash the wind blew over from the institute. No, we have the glass vial with traces of cyanide that has one set of fingerprints on it. This is the vial we found Saturday afternoon in a flower bed along the path from the house to the institute. Shortly after we were called in to Braun's death."

"Whose fingerprints?" Dr. Jørgensen asked, leaning

forward eagerly to learn the name of the killer.

"Friedrich Braun."

"No," Katrine said, her face reddening. "He wouldn't have killed himself."

"With the crowding around the coffee urn and Braun's limited eyesight, I'm afraid Herr Christiansen's demonstration was compelling. We can't be sure who the intended victim was, but we're certain the killer was Braun. It was only by accident he killed himself."

"He couldn't have. He wasn't going to kill anyone, and he didn't kill himself." Katrine glared at the policeman.

"He was going to kill me, Katrine," Andersen said. "He told me so Friday, when I threatened to tell—" He abruptly stopped speaking and backed two paces away from her.

Chapter Twenty

"That Braun was married? Not you, too, Henrik." Katrine crossed her arms over her chest and turned partly away from us.

"Katrine overheard me telling her mother about Frau Braun this morning," I told Andersen, "and then the politi came to give her the same news."

"And I was talking about Braun being married, too," Porteur said, "and could have been overheard."

"So everyone is free to leave?" Mrs. Jørgensen asked, getting back to the important point.

"Yes. We will pack up the rest of our gear, replace the coffee cups in the institute, take one more look around for the object Braun used to strike Greta down, and leave you in peace. Thank you for a delicious and thought-provoking luncheon," Larsen added to Mrs. Jørgensen. The police walked out of the room.

There were a few barely audible sighs of relief. One of them was mine. I could go home before the invasion.

"I need to finish packing," Mrs. Jørgensen said, "and I expect everyone else needs to who is joining us on the train after dinner."

"With your permission, Dr. Jørgensen, we are going to Sweden with the Becks," Nilsen said. "There will be room for us to do industrial work there with the Beck family during the war."

"Of course. You can both use me as a reference at any time," Jørgensen told him with a joyous smile on his face. "Porteur, Andersen, are you coming with us?"

"Yes, sir," they both said.

"Good. Get packed, and then help me collect the most important papers to take with us."

"I'll give you a hand with that," Christiansen said as the men all left the room.

Katrine glared at me. "You think you've won, don't you?"

"It was never about winning or losing. I want to see you and your parents, and me, safe in Britain. Will your father help the Allies win the war? I hope so, but I can't be certain. But more important, it's all about being safe from the Nazis. Your father would have been targeted by the Germans, forced to do their bidding, and it is never good to be their target."

"They're not such awful people," she told me.

"I know," I said to placate her. "But it's not their people coming here on holiday. It's the German military coming here to take over your country."

Katrine gave me a little smile with a sneer. "And when they come to take over Britain?"

"They won't succeed. We're an island nation, not successfully invaded in a very long time." I said it proudly. I'd seen the work at Bletchley Park, the gas masks, the air raid shelters. I believed we could win.

Or survive and outlast them until the Commonwealth defeated them, if we couldn't.

"You keep saying that," Katrine grumbled.

"Get packed, Katrine. We don't want to keep the men waiting," Ailsa Jørgensen said. "Will you help me pack, Olivia?"

"Of course."

Ailsa Jørgensen was efficient. She had her clothes, her husband's clothes, and a few treasured mementoes ready to go by the time dinner was served.

I was shocked when she handed me the enlarged photo of my mother with her, the one where my mother looked so happy. "I want you to have this. It will mean more to you than it would to Katrine."

"Thank you," I said and impulsively gave her a kiss on the cheek before I hurried out to pack it carefully in my luggage.

No one bothered to dress for dinner, being in our traveling clothes instead. I had on my gray wool suit that I'd wear under my heavy coat. I planned to be warm. Mrs. Jørgensen seemed to have on layers of wool for the trip.

Everyone except Katrine. She dressed formally for dinner.

"'Planning on traveling in that, darling?'" Christiansen whispered in translation after Mrs. Jørgensen spoke to her daughter in Danish.

He didn't translate Katrine's fiery response. He didn't

need to.

His eyes widened as he listened to Ailsa Jørgensen's reply. Then he leaned over and whispered, "'You need to be ready on time. We won't be able to wait, and you won't enjoy Denmark without a home or money.'"

Katrine's reply was to rise from the table and storm off.

Dr. Jørgensen looked at his wife as he started to rise and follow Katrine.

Ailsa Jørgensen said, "Olaf, is the meat cooked to your liking?" in English.

He settled back into his chair. "Yes." He ate for a minute or two before he said, "Do you think she'll be ready on time?"

"Of course. She's a sensible girl. Deep down."

"And if she's not?" Dr. Jørgensen stared at his wife.

"Then she'll stay here and live to regret her choice. That might be the best thing for her."

I was amazed at how calmly Ailsa Jørgensen could talk about leaving her daughter behind now that Braun was no longer a danger to the young woman's reputation. Or maybe she was certain Katrine liked her comforts and would be ready on time.

After dinner, we finished packing and carried our luggage to the front hall where the gardeners loaded everything into a horse-drawn wagon. Then they, and Dr. Jørgensen, went over to the institute to get the rest of the luggage, both for Mike and the chemists, and that which contained the papers Dr. Jørgensen wanted to take to Britain and keep out of Nazi hands.

I noticed one case was definitely Katrine's. Her mother had been at least partly correct. But where was Katrine?

Christiansen came back to the house to ask me to walk to the station with Porteur and Andersen. There wouldn't be enough room in the car otherwise. I started off while Mrs. Jørgensen and her wheeled chair were loaded into the car with Michelle's and Dr. Jørgensen's help.

"Think Katrine will come with us?" I asked Christiansen in English as quietly as I could.

"If the Jørgensens don't make the train into Copenhagen, this whole mission is blown," he murmured in reply.

I kept looking for the car to pass us in the village on the way to the station, but it didn't appear. We bought our tickets, and still no automobile. The luggage had already been deposited on carts inside the station, waiting to be loaded onto the train.

"The train will be here in a minute," Mike said, pacing along the pavement. "Where are they?"

"Mrs. Jørgensen was so certain they would make the train." And yet they weren't there. I was getting worried.

"All of the luggage is here, including all of Dr. Jørgensen's papers. If we have to, we'll go and take the papers with us," Mike said.

"I don't think he'd want us to do that." I could see the train's headlight at a distance coming into the station.

"We can't leave the papers here for the Nazis. It would give them the blueprints to build all his discoveries."

"Look. Headlights on the road," I said, relief in my tone. Things were working out. I hoped.

By the time Michelle and Dr. Jørgensen had Mrs. Jørgensen out of the auto and settled in her chair, a porter appeared to help get her and the chair into the station and onto the platform.

The chauffeur, whom I noticed was Berde, carried a few more cases that I guessed belonged to the Jørgensens. As he put them on the carts with the rest of the luggage, the train was pulling into the station.

"Where is Klimek?" I asked in German.

"On his way to Sweden with the Becks and the Nilsens."

"And Katrine?"

"They waited for the silly girl but she didn't appear. Finally, Mrs. Jørgensen said to leave, so I drove them down here."

It remained to be seen if the Jørgensens would get on the train without their daughter. To be polite, I asked Berde, "And you? What are your plans?"

"I'll stay here as the caretaker. Dr. Jørgensen has given me the auto to use as well." He grinned widely.

"I wish you luck."

"Oh, I'll be fine. Too old for military service and with an automobile and tasks that will be needed to be done no matter who's in charge." Humming, he climbed back into the auto.

We waited for Mrs. Jørgensen to be lifted into the train as the luggage was moved into the baggage carriage. We filed on as Dr. Jørgensen kept looking up and down the platform. At the last moment, Katrine marched over and climbed onto the train and then her father boarded.

"Where were you?" Mrs. Jørgensen asked her in English when we reached her in the first-class compartment.

"Trying to decide if I wanted to go to England with you. In the end, I came, if only to see this marvelous country you keep talking about." Katrine's voice dripped sarcasm.

Mrs. Jørgensen shook her head.

Andersen looked relieved.

The trip into Copenhagen was quick, with few others joining the train on the way into the city, but once we reached the central train station, everything seemed to slow down.

While Dr. Jørgensen, Porteur, and Michelle all endeavored to get Mrs. Jørgensen off the train and upstairs into the main hall, Christiansen found a porter to get all of our considerable luggage out of the baggage carriage and up to the main hall from where it could be moved to the platform for the train bound for Esbjerg.

When we arrived in the main hall of the station, we found Andersen by the ticket counter under one of the brick arches. "I have all our tickets," he told Dr. Jørgensen in German as he held them up. "Our train leaves from platform 5. It's there now. We need to hurry."

His tall figure loped toward the entrance to platform 5, immediately followed by Christiansen and the porter with the luggage carts. The rest of us circled around Mrs. Jørgensen as we hurriedly wheeled her toward the platform entrance.

Andersen was talking to one of the train guards on the platform and gesturing toward us while Christiansen and the porter were seeing to the luggage being loaded into the baggage carriage. As soon as Mrs. Jørgensen and her chair reached the platform, we hurried as a group toward Andersen.

The train guard helped get Mrs. Jørgensen into the first-class carriage and then the rest of us climbed on. As soon as the last of us were aboard, the guard blew his whistle and waved his flag as he slammed the door.

I settled into my seat as Mike Christiansen took the one next to me. "This will take us a good five hours to reach Esbjerg, with the ferry and all."

"What ferry?" I hadn't realized our journey would be in sections. I thought this train would take us directly to Esbjerg.

"We have to take a ferry that links the two rail lines together."

"What?" *Oh, dear.* I hoped we wouldn't lose Katrine again.

"In 1935, a railroad bridge was built between Jutland and Funen. Now the only ferry we need to take between here and Esbjerg is the ship from Zealand to Funen."

"Funen? Zealand?" I didn't know what he was talking about.

He looked at me as if I were a particularly dim schoolchild. He seemed to do that a great deal. "Jutland is the name of the part of Denmark attached to the European mainland and where Esbjerg is. Funen is an island close to it. Then there is a wide channel that takes nearly an hour to cross by ferry, and then the island of Zealand. Copenhagen is on Zealand." He gestured with his hands to explain the route.

"I hope next time Sir Malcolm gives me a chance to read up on the geography of a place before he sends me there," I said.

Mike nodded. "The trip by train and ferry from Copenhagen to Esbjerg is four to five hours. Five at night. Be glad this isn't before 1935. The trip was even longer then, with three trains and two ferries."

"Which is why we needed to catch the eleven o'clock train to Esbjerg on Sunday night to reach the Monday ferry on time." At least I figured out that much.

"There is no train after this one until tomorrow morning. Too late to catch the Monday ferry to England."

"I'm tired already." I leaned back and shut my eyes. It

was late, I was tired, and I now knew we'd go through helping Mrs. Jørgensen on and off trains three more times before we reached the ferry to take us to England. I dozed off, hoping ferries were easier to get a wheeled chair on and off than trains had so far proved to be. And that Katrine would behave.

When I awoke, the lights in the carriage had been dimmed. I kept my eyes shut, hoping to go back to sleep quickly. Instead, my ears picked up hushed Danish. The man spoke hurriedly, tension in his voice, while the woman's tone was soothing. At that moment, I wished I understood Danish, so I could learn why Ailsa Jørgensen needed to calm a panicky Henrik Andersen.

At first, I thought he was worried about the ferry ride across open water, but then I heard Andersen say a word I took to be "murder." In the next sentence or two, he said, "politi."

Something about Friedrich Braun's death still haunted Henrik Andersen. I could hear it in his voice.

I hoped after all the investigations we'd carried out, Andersen had nothing to do with the murders.

Before I could work out any more of their conversation, the lights came up and the conductor said something in Danish that made everyone gather up their belongings. We had reached the point where we switched to a ferry for an hour's crossing to reach the part of Denmark attached to mainland Europe.

We needed a porter to help with our pile of luggage.

Christiansen again arranged that while a train guard helped Dr. Jørgensen and Porteur to lift Ailsa Jørgensen down to the platform. From there, it turned out she could be wheeled over to the ferry and up a ramp into the ship.

"Well, that was easier," Mrs. Jørgensen said once we were all aboard.

"Just one more train before we reach Esbjerg," I said with a weak smile and earned several dark looks for my comment. I was tired and grumpy. I could only imagine how hard this was on my mother's dear friend. And on the people moving her and her chair.

After a few minutes in the stuffy interior of the ferry, I chose to go out on deck. The cold wind woke me up and the brilliant stars lit the sky in a dramatic panorama, but all of that and pacing didn't relieve my nervousness. Did Andersen think there was still a danger to the Jørgensens from someone in our group? Was that why he was talking about murder and the police with Mrs. Jørgensen?

The far shore, a darker strip between the lighter sea and the sky, seemed closer when Christiansen came out on deck next to me and stared out into the water. I looked in the direction he was gazing and asked, "What is it?"

"According to the captain, not a freighter."

From what I could make out by its lights at that distance, I guessed it was quite a large ship. "If it's not a freighter...?"

Christiansen glared at the distant ship and rubbed a hand across his bearded jaw. "It's a German warship headed this way as the fastest route to Copenhagen. The invasion has begun."

Chapter Twenty-One

"But the Germans aren't supposed to invade until tomorrow." My complaint sounded foolish to my ears. I guess I was surprised and frightened by their early arrival.

"Looks as if the Nazis decided to start sooner than they told us. Untrustworthy bunch of scum. It may be because they are taking the long sea route around Zealand to Copenhagen and won't arrive until late tonight or in the morning, but I don't want to give them credit for good planning. If they're traveling as far as Copenhagen." Christiansen shook his head.

"It's a good thing we've almost reached the ferry to England. The sooner we get to England, the happier I'll be," I told him.

"We're only halfway across Denmark." With a last glance at the ship in the distance, Christiansen stormed off back inside the ferry.

After one more long look at the German warship that seemed to be slowly closing the distance between us, I hurried to follow him.

I found Christiansen talking to Dr. and Mrs. Jørgensen in a low tone in Danish. Walking up to them, I murmured in English, "Is there anything I can do to help?"

"Could you take charge of Mrs. Rothberg's traveling

case?" Mrs. Jørgensen said. "It would make me easier to move if I'm not carrying it as well."

"Of course." I took the small traveling case from her and held it by the handle. Having an idea of the worth of the contents, I knew I wouldn't be able to let go of the case until Mrs. Jørgensen was settled somewhere.

Already my hand hurt with the weight of the responsibility.

I was nervous until we reached the dock, and then we were all too busy getting Mrs. Jørgensen and the luggage on board the train across Funen and Jutland to worry about how imminent the invasion was.

"I've got to make certain we get all of the luggage on board the train," Mike Christiansen told me in English as he passed me on the boat ramp.

I detained him with a hand on his coat sleeve. Having seen the German warship, I was ready to abandon everything and run. "Why you? Why can't the train porters be trusted to move all the cases?"

"Half those cases contain Dr. Jørgensen's most important papers. Formulas and notes that both England and Germany want. It's crucial that they all reach Harwich. And then Cambridge, I believe, is their final destination."

"Do you need help?"

"I've got Andersen helping me. Keep the Jørgensens moving toward the train. We've got to keep moving." He walked off, sounding as worried as I felt.

The transfer dragged on and once again, because of

Mrs. Jørgensen, we were the last to board the train. Christiansen nodded to Dr. Jørgensen, which I guessed meant all the luggage had been loaded into the baggage carriage. I made it into my seat just after the train began to roll and nearly landed on Henrik Andersen, stepping on his foot in the process.

After we apologized to each other, I asked, "Wouldn't you rather sit next to Katrine?"

"She'd rather not sit next to me. She blames me for her mother's determination to leave Denmark."

"Isn't it more Ailsa Jørgensen's determination to travel to England with her husband? She hasn't struck me as someone who wants to leave Denmark," I said. She had given me the impression when I arrived, less than seventy-two hours before, that she didn't want to leave her homeland and her children, living and dead.

That had been when Katrine thought herself engaged to Friedrich Braun. How things had changed.

"Oh, yes. Of course. Mrs. Jørgensen is interested only in being with Dr. Jørgensen, wherever he is." Andersen was nervous, speaking quickly and rubbing his thumbs over his clenched fingers. I thought he'd agree with almost anything without thinking about it, as frightened as he seemed to be.

"Are you worried about our ferry ride to England?"

"No. I'm a good sailor. Most Danes are. The coast is always nearby and we learn to sail as children."

He sounded so intent on assuring me that he had no

fear of the sea that either it was the truth or he was terrified. "That must have been a marvelous childhood."

"It was." He smiled and stopped rubbing his fingers.

"I imagine you're going to miss your homeland."

"I will, but I know it's only for a short time. And Dr. Jørgensen's work is so important, and so exciting to be a part of, that the time will fly by."

"You'll be working in Cambridge, too?" Christiansen had told me a little of the government's plans to support Dr. Jørgensen's research.

"I am. Mikkel Christiansen has told us there is a laboratory ready for Dr. Jørgensen outside Cambridge with a cottage nearby for the Jørgensen family. Porteur and I will be able to work as his assistants. We still have to find lodgings in the town, but Mikkel thinks that will be a small matter. Everything will be smaller than we had in Denmark, but we'll have to make do."

"At least you'll be able to work on research without fearing the Nazis constantly interfering with your work. People such as Friedrich Braun."

Andersen looked into my eyes, showing anger, and possibly fear, in his. "I never want to hear that name again."

"What are you so afraid of, Henrik?" I asked. "Are the Jørgensens in some sort of danger?"

He frowned at me. "If you'll excuse me, I'm going to try to get some sleep. We have already traveled for half the night and I'm tired."

It had been a long night. I was weary, made more uncomfortable by the thinly padded seats. I tried to get comfortable with the traveling case in my lap, but I kept fearing it would fall to the floor with a loud thud, waking everyone up.

I finally set it on the floor and put my feet on top. I wasn't in a great position, but this was a little more comfortable. I nodded off, but every time I did, I moved and woke myself up.

Finally, I was stiff and sore and tired enough that I needed to walk the aisle to stretch my muscles. If I woke Andersen, he didn't show any sign as I carefully climbed around him and reached the passageway.

I reached the end of our carriage and was about to open the door that led to the next carriage when a voice said behind me in English, "Where are you going?"

I jumped, grabbing at the wall for support and banging the traveling case that I couldn't let out of my sight on the door. I realized how tired I must have been to let anyone sneak up behind me. Facing Christiansen, I answered, "Nowhere. I couldn't sleep and had to get up and move around."

"Same here. The clock is ticking down, we're surrounded by danger, and no one seems to realize how perilous this journey is." He sounded disgusted.

I tried to sound positive in the hopes of cheering him up. "Surely we'll reach England before Denmark gives in."

"Maybe. And maybe we'll meet up with a U-boat

somewhere in the middle of the North Sea. Or maybe a destroyer will chase after us, intent on getting back Jørgensen's papers. They are brilliant."

My heart jerked so badly I thought the train had hit a rough patch in the tracks. But no, that trembling was only me. "I didn't think the U-boats were going after passenger ferries. And how would they know Jørgensen and his papers are aboard?"

"They don't routinely target ferries, but the submarines sail from north German ports. We could just get in their way, and we're large enough not to be mistaken for a fishing boat. We could be unlucky. Or someone might have sold us out, and that would mean a destroyer being send out to pick all of us up."

"Wonderful. Remind me not to talk to you if I want cheered up."

"We're facing multiple perils and I don't think anyone realizes it. The Jørgensens just make this journey more dangerous without thinking how they are putting their own lives at risk. And everyone else's." Mike shuddered.

He really was in a panic. And the only thing I could think of to say was, "Just keep moving forward. That's all we can do."

He gave me a weak smile. "It will soon be dawn. Maybe I won't be so gloomy then."

The sky seemed to be lightening from starry black to deep pearly blue. "Maybe," I said. "A night without sleep, and tonight we'll be on the North Sea."

"A night none of us will want to sleep."

I didn't see how I'd be able to keep my eyes open. "What time are we scheduled to arrive at Harwich?"

"Very early in the morning. About dawn on Tuesday, 9 April. Invasion day."

"Then I'm going to want to get a few hours' sleep before we land." I didn't see how I could avoid it. I wouldn't be able to hold my eyes open. "I am looking forward to sleeping in my own bed tomorrow night after we land in England. The whole night."

Christiansen thought for a moment before he said, "You're right. Tomorrow night we'll be in Britain. We'll be home." He smiled, apparently cheered by the thought.

"What are you looking forward to the most when we return?"

He studied the ceiling of the carriage for a few clicks of the rails before he looked at me and said, "Fish and chips from a little shop around the corner from my flat. You?"

"My cousin lives with four growing boys in a manor house surrounded by farms. I was married there last summer." I stopped then in surprise. "Was it only last summer? It seems so long ago. Anyway, I can't wait to visit them for a weekend and eat lots of fresh vegetables and eggs and cheese."

"Sounds tasty."

"It is. And the boys are so full of energy. So much fun."

"You make it sound idyllic. Are any of the boys

conscription age?"

Suddenly, my wonderful daydream turned to dust. "The oldest will be in a year or two."

"Maybe the war will be over then." He didn't sound like he believed it.

"Maybe. I'm going back to my seat." I didn't want any more of Christiansen's company. Or his lack of cheerfulness. Or his dark suggestions.

Andersen was still asleep when I returned to my seat, but Porteur and Michelle were whispering in French in the aisle. "How are you doing?" I murmured in French as I passed them.

"Mme. Jørgensen has been uncomfortable this train ride. It's been bumpy and she can't sleep. Which means nobody sleeps. I'm hoping I'll be able to settle her once we're on the ferry," Michelle told me and sighed. "I'm exhausted."

"How much longer until we reach the port?" Porteur asked.

"It should be soon, I think." I sat and tried to relax all of my muscles in an attempt to get some rest, if not sleep. As soon as my head began to nod, the conductor came by to say we'd be in Esbjerg in ten minutes.

Then it was a matter of organizing our belongings and waking Katrine, who seemed to be able to sleep anywhere and through anything. As we pulled into the station, Christiansen walked over to our seats and said to Andersen, "I need your help with the porters again."

"Will we have help with the papers once we reach Britain?"

"I suspect we'll have an entire welcoming committee after we get off the ferry," Christiansen told him and then grinned.

"Have you told them how many of us are arriving?" I asked.

"I sent a telegram while everyone was packing," Christiansen told me. "They'll be expecting us."

"I would guess they'd have some leading chemists from Cambridge there to greet us," Andersen said. "To greet someone of Dr. Jørgensen's stature."

"Possibly, although I'd expect the chemists will greet Jørgensen on arrival in Cambridge. I think we're all going to London first to arrange paperwork and funding. All that tedious stuff." The train clanked to a halt. "Ready? Let's find some porters."

Once again, we all filed off the train with Dr. Jørgensen, Porteur, and the train guard helping to get Mrs. Jørgensen and the wheeled chair down to the platform. I looked toward the sea and found the path to the dock to be smooth pavement. While this had no doubt been designed to move freight between the ferry and the train, it would make life easier for Mrs. Jørgensen and all the baggage containing Dr. Jørgensen's papers.

A crowd had formed on the dock before we reached the ship. No one seemed to be boarding. I felt a shiver of terror flow through my veins. I didn't want to be stuck here, in a country where I knew no one, where I didn't speak the language, for an entire war being waged against my country. And this would be the last ship sailing to England before the invasion.

"Dr. Jørgensen and I will see to the tickets and find out what the problem is," Christiansen murmured to me in English as he walked past where I stood.

All we could do was wait with the luggage and try to keep anyone from pushing into Mrs. Jørgensen. The sun rose behind puffy white clouds, keeping the day from becoming bright or warm. I set the traveling case on top of a stack of cases on the cart, glad not to have the weight on my arm for the moment.

From the restlessness of the crowd, I knew we should have already been boarding. And still we waited.

Finally, when fatigue had worn us all down to silent, brooding individuals, the two men returned. "Good news, bad news," Christiansen said to me in whispered English. "We have seats on the ferry. We're lucky. They don't appear to have enough space for everyone here, and some people have been waiting on the dock since late yesterday. We got a cabin for the Jørgensens, but the rest of us will have to make do with chairs."

Our group had tickets. We'd get on board. I felt immense relief. "Sounds as if it's pretty good news," I told him.

"I'm not certain how things will work out when we can finally start boarding. There was a delay in issuing tickets, and meanwhile the tide went out. It will be some time before the tide comes in enough so we can board and sail. And if people who've been waiting don't have tickets…?"

Chapter Twenty-Two

"Any idea when we can start boarding the ferry to Harwich?" I asked.

"When the ramps up to the ferry are at less than some particular degree and angle. Even then, it will be challenging enough to get the freight loaded, much more so passengers such as Mrs. Jørgensen," Mike Christiansen told me.

"Why is it all off schedule today?"

He shrugged. "The moon. The tides. The weather. That's what they say. More people want to take this ferry than usual and the officials weren't prepared for it. They don't know how many they'll have to leave behind."

That was a frightening thought, even if those left behind wouldn't be us. "I hope they don't have to leave anyone here. Thank you for letting me know. Everyone else was speaking Danish, and I knew something was going on, but not what," I told him.

Mike looked around. "This delay could be in someone's favor, but it isn't in ours."

"What do you mean?" He was definitely frightening me.

"If the ownership of the ferries wanted to keep the ships here within reach of the Third Reich, delaying the sailing a day would keep us in port. I don't know that is what's happening, but our not sailing might be in German interests that have nothing to do with us."

"There might be famous people on board besides the Jørgensens that the Germans want to find here when they arrive?"

"It's possible. Where's Andersen?" Christiansen asked, looking around.

"Whispering in Mrs. Jørgensen's ear. Did you know they were that close?" I asked.

"No. He isn't Dr. Jørgensen's or Katrine's favorite. I wonder what he and Mrs. Jørgensen have to talk about."

As I watched, Mrs. Jørgensen murmured in his ear as she patted his shoulder. "Maybe she's still trying to calm him down. She's been trying all trip."

"Why? Is he a poor sailor?"

"He says he's not," I told Christiansen.

At that moment, officials near the boat started to issue directions. "They're starting to load freight. Andersen, come help me with this," Christiansen called out in German.

I took the traveling case off the top of the huge stack of luggage on the large flat wagon and Christiansen, now aided by Andersen, began to maneuver the unwieldy wooden cart around the outside of the crowd toward the ferry. They had to do it on their own. The train porters had abandoned us as soon as we reached the dock area and the ferry porters were busy loading freight.

I watched the two men until I lost sight of them in the throng.

"When are they going to let us board? It's cold and windy out here," Katrine said in English, pulling her fur-trimmed coat tighter around her.

"It's cold and windy for all of us," her father said, sounding vaguely annoyed. He kept scanning the crowd, but I couldn't imagine who or what he was looking for.

"They're moving crates of produce and the luggage onto the ship. Soon we'll be on board and you can warm up then," her mother said in a distracted tone. She sank farther down into her wheeled chair, looking pale with cold and fatigue.

Michelle tried to bundle the older woman up by shifting her blanket to cut down on the wind, but I didn't think it would help. Nothing would.

Porteur stood at the edge of our group, the frown on his face making him look as if he was meditating on his discomfort.

I tried to focus on the tang of the salt air to make standing around in the cold sea breeze more pleasant. It didn't work.

We were not a happy group amid the crowd of impatient, grumpy people. We fit right into this sea of misery.

Then another announcement was made in Danish and the message was passed from group to group.

"That is us, dearest," Dr. Jørgensen said to his wife.

"We'll see the rest of you on board." He began to push his wife's wheeled chair toward a long line forming to one side.

I looked at Katrine, but she was looking away from the ship. "What was the announcement?" I asked.

After Porteur and Michelle exchanged glances, Michelle said, "Those who have cabins can go aboard. Ticketed passengers need to wait until those with cabins have boarded."

"Then it won't be too much longer," I said, putting false cheeriness into my tone.

"Once more, it's Dr. and Mrs. Jørgensen's comfort that must be considered above all. They don't care if I'm cold or tired. Just 'Come along, Katrine, and don't make a nuisance of yourself.' I'll show them a nuisance." Katrine began to walk away.

"The way you did when we left the institute?" I asked. It was my first chance to speak to Katrine since we began our travels.

"I wanted to see if they would leave without me. I wanted to see if they cared about me." Her face showed her anguish. "They don't. They would have left me behind. There's no point in my traveling with them."

"Don't forget that your support, your clothes, your money, everything, is going on this ferry," I said, "and we'll have sailed before anyone knows you didn't get on board. No one will be able to do anything about it then, so if you want to be a nuisance, choose your place and timing well."

"You think you're so smart." Fortunately, Katrine was speaking English, but we were still being stared at.

"I have a father who makes yours look sympathetic. I've learned the value of timing."

"I doubt anyone could make my father look better by comparison."

"He criticized my hairdo and my gown as he walked me down the aisle at my wedding." The memory still rankled.

Katrine looked at me, her eyes widening. "Really?"

I nodded.

Before I was called on to tell more stories about my father's horrid behavior, another announcement was made in Danish.

"That's us," Michelle said in French and picked up the case she was carrying for Mrs. Jørgensen. Porteur followed her closely, and Katrine and I straggled behind.

The line creeped along as the sun rose higher into the sky. I hoped Christiansen and Andersen had got all the luggage on the ferry and been able to embark themselves.

My stomach hurt, and I realized I hadn't had so much as a cup of tea since dinner last night. My body was ready for breakfast, but I had a feeling food was still a long way off.

Far in front of us, I saw the Jørgensens enter by the ramp with people walking closely in front of and behind them. At least I could see the line was moving, but at this rate we'd still be here tomorrow when the Nazis arrived.

Katrine said, "I'm hungry. You don't have anything to eat on you, do you?"

"No."

"I'm hungry, and I'm tired, and this line isn't moving fast enough. Why isn't it? My parents are already on board and comfortable. It's not fair."

As the line shuffled forward, Katrine kept up her litany of complaints.

By the time we reached the passenger ramp from the shore to the ferry, my arms were ready to fall off from carrying Mrs. Rothberg's traveling case. What had started off so small and light had become a trunk full of bricks. If Katrine grumbled one more time, I was willing to use my last bit of strength to push her into the harbor.

Instead, I had to dig out my ticket and my papers for the customs officers at the foot of the ramp, as did Porteur, Michelle, and Katrine.

All of our papers were scrutinized closely, Porteur's most of all. No one's papers had been more than glanced at when we arrived on Friday.

Then one of the officials waved Porteur to the side. I thought he was going to make a run for it.

"What are you doing?" I demanded in English.

They looked at me blankly.

"German? French? English? Anybody?"

One of the officials answered me in German.

"Dr. Porteur is Dr. Jørgensen's right-hand man…"

Katrine snorted delicately, and I kicked her, hoping

the small case she carried hid my action.

"And surely you know who Dr. Olaf Jørgensen is," I went on.

"Of course. Is he traveling with you?" the official asked.

"Yes. He should be in his cabin by now. Unfortunately, you didn't have cabins for all of us. Most distressing. I shall have to report this unfortunate state of affairs."

"And who are you?"

"Mrs. Redmond, first secretary to the Royal British Chemical Society. I'm shepherding Dr. Jørgensen and his family and colleagues over for a conference in Cambridge."

Katrine choked and then coughed. She was probably as surprised at how quickly I came up with a lie as I was.

"His daughter sounds unwell. Standing around in this wind can't be good for her. Or for any of us. May we get on the ship, please." I didn't make it a question.

"But Dr. Porteur's papers are French. Not British or Danish."

"And in perfect order. Chemistry is an international discipline. We have scientists from several countries coming to this conference. May we get on the ship, please." My tone was growing authoritative.

Another official, I suspected the leader, nodded and the man handed Porteur back his papers. Only then were we all allowed to climb the ramp into the ferry and the line could move once more. They had barely looked at

Michelle's papers, which were also French.

When we all set foot on the ferry and walked up the stairs to the main level, I breathed a sigh of relief.

"What if they had checked your little lie?" Katrine whispered in my ear in English.

"They didn't have the time nor the facilities. They have too much to accomplish in too short a time with all those people still waiting to board. The captain has already been held up. I'm sure he wants to leave." I would in his place.

We found Mike Christiansen and Henrik Andersen seated in the massive lounge area. I was glad to see they'd saved us two more large chairs similar to the ones they sat on. There was also a padded bench across a table from them. The area was only partially filled up, but all the comfortable chairs were already claimed and I didn't think they'd be able to get everyone on who wanted to sail.

Andersen moved his legs to let Porteur sit in one of the chairs, and Christiansen gestured me to sit next to him. "Any problems?" he asked as soon as I collapsed into the chair and dropped the traveling case onto my lap.

"They didn't like Porteur's papers. French." I rubbed my hands and arms, trying to rub the ache out of my muscles.

"I don't think we can get any coffee until after we sail," he told me. "They'll probably have some lunch for the passengers early in our voyage as well."

"Thank goodness. I'm famished," Katrine said, sitting

on the bench across from us. "I may thaw out before we reach England. And you should hear Mrs. Redmond lie."

Christiansen looked at me and grinned. "Good for you. I didn't know you had it in you."

"Oh, I'm a woman of many talents."

Katrine looked from one of us to the other with a calculating expression on her face. "What are you two involved in? Who do you really work for?" Fortunately, she was still speaking English, so there was less chance we'd be overheard and understood.

Christiansen and I looked at each other. I shrugged. I had run out of lies. Christiansen smiled a smile I wouldn't have trusted. "We work for the British government, helping people come to Britain who have special talents."

"So you can use my father." She was glaring at us now.

"No. So your father's brilliant research doesn't fall into the hands of the Nazis and lengthen the war," Christiansen said, still smiling.

"Your parents wanted to come, Katrine. It was only you who insisted on making difficulties," Andersen said.

"So it's all my fault, is it?" Katrine rose from the bench.

"Where are you off to?" Christiansen said as the men half rose, showing good manners.

"What's it to you?"

People were still entering the increasingly crowded lounge we were in. The ramp must still be attached to the shore. Was she planning to leave the ship at the last moment? As tired as I felt, I'd never be able to catch up with her if she made a run for it. I had no intention of leaving the ship, but had that been her plan the entire time? To leave the ship and force her parents to show their love for her by chasing after her?

Fortunately, they didn't know where she was at that moment, since they were safely in their cabin.

"Why don't we find your parents, Katrine?" Michelle asked, also rising from her side of the bench.

"We could find out if they're coming up for luncheon or if we should take it down to them," I suggested, struggling to get out of the comfortable chair.

Katrine gave a muffled shriek and stalked off, shoving her way through the crowd coming up the stairs toward her. Michelle and I followed her but had little success moving against the tide of passengers.

I saw a sign on a side staircase in English and probably Danish pointing to the cabins. They wouldn't have made Mrs. Jørgensen come upstairs just to go back down to her cabin. There must be another way, a faster way, to the ramp.

"Come on." I dashed to the side and Michelle followed me, possibly still thinking I was going to find the Jørgensens.

At the bottom of the stairs, the corridor went to the cabins. A door to one side led to another passage where at the other end I could see people embarking from the ramp. I went through the doorway and stood to the side of the ramp, Michelle next to me saying in French, "What are we doing?"

"Stopping Katrine," I replied. I looked up the stairs and down the ramp, but I didn't see her. Had she already made it past me and on to the shore?

Chapter Twenty-Three

I spotted her more than halfway down the stairs when she cut around a tall man and rushed down the next three steps. When she saw me, her steps faltered for a moment.

Then she stalked down the rest of the staircase and walked up to me, smiling smugly. "You can't keep me on this ship against my will."

"Where do you plan to live? Where will you get the money to take the train back to Copenhagen?" I asked her.

"I'll—I'll think of something," she said, sounding more assured as she went on, holding her head high.

I needed to keep her on the ship without causing a commotion. "Your life will be easier if you come with us. Your parents will be able to provide for you very nicely. You have the clothes you packed to take with you into new adventures. You could—"

"I want to study art. You can't do that in England."

"Of course you can. London has great galleries. And France is right across the channel."

She looked slightly mollified. Then her expression changed again, obstinately. "My father will never allow it."

I put my hands up. "That's something you have to argue out with him. Although I would think your mother would be on your side if you want to study art."

She looked down the hall to where Michelle stood. "He doesn't listen to her, either. We come in second to chemistry."

"That's something you need to work out with him."

"And my mother. Don't forget my mother." Katrine sounded bitter. "She just doesn't care what I do, as long as it doesn't disturb her tranquility."

Wordlessly, a ferry officer nudged us over to the side while they brought up the ramp. I could hear men calling to each other as they loosened the ropes holding us to the pier.

Katrine turned to face the still-open doorway and took a step forward.

The ferry officer put up a hand and said something in Danish.

Katrine replied in the same language and then said in English, "I want off this ship."

"I'm sorry, miss," he replied in heavily accented English. "It is not possible. We are setting sail."

She stomped her foot. "I want off this ship."

The engines, which had been rumbling for some time, changed to a higher pitch and the ship jerked slightly. Two deckhands jumped in behind the officer and shut the door.

"I want off this ship!" She sounded a little hysterical.

I'd heard her do much worse in Copenhagen. I wondered how bad this would get. "You said you wanted to cause a commotion," I pointed out. "You just picked your time wrong. Let's go find your parents and you can complain to them. I'm sure this officer has more important things to do."

Katrine glared in my direction and then turned to stalk up the stairway away from Michelle and me. I muttered apologies to the ferry official and headed up the stairs after her, Michelle trailing me.

When we reached the men, Katrine had taken my comfortable chair and left the bench seat for Michelle and me. She gave me a smug smile that made me wonder if the whole point of her running off was to get my chair.

We, and all our luggage, were underway to Harwich, and I felt I could relax for the sailing. If it made her feel better to think she'd bested me, that was fine. It didn't matter to me. Once we reached England, others would be taking care of the Jørgensens, and I would be free.

I could handle a little discomfort until then. Or quite a lot of discomfort sitting on this bench.

"I learned the Jørgensens' cabin is number 16," Christiansen told us.

"I'd better see if Mrs. Jørgensen needs anything," Michelle said with a sigh and left the table, the men half rising from their chairs before settling down.

"Did they have to leave anyone behind?" I asked Christiansen.

"No, they squeezed everyone on. We're a little crowded and luncheon will be late, but we're leaving the harbor and there aren't any storms out in the North Sea." Christiansen stretched in his chair. I felt sure he was as pleased to be on the way to England as I was.

* * *

More than an hour later, they began to sell coffee, tea, sandwiches, and apples. "I'll see what the Jørgensens want," Porteur said and left the table. Christiansen and Andersen went to buy food for the four of us, and I was left holding their seats with Katrine.

"Aren't you going to check on your parents?" I asked in English.

"Why? They aren't checking on me."

Her snide tone told me all I needed to know. There would be no point in me trying to start a conversation with her. Still, she had said things I didn't understand. "You said you knew Braun would never murder anyone. How can you be sure?"

"What do you care?"

"I want to know the truth, even if I'm in no position to do anything about it at this point."

"What difference does it make if you know the truth?" Katrine was angry and probably as tired as I was.

"I don't want to think badly of Braun if he was innocent. And I don't like bringing a killer to England who might strike again."

Katrine sighed. "Yes, he was married, and yes, he was a Nazi thug. Although better educated than most of them. But if you sat down and talked to him, you'd discover he was a young man who loved his country and those he considered his countrymen. To his way of thinking, everything was going well."

"Your father, the prize Braun was getting for Germany, was threatening to leave. His fellow chemists knew he was stringing you along to keep your father in Copenhagen until the ports were closed. That's hardly going well."

"Fritz was certain he could convince my father to stay. He was a lot of fun, but I don't want to marry yet, and Fritz knew that. He knew I planned to tell my father that, too."

"If he was married and you didn't want to get married, why say you were engaged?" I asked, definitely puzzled.

"If I said I was having an affair with a married man for the fun of it, my parents would have had kittens. They want me to be respectable."

"So the engagement was just a pantomime?"

"Of course. Designed to make them happy." There was Katrine's smug smile again. "It suited both our plans, and my parents never guessed it was a lie."

With Katrine, I wasn't sure what to believe. Had she known he was married? Did she love him? It was impossible to know the truth. I didn't think I could believe anything she told me. "Then why did you carry on when you heard he was dead?"

"Because I loved him. I'd have grown tired of him quickly, but I did love him at the time and I'm very sorry he's dead."

"But all that wailing." Was that how Katrine expressed herself? I would grow tired of her lung power quickly.

She leaned forward close to my face and said loudly, "I was upset. A friend had just been murdered."

"You said you knew, not thought, but knew, Braun wouldn't kill anyone." I studied her until she looked away.

She lowered her voice. "Not with cyanide."

"What do you mean?"

"He told me several months ago a classmate of his had killed himself with cyanide. It was a short but violent, painful death. One he said gave him nightmares months later. He never wanted to experience that again." Then she looked at me, her eyes wet. "I hope he didn't realize that was what someone had done to him. That was why I was so upset."

Maybe, maybe not. Katrine was so changeable that I couldn't tell what was the truth. I wondered if she knew anymore.

Mike and Henrik came back with sandwiches and coffee then, and we changed the subject.

We had finished lunch and taken back our used dishes before Michelle and Porteur returned. They carried on a short conversation in Danish, and by her head shakes, everything they said was negated by Katrine.

"Apparently, the Jørgensens have had luncheon in their cabin and want to see Katrine. Katrine doesn't want to see them," Christiansen translated.

"That's not what I said," Katrine told him.

Christiansen smiled. "It's what you meant."

Katrine gave a sniff and turned away from us in her

chair. If I had been smart and known she'd never get off the ship and make her own life more difficult, I'd still be sitting in that chair.

No matter what, there was an end in sight to dealing with her, and that was the dock in Harwich. And if I weren't so blastedly tired, none of this would have bothered me. At least the coffee helped.

"You seemed more relaxed," I told Henrik Andersen in German. He wasn't clutching at his fingers or looking around fearfully. "You really are a good sailor."

"I told you so," he replied with a smile. "I was just anxious to get moving. The last few days with the politi were difficult. Unnerving."

"I'm glad they figured out what happened and let us go." I watched him closely as I said that.

"Yes," Andersen said, drawing out the word as if he were considering its meaning.

I'd thought he was the target, but the look on his face, anxious, thoughtful, made me wonder if we'd all come to the wrong conclusion. Who did Andersen think the murderer was? Was Katrine right that Braun couldn't have been the murderer?

Chapter Twenty-Four

The afternoon passed slowly as people wandered around the lounges or out on the deck. I tried to doze, annoyed to see Katrine was curled up, sleeping peacefully, in that comfortable chair while I was stuck on the hard bench.

The men were sprawled out in their chairs asleep as well. Michelle had gone down to the cabin with the Jørgensens, where she might be sleeping in an upper berth if their cabin had one.

I went out on the deck to try to find someplace where I could sleep. The sunshine and fresh sea air was restful and the deck chairs, while sloping and wooden, were not uncomfortable, but it was too cold to stay out there for long without a blanket. I was glad to have a thick woolen one brought to me by one of the stewards.

Afterward, I got a good nap, or at least enough sleep to keep me from strangling Katrine. Even after I woke up, I stayed in the chair and enjoyed the sun on my face with my eyes shut. I found it pleasant not to be crowded in with too many bodies in too little space with too much noise. Even the odor of coffee in the midst of all those people in the lounge was overpowering.

Suddenly, the smell of coffee was strong out here on

deck. I opened my eyes and found a hand holding out a steaming mug to me. I slid one hand out from under the blanket and took the mug, tasting the hot, bitter brew.

"Thought you might like some," Christiansen said as he pulled up a chair and sat down beside me.

"When do we get in tomorrow?"

"After sunrise. We're running hours late, but it's the night hours that worry me."

"Why?" He didn't tend to be concerned about unimportant things, not when he could find so many dangers to worry about.

"The U-boats sail from north German bases. If we cross paths with one in the dark, they won't know we're a ferry. In daylight, they'll be able to tell what we are. A commercial passenger ferry. A target they don't want to attack for propaganda reasons."

"It's a big sea. We'll be all right." I gave him a smile and took another sip of the rapidly cooling coffee.

"There's another thing." He studied my face before he said, "The ownership of this ferry is Danish. Depending on how quickly the Nazis take over Denmark in general and Esbjerg in particular, we may be hours from Harwich when the control of this ship is in German hands."

I stared at him, unable to see where his thoughts were leading him. "But surely that won't affect us. We sailed hours ago."

"I fear the captain will be ordered to turn around and head back to Esbjerg without landing in England, where the ship will undoubtedly be confiscated by the British government."

"You said we were overloaded."

"A little. Why?"

I crossed my fingers and said, "Perhaps the captain will say he doesn't have enough fuel to make it back if we're more than halfway."

"Whatever happens, we'll have to make sure the captain doesn't turn the ship around."

"'We'?" I knew nothing about ships or maritime law. "Can we do that?"

"We have to." His eyes narrowed and he leaned forward slightly. "Can you imagine the greeting we'd get in German-occupied Denmark? British citizens? They'd shoot us without a second thought."

"At least you're traveling on a Danish passport," I said.

"Katrine would tell them differently." His expression was grim.

"No doubt. She does think of us as the enemy." I thought of Oberst Bernhard. While he'd been helpful enough before war was declared, he'd made clear in Copenhagen that he couldn't do anything to help me now if I was in Denmark after the invasion.

I stared at Christiansen before I said, "What are we going to do?"

"Get onto the bridge at about five in the morning. That will be six back in Denmark. And then we'll have to make sure we sail directly to Harwich." He smiled grimly, took my empty coffee cup, and left.

I went inside a little while later to find the lounge had taken on the odor of unwashed people and food and tobacco smoke and beer. Michelle was nowhere in sight. The three men and Katrine were drinking beer, the traveling case of Mrs. Rothberg sitting among the glasses. I had been so tired I'd forgotten all about the small case.

"Any idea if they make a good pot of tea?" I asked.

"No idea. Dinner is rumored to be fried fish and sausages," Henrik told me.

"At least we won't starve," Katrine said in a dismissive tone.

Eventually, Porteur went downstairs to help Michelle bring dinner to the cabin. I sent him down with Mrs. Rothberg's traveling case to put in Mrs. Jørgensen's hands. Andersen and Christiansen went to get food while Katrine and I saved their chairs.

After dinner was cleared away, people played card games and children were read to and played with their stuffed toys. With nothing except darkness outside the windows, people began to settle down for a long, restless night. Stewards handed out the blankets from the deck chairs to passengers who wanted to try to get a decent night's sleep. They smelled of damp wool, but at that point I was beyond caring.

When Porteur came back without Michelle, I gave him back the chair and stretched out along the bench with my hips to my head prone under a blanket and my feet resting on the floor. It wasn't comfortable, but I was tired enough to try anything.

* * *

I must have fallen asleep because I was roughly shaken awake. I sat up in surprise before my eyes focused. I discovered now that the blanket didn't cover my eyes, the lights in the lounge had been lowered, and it was Christiansen who leaned over me. "Time to get up," he whispered.

I struggled to my feet, blinking my eyes and trying to regain circulation in those limbs that had been pressed into the bench and were now numb. "What time is it?"

"After five."

"Then the occupation has already begun." I kept my voice low.

"Yeah."

I could hear the anger and sadness in Mike's voice. "I'm sorry."

He gave me a wry smile. "Nothing to do now but get back to Britain and win this war."

"Do you know how far it is to England?" Dawn's colors were beginning to lighten the sky and people around me were beginning to stir.

"I'd guess a couple of hours. Come on."

I followed Christiansen through a dining lounge full of people trying to sleep in wooden captain's chairs with their heads on tables and past the kitchens to a narrow hallway and a staircase. This wasn't paneled or carpeted the same way as were the areas the passengers saw.

Without hesitation, Christiansen marched up the staircase with me following and entered a door at the top. When I squeezed inside, I looked past Christiansen's greater height and broad shoulders to the equipment and wheel and radios of the bridge with its huge windows. A half-dozen men faced us, looking in equal parts surprised and belligerent.

"I'm Mr. Christiansen, representing the British government, and I'm here to make sure this ship goes directly to Harwich, no matter what orders you might receive from your home office."

He sounded official. I believed him.

Then he spoke in Danish, words I suspected were something along the same lines. A barrel-chested, gray-haired man, whom I suspected was the captain because he was wearing a uniform similar to a Royal Navy uniform with gold braid, replied in heavily accented English, "I have received no orders contradicting my mission to sail to Harwich."

"Well, we'll just stay with you and make sure all is well." Mike gave the captain a nod.

"That's really not necess—"

One of the men, dressed as an ordinary seaman, said something in Danish and handed a piece of paper to the captain.

The captain glanced at it and said, "I'm afraid we've received new orders, sending us back to Esbjerg."

"Do you have enough fuel?" Christiansen asked.

The captain shrugged. "We have to try."

"No." Christiansen pulled a very large handgun out of the waistband of his trousers and pointed it at the captain. "Tell them it's impossible without stopping first for fuel."

The gasp that was heard when Christiansen pulled out his pistol came from me, and I found everyone except Christiansen looking at me.

Where had he been hiding it?

"I'm—I'm Mrs. Redmond of the British Security Services and you are not to sail this ship anywhere except to Harwich," I said. "Feel free to answer that cable any way you want, but you are not going back to Esbjerg."

"But I must. Those are my orders," the captain said. The other men sat or stood at their stations, none of whom appeared willing to get in the middle of this confrontation.

"Are you a Nazi?" I asked.

He jerked back and glared at me. "No. I am a loyal Dane."

"Well, Denmark is being overrun by the German military today because you are between Germany and Norway. Your neutrality has been ignored. Your king has been told to accept that Germany is in charge of your country or you'll have your people butchered as they were in Poland. If your loyalty is to Denmark, you will sail to Harwich." I hoped I was convincing. Or Christiansen's pistol was.

"Put that away," the captain said to Mike. Then he turned to the radioman. "Send a cable saying we are short of fuel and must take some on before we can head back to Esbjerg."

The man who had showed him the cable went back to his desk to send another cable. I followed him and listened to the dots and dashes going out, jotting down each letter on a sheet of paper I grabbed off a desk to make sure that he sent the message the captain had ordered.

"What are you doing?" the man asked in accented English, pausing partway through.

"Thanks to the Girl Guides, I had three years of practice with Morse code. Keep going."

He did, and as best as I could listen to Morse code relying on my school days, he sent the right message. Once again, I was thankful to the teacher who'd run our Guides group and drilled us on Morse code until we could do it in our sleep. She had believed it would save us if we were lost in the woods. As ridiculous as that thought was, the skill had been lifesaving more than once.

"All right?" Christiansen said, running a hand across his beard.

"Yes." I'd recognized "petrol" and "Harwich." Written Danish had some similarities to German. They didn't need to know I didn't speak Danish.

I handed the paper to Christiansen, who glanced at it before putting away his pistol and leaning against the bulkhead with his arms folded over his chest. I stood near him, knowing if anything needed to be translated for me to understand, he'd keep me informed without alerting the others to my handicap.

"How far is Harwich?" I asked.

"We should be able to see it in an hour or so," the captain replied.

The ship continued to sail straight ahead at what seemed to be the same pace. The engines sounded the same. I was beginning to relax when I heard another cable coming in.

The man operating the wireless transmitter wrote down the message and passed it to the captain. Christiansen stood behind him to read over his shoulder.

"The captain is ordered to refuel without letting any of his passengers off and return to Esbjerg," Christiansen said in English.

"I would think the passengers will have a great deal to say about that, not to mention the British officials in the port," I said, looking at the captain.

"How can I disobey an order?" the captain asked.

Christiansen walked over and fired his gun once into the wireless. First, the noise made all of us cringe and duck. Then sparks and a hissing sound along with a little flame flashed from the device, making everyone jump clear.

"What order?" he said with a smile.

Chapter Twenty-Five

The captain looked at me with a panicked look on his face. I didn't blame him. At this point, Mike Christiansen scared me, too.

I could understand his action. We'd gone to Copenhagen to bring back a Nobel Prize winning chemist. Britain needed his research. To keep him out of Britain when we were so close was not to be borne.

"Well, you can't respond," I said, "so you might as well sail to Harwich and let us off. Who's to say you received their message?"

"How can I sail without a working radio? It is against regulations," the captain said.

"Then you need to get to a port where you can get it fixed. Harwich would serve the purpose," I said.

"I will lodge a formal complaint." The captain gave his words the aura of an ultimate threat.

"I would expect you to," Mike said, not at all impressed after the threats we'd faced in the past few days.

The captain said something in Danish to the helmsman, who continued on his steady path to England. Christiansen put his pistol out of sight and stood in a corner, watching. I stood near him, in part to see where he would aim the pistol next and stay out of the line of fire.

We were in luck. Before anything else happened, we could see the coast of England from the bridge. The captain gave various orders in Danish that didn't appear to worry Christiansen. The harbor slowly came closer.

* * *

We came down the ramp as a group, Porteur pushing Mrs. Jørgensen's wheeled chair, Christiansen leading us toward the officials who were there to greet Dr. Jørgensen, and Andersen, Katrine, Michelle, and me bringing up the rear.

I didn't know the officials greeting us, but I did recognize Sir Malcolm in the background. I walked over to him and said, "We've returned with Dr. Jørgensen and his family, his wife's maid, and two of his research assistants on the day we said we would. Now please tell me, did the Germans attack?"

"The Danes are already negotiating a peace treaty. They offered little resistance and suffered few casualties." He shook his massive, balding head. "I can't see King George giving in without a fight. What a way to run a country."

"It must work for the Danes." I gave him a cheery grin.

He grumbled in reply. I didn't want to know what he said.

Christiansen came over and said, "We were successful, as you can see."

"Did you have to employ the pistol?"

"Yes, but only on the ship's radio."

"We did have two deaths," I told Sir Malcolm. "It was the German chemist who was supposedly engaged to Jørgensens' daughter and one of the Jørgensens' maids. The police eventually decided the German chemist accidentally died by his own hand, while trying to poison someone else, after killing a troublesome lover."

"That was convenient, mistakenly poisoning himself," Sir Malcolm said, eyebrows raised.

"Yes, it was," I said, feeling vaguely uneasy about the police's conclusion.

"Don't tell me you're having second thoughts," Christiansen said. "You were the one who figured it out and convinced the politi."

"It's the only solution that fits the facts and the evidence," I told both men. "But Braun—that was his name—was apparently meticulous. He wasn't the type to accidentally poison himself."

"He was also blind in one eye. That's what caused the accident in the middle of a great deal of activity in a very small area," Christiansen said. "And the only fingerprints on the vial of cyanide were his."

"The police were satisfied and let you and the Jørgensens go, so that is the end of it," Sir Malcolm said. "I'd hate to think you accused the wrong person twice, Olivia. You did that just a few months ago and almost got yourself killed for your efforts. Don't disappoint me."

"I'm not accusing anyone," I said, sounding defensive

to my ears. "There were so many who wanted him dead. That he died from an accident seems—odd."

"But fortunate. That accident allowed us all to leave Denmark ahead of the Nazis," Mike Christiansen said.

Before I could respond, an official came up to Sir Malcolm about plans for the Jørgensen party. It turned out we were to ride together, in a first-class carriage, to London where they would be put up in a hotel. And I could go home, finished with the problem of Katrine's sulking and Braun's and Greta's murders.

"I'm glad we don't have to work out the details of Jørgensen's living and laboratory requirements," Christiansen said.

"Whatever they come up with, one of them will object," I replied.

"It won't be him doing the objecting. It'll be one of the women." Mike shook his head sadly.

"I wonder if they'll let Katrine live on her own in London," I said. "She'd probably be happier."

"Her parents won't, unless Miss Jørgensen can come up with a really compelling reason for her to stay there."

"She'll scream the roof down if they don't let her?" I asked, putting on an innocent expression.

Mike burst out laughing. "Too true."

Porters were moving all the baggage to the baggage carriage and officials were helping get Mrs. Jørgensen and her chair into our carriage. The officials were not nearly as efficient nor as gentle in moving her as the train porters had been.

Once we were all inside with several other important Danes who'd escaped at the last minute, Mrs. Jørgensen said, "Olivia, would you take this to Mrs. Rothberg's daughter when we reach London? Here is her address. It is not a place I am familiar with." She handed me the traveling case.

I looked at the address. Bloomsbury. "Of course. I'd be glad to." Fortunately, Mrs. Rothberg had included a telephone number for her daughter as well.

Once more, I hadn't shaken off my responsibilities. I was obligated to safely deliver a fortune in jewels.

When I moved down the carriage full of wide blue cloth seats, away from the important people in the world of science, Sir Malcolm signaled me to sit next to him. I walked up to him and sat with the traveling case on my lap.

"What is that?"

"A delivery for a friend of Mrs. Jørgensen."

"Anything of interest?" Sir Malcolm looked at everything from the point of view of espionage.

"The family jewels. The family in question is Jewish and the mother wants her daughter to have the valuables the Nazis would like to keep for themselves."

"You're certain?" Sir Malcolm sounded as if he didn't believe me.

"I have the key. I'll check it again before delivery," I told him. I wasn't stupid, and I wasn't trusting. At least not since working with Sir Malcolm.

"Be sure you do. Did you get any sleep on the ferry?"

"A little. They were overbooked, so I was on a bench all night."

"And Mike Christiansen?"

"He was in a chair."

"What a shame." Sir Malcolm didn't sound the least bit concerned with our travel arrangements, but I was used to that.

Just as I drifted off to sleep, I awakened to find Sir Malcolm gently removing the traveling case from my lap. I glared at him as he held out his hand for the key. "You won't need to check it later. I will be glad to verify the contents with you now."

For a large man, Sir Malcolm moved with delicacy and grace. Another five minutes and I'd have been sound asleep. I'd have to watch him even more closely now that I was aware of his light-fingered tricks.

Once I unlocked the case, it took him under a minute to check the inside of the case and pronounce it safe for me to bring into the country.

As much as I wanted to keep an eye on Sir Malcolm, I fell asleep again within minutes, and I didn't awaken until we reached London.

Sir Malcolm shook me awake. "Get your case and go home. If I need you for anything else about this task, I'll call you. Otherwise, you're released until your next assignment."

"Thank you." I knew Sir Henry Benton, my employer at the *Daily Premier,* would be glad to have me back at work. I didn't write good newspaper copy, but I did find some newsworthy stories.

As we began to disembark, Mike Christiansen came up to me. "Considering you don't speak Danish or know anything about chemistry, you did very well. I'm glad you were there to help me."

"Copenhagen is beautiful. What I saw of it," I told him. I needed to be as generous as he was. "Thank you for quickly translating for me so I could be of some use. I'm glad we got the Jørgensens and the important papers out of Denmark."

He nodded. "I suspect after they get settled in Cambridge, Katrine and Andersen will be making frequent trips to London. If they call me, I'll call you to help entertain them. Or separate them," he added.

"Why would Katrine come to London with him? She can't stand him." I murmured because I did not want to be overheard.

"The Jørgensens can't come to London with her, and they think Andersen will keep an eye on her the same as an older brother."

"In which case," I told him, "Katrine will get away from Andersen as quickly as possible."

Mike shook his head. "I don't think so. That's the one thing that would make her father stop her from coming to London. And he would, too."

"Then we should expect to see them in London soon?"

"Yes. And when they call me, I'll call you to join us."

"Don't you have a girlfriend to make up a foursome?" He hadn't mentioned a wife or girlfriend, but then, I hadn't mentioned Adam any more than necessary.

"No. I want to avoid getting trapped until the war is over. Then maybe…"

"It might be a Danish girl rather than an English one," I finished for him.

He grinned at me. "It just might."

"Anyone in particular?"

He shook his head, but I didn't believe him. Mike kept everything private. With many things, this was good, but not when it was information I also needed to carry out our assignment.

Chapter Twenty-Six

I went back to my flat and found there was no note from Adam, so I knew he hadn't been given the weekend off. I'd have been upset if he'd been home while I was in Denmark since I saw him so seldom. I unpacked quickly and crawled under the covers for the first good sleep I'd managed in a few days.

When I awoke it was midafternoon. I called Sir Henry Benton at the newspaper and told him I'd be back at work in the morning, released from Sir Malcolm's latest foolishness. Sir Henry sounded pleased and asked me to write up those details of my experience that wouldn't give any hint of my assignment.

In other words, he wanted something in return for lending me to Sir Malcolm for a few days. I told him I'd do that as soon as I arrived at the newspaper in the morning.

Once I looked around my kitchen, I knew there was nothing to eat and dining out at a restaurant was my only option unless I grabbed my ration book and picked up a few things at the shops. Knowing I'd face the same problem the next day, I put on my hat, coat, and gloves and headed out.

* * *

When I returned from the shops, I called Mrs.

Rothberg's daughter at the number she'd given us. When Mrs. Anne Bannacloss was brought to the telephone, she sounded eager for news of her mother and invited me to come over immediately. I agreed. The sooner I was rid of the traveling case and a fortune in jewels the better.

The house was a four-story brick-fronted row house facing one of the parks around Bloomsbury. Mrs. Bannacloss was in her mid-twenties, but she appeared to be wearing her mother's old clothes, out of date and dreary. Either she'd lost weight or her dress, a dark blue print, had belonged to someone else.

What I could see of the ground floor, the hall followed by the drawing room I was shown into, was plainly furnished but scrubbed clean and polished.

After we introduced ourselves, I said, "Are you living here on your own?"

"No." She sounded startled by the question. "My husband and I live with his parents and his sister and her family and some relatives of theirs. We all came over in 1938 from Vienna. When the men were thrown out of work after the Nazis came into power, we all escaped."

"And no doubt had to leave everything behind." I had seen Vienna in those days.

"Except our lives. Our loved ones. We were lucky. I'm surprised my parents didn't come with you."

"They didn't want to, from what your mother said. She sounds as if they have plans to go to Sweden if the situation gets worse in Copenhagen."

"As nice as the Danes are, things will get worse with the Nazis there." She shook her head. "But you have something for me?"

"Your mother wanted you to have this." I held out the traveling case and the key.

She set the case on an end table and opened it. "Ah. This was my grandmother's. And this her grandmother's." She fingered the old-fashioned necklaces and rings before she looked up at me with a smile. "You have no idea how much this means to me."

"I was glad to bring it to you."

"What were you doing in Copenhagen?"

"Escorting Dr. Olaf Jørgensen and his wife and daughter and some other chemists to England before the Nazis arrived."

"Let me guess. My mother asked Mrs. Jørgensen to bring this to me. She agreed and then had you take care of it for her."

"That sums it up," I admitted.

"Is she really ill or is this just another of her little ploys?"

That surprised me. "She really is ill, I believe."

"Then I feel sorry for her." Anne Bannacloss turned her attention back to the jewelry I had brought from her mother.

"What has your mother said about Mrs. Jørgensen? They seem to be good friends." I was curious to hear what someone who'd known her for a long time thought of the woman who'd been my mother's friend.

"She has always needed to be waited on, even when she was healthy and walking around."

"Really?"

"Oh, yes. She's always needed to be the center of attention, to be catered to. If someone rose to fetch something, she always had something for them to get for her, too, even if it was in the wrong direction and she was otherwise capable of walking for miles."

"Perhaps her disease had begun but nothing had been mentioned to anyone outside the family." She had been kind to me, or at least to the memory of my mother, and I wanted to be fair to her.

"Oh, no. It started suddenly when Vilhelm became sick and died. As soon as it began, everyone was treated to all her trips to the doctors and the loss of her son. No one had ever suffered before the way she had. The odd thing is, everyone believed all her protestations of not wanting to be a bother. All her gratitude. Even without a diagnosis." Anne stopped and then added, "Katrine can't stand her."

"Your mother said you went to school with Katrine."

"We grew up together. We were close friends. I'd been in Vienna less than a year when the Nazis came and we had to leave. For years before that, I was there to see her mother use Katrine as if she were an extra servant. 'Oh, I know you want to spend time with your friends, study, whatever, but I need you here. It's just one evening.

A few hours. And I won't be here much longer.'" Anne changed her voice to a passable impression of Mrs. Jørgensen's.

"I suspect Katrine didn't like it." This went a distance toward explaining Katrine's attitude toward traveling with her parents.

"This has been going on since 1934. By the time I married, Katrine had suffered more than enough at the hands of her mother. For all her protestations, the woman never gets any worse. Any sicker. She goes on, year after year, always the same."

"What about the servants?"

"None stayed for very long. Mrs. Jørgensen has a way of pushing people too far."

"And Katrine has learned it from her." She'd certainly pushed me too far.

"Katrine is here in London? Tell her to come and see me."

"When next I hear from her, I will. But tell me. What do you mean, without a diagnosis?" It seemed an odd choice of words.

"No one knows what is wrong with her. Both she and Dr. Jørgensen give vague answers. In fact, Dr. Jørgensen admits he really has no idea what is wrong. He says the doctors say it is unlike anything they have seen before."

"That uncertainty must be difficult to live with."

Anne gave me an appraising look. "Is it?"

"What do you mean?"

"Why do you think she has that cane with a dragon's head?"

"What? What cane?"

Anne shook her head. "When the wheeled chair was designed for her, she had the cane built of the same metal tubing with a dragon's head for the hand grip. It fits neatly into the back of the chair so if you don't know it was there, you'd never notice it."

"I saw it, but I thought it was part of the chair." And all this time, it was a cane. Detachable from the wheeled chair.

"One afternoon shortly before I was married, I went over to the Jørgensens. The maid said Katrine would be home soon and for me to wait in the music room. I walked down the hall, and as I passed the library, I saw the door was open. I looked in and saw Mrs. Jørgensen standing, walking around, getting a book from a shelf. Her wheeled chair was nowhere to be seen, and she had her cane propped up against a bookcase."

"Could her paralysis come and go? Had Mrs. Jørgensen regained her strength?" I was amazed. I was also seeing the possibility of a different killer for both victims.

Anne shook her head. "No. According to my mother, she's supposed to be as stricken as she was six years ago."

"Did you tell your mother what you saw?"

"No. For some reason, I decided that would not be wise."

"So your mother doesn't know."

"No one does. Not even Katrine."

That was something Katrine would never have been quiet about if she'd known. Ailsa Jørgensen could walk. Suddenly, everything I knew about the trip to Denmark, and carrying Mrs. Jørgensen on and off the trains, changed.

* * *

Life returned to normal surprisingly fast. Adam and I wrote to each other nearly daily, our letters crossing in the mail. I wrote my cousin Abby Summersby to find out how her four boys were doing in school and with their numerous projects around the large farm. I phoned Esther, Sir Henry's daughter and my best friend for ages, to hear about her two children and to set up luncheon dates for the two of us in hotel restaurants and tea shops.

My father and I reestablished our habit of having Sunday dinner together at a hotel restaurant. At our first meal, my father said over the roast course, "Where have you been? I tried to reach you last Sunday and never heard a word."

"I was out of town on assignment."

"For Sir Henry?"

"For Sir Malcolm."

"Oh, Olivia, really. Is that wise?"

I ignored his question. "Was Mother a good baker?"

I had to wait until my father finished his bite before he answered, "Fair, I suppose."

"And good at needlework?"

"She never went near the stuff. Told me if I expected my wife to do any of that, then I should marry a seamstress." My father looked at me and set down his fork. "Why all the questions?"

"I spent the weekend with a friend of Mother's. Ailsa Jørgensen."

"Oh." There was a world of meaning in his repressed "oh."

"Oh? I'm sure you knew her."

"Oh, yes."

Well, that wasn't informative. "Was she a good friend of Mother's?"

"Sometimes."

"'Sometimes'? That's cryptic." And unhelpful.

"Ailsa always wanted things her way. For everyone to follow her plans. To do things her way. To go where she wanted to go. To be the center of the universe. Your mother was not a natural follower. If Ailsa's plans fit in with your mother's, she was happy to go along. She said Ailsa was fun to be around."

"And if my mother wanted to do something else?"

"Then she would politely decline and do whatever it was she wanted to do." He took another bite.

"Did that ever cause friction between Mrs. Jørgensen and my mother?"

After he finished, he said, "Sometimes. Sometimes she didn't find out your mother had gone out without her."

"And if she found out?"

"'Oh, Phyllida, I thought you were my friend' and other complaints of a similar nature. Your mother never paid any attention to her whining. She just asked Ailsa what she wanted to do that day." My father shook his head and continued eating.

"Why would she have said my mother was good at embroidery?"

When he finished that course, he replied, "I suspect she wanted her to be, and so she rearranged reality to fit what she wanted. Her memories probably now match what she wished people to have been like."

After we finished our meal and were waiting for our coffee, I asked, "What did you think of Mrs. Jørgensen?"

"She was a neurotic, spoiled, selfish pain. I couldn't stand her. I told your mother if she wanted to go around with her, fine. But she shouldn't expect me to tag along."

"So you didn't have anything to do with her?"

"It was unavoidable at the opera or at concerts or large parties thrown by my Danish counterparts. But there were always so many people present that her effect was diluted." My father gave me a brief grim smile. "And she wasn't so demanding at a large gathering."

He stopped and thought for a moment. "And you need to understand, Olivia, that Ailsa disliked me as much as I disliked her. She felt I wasn't good enough for your mother. Fortunately, your mother didn't think that."

Our coffee arrived and I waited until our cups were prepared before I asked, "Did my mother like her? Truly?"

"Truly? I think she liked her. She thought she was fun to be around, which was important when we were young. She just didn't let Ailsa run her life, and that was frustrating to Ailsa."

* * *

As reporters at the *Daily Premier* were leaving, either being called up for military service or to work in government departments, Sir Henry was not replacing them. There were no replacements to be found. He began to send me out to various departments to pick up the latest announcements and to question anyone I could about what the carefully worded governmental statements actually meant.

Frequently, what I learned or surmised wouldn't pass the Ministry of Information censors.

The *Daily Premier* was full of articles on how well the defense of Norway was going for Allied troops, how many German ships were being sunk without much mention of our own ships going down, and how, despite rationing, there was plenty of food, plenty of fabric, for everyone. If what we printed didn't quite match what we saw or didn't make sense if studied too carefully, no one said so.

It would have been unpatriotic to question the government too closely.

The news from Norway made me nervous. I didn't know where Adam was, but his letters arrived with such infrequency, arriving several at a time, that I suspected someplace cold.

To calm myself, I started to sketch the fashions I saw on the street. Skirts were shorter and slimmer, jackets had epaulets and fake belts. Cuffless trousers, boiler suits, wildly decorated hats, there was much to catch my eye as I walked around London.

* * *

Almost two weeks after our return, I received a telephone call at the flat shortly after I returned home. "Olivia Redmond?" a male voice asked.

"Yes." My heart stopped. Had something happened to Adam?

"Mike Christiansen. Katrine Jørgensen and Henrik Andersen are in town and asked us to go out to dinner and dancing with them."

Once my heart began to beat normally again, I asked, "When?"

"Tonight."

We agreed on a time and place. Once I hung up, I looked through my prewar dinner gowns and chose one in lavender that I seldom wore. I paired it with black heels and jet jewelry that matched my mood. Katrine was not one of my favorite people, even though I'd been out of her presence for a while and was back to my ordinary life.

I hoped that now we were in Britain and she was settled, Katrine wouldn't be so combative or self-centered.

As soon as I walked into the place where we were to meet, I realized that she meant to enjoy herself. It had a huge dance floor, dim lighting, a jazzy orchestra playing the newest hits, and strong drinks. Dinner did not seem to be part of the equation.

I felt cheated, and I suspected Katrine was behind the choice of venues. She seemed to enjoy looking for trouble and this appeared to be the type of place where she'd search for calamity and which would deliver it in spades.

Chapter Twenty-Seven

Just as I turned to leave, I discovered Mike Christiansen had been watching for me, and he greeted me with a hug as if I were a long-lost friend.

"I thought you mentioned dinner," I told him.

"Sorry. This was Katrine's idea." He had the grace to look embarrassed.

"Have any of you had dinner?"

"No." Then he added, "The brat is determined to cut loose tonight, away from mummy and daddy."

"And why I am here?"

"For reinforcements. And because you're a good person." He gave me a smile.

"Oh…" I said in disgust before I gave in. "Lead on."

"Thanks. You're a pal."

When we reached the little round table, Andersen was there slumped over his drink and Katrine was out on the dance floor with some young man in uniform.

Andersen looked up at me and said, "Why will she dance with every man in the place but me?"

I sat down next to him. "Because she's an idiot and you need to look for a woman who will appreciate your good qualities."

"I don't have any."

"Not when you're whining that way," I nearly shouted over the crescendo of quick notes in the music.

"Thanks." He made a face and took another sip of his drink.

"You're stable and kind and hard-working. Many women want that. Katrine doesn't. She wants all flash and glamour."

"I'm not handsome enough."

"Nonsense. You're not silly enough. Not for her."

"Maybe I should enlist."

"Why? You're needed to find out how to make synthetic rubber and...and other important chemicals. That's your contribution to the war effort. That's more important than anything you could do on the battlefield."

Katrine danced by with a different partner, also in uniform, and Mike came over with beers for himself and me. "Why don't you dance with Olivia?" he asked Andersen.

"She doesn't want to dance with me."

"How do you know that?" I demanded. "How do you know that about any woman until you ask her?"

"You want to?" he asked, turning sad dog eyes toward me.

I didn't want to, particularly, but I lied well, and we went out on the dance floor among the kicks and twirls. All of this seemed just about beyond him, but I tried to coach him and we managed a respectable turn on the floor despite my long gown. Most of the girls Katrine's age wore shorter dresses to be able to do all the fast dance moves.

"Now," I said when the music stopped, "why don't you walk over to one of those girls over there and ask her to dance?"

"But I don't know her."

"Would you prefer for me to introduce you?" I thought Andersen was being as difficult as Katrine.

"Katrine's back at our table." Speaking with an eager tone that I found pitiful, he strode off, leaving me to catch up. *Wonderful.* The band was taking a break. I had a feeling that was the only reason she had come back to sit with us.

"I'm thirsty. Get me another drink, Henrik," she told him.

"Do you really think—?" he mumbled.

"Yes. Go get it."

Andersen walked off, shoulders slumped.

"Why did you come to London with him if you don't like him?" I asked.

She looked at me as if I were stupid. "Because that was the only way I could convince my parents to let me come here. And because he likes me, he'll do what I want him to and won't tattle on me to my parents."

"That's not fair to Andersen," Mike said, anger in his tone.

"Life's not fair. I'm here, aren't I?" Katrine glared at him.

"You don't like this dance club? We could leave," he said, deliberately misunderstanding her.

"The dance club is fine. Cambridge is dull, and the only way I can escape is by coming here with Henrik, even though I can't stand him. He's as dull as Cambridge. Henrik is all tea and biscuits, but I want Champagne."

Andersen was standing behind her. She took the drink he held out without a thank you. If she had looked into his face, she'd have seen his pain and sorrow. Though I doubted she'd care.

"I saw Anne Bannacloss here in London."

Katrine looked at me. "Who?"

"Anne Bannacloss. Used to be Rothberg. School friend of yours."

"She's living here in London? How did she get to be so lucky? This is a wonderful city. It's huge." For once, she sounded enthusiastic about something.

"She came here with her husband and his family. They're all refugees from Vienna."

"That sounds so dreary. Is she doing anything interesting? Does she go dancing a lot?"

"Not that I know of. You could ask her."

Katrine ignored me and started commenting on the frocks worn by other young women in the club.

As the band began to play again, Katrine finished her drink, set the glass down, and walked off without a word to any of us. Within a minute, she danced past with a different dance partner, this time in a lounge suit.

Henrik Andersen sank into a chair. "What will I tell her parents?" he moaned.

"The truth, but only if asked," I suggested. "By the way, your English is very good for someone who just arrived here."

"I've been studying it for months from Mrs. Jørgensen. Since we knew there was a chance we'd come to England. Both Dr. and Mrs. Jørgensen wanted me to come with them. They find me useful."

"Why didn't you tell us?"

He shrugged. "We thought you'd find it strange that I could speak English when hardly any of my countrymen could."

"'We'?" Mike Christiansen asked.

"Mrs. Jørgensen and I."

"Is this how they find you useful? To chaperone Katrine?" I asked. I must have sounded astonished. It was a terrible waste of a talented man.

"What's your role here? Are you her bodyguard?" Mike asked.

"I'm to try to, but I don't know how successful I'll be." Henrik finished his drink. "I love her so much, and she wants nothing to do with me." He rose then. "Anyone want another?"

Mike and I shook our heads. I'd barely touched my beer.

He returned with a glass and a pint bottle.

As soon as Henrik sat down, Mike asked, "So what is our role in this farce?"

"Help me keep her out of trouble." He tossed off a

shot of whisky.

"Who's going to keep you out of trouble?" I asked. "Drinking that much won't help."

"It doesn't matter what happens to me." He looked at me then with the saddest expression and said, "Haven't you figured it out? I don't matter. Not to Dr. Jørgensen, not to Mrs. Jørgensen, certainly not to Katrine. I've never mattered to any of them. They just use me."

"Dr. Jørgensen considers you his lead researcher," Mike said.

"But he makes all the rules. All the decisions on what we try next. He keeps me around to keep an eye on Katrine. She is all that matters to him. And to me." He curled his fingers into a fist and pounded it on the table. It was so loud in the dance hall that no one heard it.

I looked at Mike to do something, but he shrugged.

"And Mrs. Jørgensen?" I asked.

"She's the worst of the lot. Made me think she was my friend. That she needed my help."

"She needs everyone's help," I pointed out, trying not to think of what I'd learned from Anne Bannacloss. "She's in a wheeled chair. She's frail."

"But her mind is sharp." Henrik tapped his temple with his right hand.

"Yes, it is. And that must make it harder for her."

"And for everyone around her," Henrik replied.

"Particularly Dr. Jørgensen," Mike said.

Henrik held up the bottle toward Mike, who shook his

head. Pouring himself another drink, Henrik said, "And for those little chores that she can't call on Dr. Jørgensen for, who do you think she calls on?"

"You?" I asked. At this point I thought the sooner he voiced all his grievances, the sooner he'd stop drinking so heavily.

"Yes. Me."

Katrine danced past with yet another man in uniform. Henrik watched her, glaring at her partner.

"You need to find yourself a nice girl. Someone who appreciates you. Appreciates a nice, stable, quiet man," I told him.

"Where?"

"Not here." I looked around the cavernous room, music bouncing off the distant walls, people dancing maniacally. "Look around Cambridge. Talk to your neighbors. Introduce yourself to the vicar. Someone will know the perfect girl for you."

"It's too late."

"No, it's not. You're not married to Katrine." I spoke with heat.

"No, not Katrine. She doesn't know about it."

"You're married?" Mike said, confusion written on his face.

"No. Not me. I'm a bachelor."

I was rapidly growing tired of guessing games, and I was hungry. Mike had promised me dinner, which wasn't going to happen that night. "Then it can't be too late."

"It is. It is."

I remembered my thought that Andersen was aware of a danger to the Jørgensens. Did he, or was this a flight of fancy? "Is there a danger to the Jørgensens from their immediate circle? What is the danger they're facing?"

His expression made him appear stricken with guilt. In an anguished voice he said, "You know?"

Mike and I exchanged glances. "I want you to tell me," I said.

"Promise you won't tell."

We both promised. It was so loud in the dance club no one else would have been able to hear his confession or explanation or crazy theory. Whatever we were about to hear.

"Promise."

"Yes."

"I'm an accessory."

Mike raised his eyebrows.

"To a crime?" I asked when I could speak again.

Andersen downed another drink. Much more and he'd be making no sense at all. And I wanted to know what he was talking about. This would be my best chance of learning if he had anything to do with Braun's death.

"Yes."

Mike sat forward slightly and glanced at me, his eyes narrowed. "What crime?"

"Whaddayu think?"

"You didn't kill Braun," I said.

"No. I didn't."

"Who did?" Mike asked.

"Not for me to say. No limitation on being charged for murder."

"But you know who did it," I said, certainty in my words.

"'Course." Henrik's arm slid off the table and he nearly fell out of his chair.

Mike grabbed the bottle and put it out of reach and out of sight below the table.

"Hey."

"Henrik, what did you do?" I asked. It took me a minute to get his attention since he was focused on finding the whisky bottle. "I know you feel badly used, but what happened?"

"It all made sense. And I could trust her. Then I had to clean up afterward."

"Clean what up?" We were so close to learning the truth, if I could just get him to make sense.

"When I found the vial, I kept it. I didn't want Katrine to know. She didn't believe he would kill someone, but he really did plan to kill me."

"You found poison on Braun and thought he planned to kill you?" Mike asked.

"Then when you kept saying it had to be murder, I threw it in the flower bed. That confused you, didn't it?" He seemed a little confused himself. He also appeared to have some trouble focusing as he addressed his comments to me.

"You removed the vial from Braun's body when you found him dead and threw it in the flower bed so we wouldn't know how it got there." Mike looked at me. "Brilliant."

"Henrik, you wouldn't get in a lot of trouble for doing that. The politi would be angry, but that doesn't make you an accomplice in his death." I patted his shoulder.

Good. I was glad that the official version was proving to be the correct one. I didn't want to think there was someone else who had been involved in murder, someone we'd helped escape justice as well as escaping the Nazis. It explained why the vial had been found where it was.

But not the folded paper by the front door.

"But I am," he insisted.

"You found and threw away an empty vial. That isn't a big crime," I told him.

"No." He shook his head and then held it in his hands. "I emptied it first. In the flower bed."

"You emptied the cyanide into the flower bed and then threw the vial in there?" Mike said, leaning forward.

"Thaswha I said."

"Then where did the cyanide come from that killed Braun?" I asked, looking at Mike. This was getting more confusing.

"I put a little in a folded paper."

Mike and I looked at each other and then we turned to look at Henrik who still sat with his head in his hands.

Had he killed Braun? Keeping my voice low, below the level of the music, I asked, "What did you do with it?"

"Gave it to Mrs. Jørgensen. She wanted a way out, you know, if her disease got too bad."

"When did you give it to her?" Mike asked, equally quietly.

"The day before Braun died."

"Why didn't you tell the politi?" I asked.

"She'd have killed me. She expects absolute loyalty. Braun wasn't loyal to Olaf or Katrine. She told me later he had to die." Then Henrik began to sob.

We finally managed to get Henrik to tell us where they were staying and produce his room key. Mike got him up and moving while I stayed behind, waiting for Katrine to make another appearance.

She came back to our table when the band next took a break. "I want another drink."

"Get it yourself." I was not in the mood. I didn't know if Henrik or anyone else's life was in danger. And puzzling it out in the din of this dance club was impossible.

"Henrik will get it. Where did he go?"

"He and Mike left. It's just us now." I gave her a tight-lipped smile so she'd know I wouldn't go out of my way to do anything for her.

"Lend me some money."

"No."

"You know my father's good for it."

"I don't care. You have your hotel room booked

already." I didn't make it a question. "You don't need any money. Let's go."

"But I want another drink. And I want to dance."

"Now aren't you sorry you treated Henrik so badly?"

"Where is he?"

I shrugged.

"Fine. I'll get someone else to pay for my drinks." She started to walk off.

"Don't be a fool, Katrine. They'll take you for a tart."

Chapter Twenty-Eight

Ignoring me, she walked over to a couple of men in army officer uniforms. "My friend left and took my money. Could one of you big, handsome men buy me a drink?" She tilted her head as she looked at them and gave them a big smile.

They just about fell over each other in their haste to buy her a drink. I was certain the management didn't allow any outright solicitation on the premises, but Katrine had definitely given those soldiers the wrong impression. Now I was stuck keeping an eye on her. And worrying about Henrik.

Fortunately, it was late. I knew the dance club would be closing down soon. I watched as Katrine danced with both men. When she tried to dance off with someone else, and a naval officer at that, they pulled her back. The naval officer objected, but the two army officers convinced him that would be a mistake, and he moved on.

Finally, they turned the lights up high as the orchestra finished their last long, jazzy tune. People began to gather up belongings, claim coats, and leave by the main entrance. I remained in my seat, watching the two men with Katrine at a table twenty feet away.

When she tried to walk away, one of the men pulled

her arm tightly behind her and said something. She shook her head, smiling, trying to talk her way out of the situation.

Then they started to march her toward the door, one of them on either side of her. I rose and tried to block their path. "Out of our way, honey, we have a date already," one of them said as they pushed me out of the way.

I followed them out the door where Katrine, who'd been struggling to get free, screamed. People turned and stared, but there was a crowd on the pavement of laughing, rowdy partygoers who blocked any attempt to interfere.

But there had to be a bobby nearby on this beat. I stood directly behind them and screamed, and Katrine joined in. That drew the attention of more people up and down the street, including a bobby who hurried over.

While Katrine and I said they had tried to take her away against her will, the two young army officers insisted we had tried to extort money from them with promises of sex. We all spoke at once, loudly to be heard over the others, until the bobby blew his whistle and quickly had us all inside a police wagon going to the local police station.

At the station, the two officers crowded around the desk, saying they had to be released so they wouldn't be late and considered absent without leave.

"You should have thought of that before you tried to spirit this young lady away to some dark alley," I said loudly, indignation attacking with every word.

"Lady? Ha! She's nothing but a common slag."

Katrine slapped the man who had spoken. He in turn began to throw a punch when two bobbies stepped in between them.

"Did you see that? She struck me."

"You called me a whore. I am a virgin," Katrine declared.

Her words caused everyone in the police station, including strangers there due to some other complaint, to freeze in complete silence. Including me.

Unfortunately, she'd told too many stories. I didn't know if I believed her.

The two army officers looked at each other in amazement, knowing their case had grown weaker. If they pressed their case, this was provable evidence against their claims. They looked a good deal more sober. And a good deal more frightened.

"And that lady's a newspaper reporter. Do you want to see your names in the paper?" Katrine continued.

I'd never seen two men break out in a sweat as quickly as they did at Katrine's threat. I silently vowed to never, ever go anywhere with Katrine again. I promised myself that before. This time I really meant it.

Katrine turned to the police sergeant. "May we go now?"

"I don't know what you're doing here." He looked more than ready for us to leave.

She grabbed my arm and the two of us hurried away.

When we were halfway down the street, she said, "How dare they treat me that way."

"If you treated Henrik better, none of this would have happened."

"There you go, blaming me. Everyone blames me. All the time. Mother blamed me for Fritz carrying on with Greta. Said I should have kept him in line better."

I looked at her in shock. "You knew about Braun and Greta? Your mother knew? Did your father?"

"Father was blissfully ignorant as always. As long as nothing happened to interrupt his experiments or his dinners, he was happy."

"What was your mother going to do if you didn't keep him behaving properly?"

Katrine shrugged. "I don't know and I don't care. She said she'd deal with it."

"When was this?"

"A few days before Greta died." She gave me a puzzled look. "And then the day after Greta, Fritz died."

And the day before Fritz died, Henrik Andersen gave Mrs. Jørgensen the cyanide.

* * *

A week later, I received an invitation to tea from Mrs. Jørgensen at her cottage outside Cambridge. I wrote back, suggesting a day and time. She wrote back, suggesting a different time and date. A few days after that, I found myself getting off the train at the Cambridge station. Following her directions, I began to walk out of town toward the countryside.

There was no one around.

I was not looking forward to this visit. Since I'd returned from Denmark, I'd learned details that I found troubling. Details I didn't want to face. She had been my mother's dear friend and she'd been kind to me.

Or if my father was correct, she wasn't such a dear friend to either of us after all.

The house the Jørgensens had relocated to, when I found it a short way down a lane, was a substantial two-story stone cottage that had been there for centuries. Michelle answered the door and greeted me in French. "The doctor is at work, Katrine is out, and I have been instructed to pour the tea and leave."

"It's good to see you again. How is Porteur?"

"Glad to be here. He has left Dr. Jørgensen's employ to help run a chemical factory nearby. The British government needed someone there. He is happy to take charge."

"And you, Michelle?"

"Glad to be here with the Jørgensens." Then she whispered, "For now. Not for long."

We went into the drawing room and I greeted Mrs. Jørgensen while Michelle poured the tea and left on "Thank you, Michelle."

"Sugar? Milk?"

"Sugar." I watched her closely, knowing Ailsa Jørgensen could slip something in my tea as easily as she must have added something to Braun's coffee. Then, just for an instant, she had her wheeled chair between me and the teacup before she handed it to me and I knew she had poisoned my tea.

My mother's good friend was trying to kill me.

Suspicious, I looked into her cold eyes as I took the cup, determined not to taste it.

"How is your husband? Have you seen him?"

"No, he's been away with his unit. I've seen my father, who sends his regards."

"Ah, Sir Ronald. Such a handsome man when he was young. But so stern. He was not fun loving."

"He hasn't changed."

"That is a shame," Ailsa Jørgensen said and then added, "I wonder what you have made of our last days in Denmark with two murders at the institute. Not the weekend I'd hoped you'd have with us."

I feared our conversation would devolve to this, her curiosity concerning what I'd figured out about the murders. I hadn't thought our visit would begin there. "I keep wondering how you poisoned Braun without anyone noticing," I told her.

"What a strange thing to say. The politi are convinced Friedrich Braun accidentally killed himself with cyanide," Ailsa Jørgensen said. She took a long sip of her tea, perhaps hoping I would do the same.

"But that's not what happened," I replied. "No one believed Katrine when she told the police that you had paid one of the assistants to bring you the cyanide, but she guessed right. While I don't think you paid Andersen, did you tell him this was to make it possible to kill yourself in England if your disease grew too difficult?"

"Not only are you accusing me of murder, but you are also saying Andersen was an accomplice. I thought you were my friend, Olivia, as your mother was." Mrs. Jørgensen wheeled herself away from me, her head held high.

Perhaps I am the friend my mother was. Only following your lead when it suits my plans. "Now that we've arrived safely in Britain and there is no danger of either of you facing criminal charges, it shouldn't be hard to get Andersen to privately admit what happened."

She made a scoffing noise and looked away, not knowing he already had.

"He holds you in very high regard. He never would have told anyone in Denmark, where the crime took place, but here in England? There's no body, no evidence, and now Denmark is part of the Third Reich and we are at war with them. No British judge or jury would get involved in such a tale."

"You're every bit as smart as Phyllida," Mrs. Jørgensen told me as she glanced at me again. "She was a clever woman. And determined. You've inherited that."

"That doesn't answer whether you killed Friedrich Braun." I wanted her to admit it, if only to acknowledge to another person what she had done. She wouldn't face justice in this world, but it wasn't too soon for her to prepare for the next.

"You've already guessed what happened. Why should I have to say anything?"

"I've been honest with you. If this isn't true, tell me. Please. I don't want to go through life thinking my mother's good friend was a murderer." There was anguish in my tone. I'm not certain it was real, but it was there.

"I never thought I would be." She wheeled herself over to me. "But then that horrible Nazi arrived and stole Katrine's heart. I heard Porteur telling Andersen about Braun's wife and I became extra vigilant. I couldn't have my daughter ruin her life with such a man."

"So then you plotted his murder?" I asked.

"No. Not until Canaris announced to our government that the Germans were invading. There was obviously nothing we could do to stop them. And Braun began to goosestep around as if he owned the institute. He wasn't even a good scientist." She sounded disgusted.

"I knew Andersen was sympathetic to both Katrine and me. I explained to him that I needed some way to assure I could end my life if we had to leave the institute and I became too much of a burden on Olaf and Katrine. He brought the cyanide over in a folded paper."

"And that was the paper found on Sunday morning outside in your flower beds?" I asked.

"Yes."

"The police thought that paper had simply been

blown over from the institute since it didn't show up until the next day."

She smiled. "I couldn't get away from Katrine and Olaf and all of you long enough to throw it out of the door. I hoped it would confuse the politi and keep them from arresting anyone."

"It confused them," I agreed. "Since the paper was still crisp, and since they'd already searched the area, they knew it couldn't have been out overnight."

"Yes." Ailsa nodded. "I was trying to widen their choices, when I should have been following your lead and pointing them toward Fritz."

"Why didn't you?" Mrs. Jørgensen was intelligent. I would have thought she'd grab on to that theory faster than she did.

"For too long, I couldn't see how Fritz could be both victim and killer. That was clever of you, seeing that possibility."

What I wasn't was clever. I hadn't seen how Ailsa Jørgensen could be the killer for a long time. Too long. "I understand how you got the poison, but I don't see how you put it in his coffee cup."

"I did it right in front of you and everyone at the table, and no one noticed. He came around my chair with his filled cup. I contrived to get him to pause for a moment, not enough that anyone would remark on it but long enough to tip some crystals into his cup while I drew his attention to my face and what I was saying. The coffee was steaming. The crystals dissolved immediately."

"It's handy that you knew they would do that."

"My dear, I've been married to a leading chemist for over a quarter century. I'd be pretty dim to not learn anything in all that time."

"I was sitting next to you, and I never noticed you put anything in Braun's coffee cup. I barely noticed you speak to him. And I never gave that conversation any importance." How could I have been so blind?

"You—you won't tell Katrine or Olaf what I've done? I've lost so much, and I have so little time left. Please keep my secret."

I looked into her eyes. I was surprised not to see pleading there. She was too proud to plead. And too certain that having got away with murder in Denmark when the police agreed with my conclusion, she could convince her family and everyone else of her innocence if she killed me.

I helped make it possible for her to escape punishment for murder. She'd easily be able to convince her family that I was wrong if I told them my conclusions. "No. I won't tell anyone. And I won't tell anyone that you aren't as ill as you have made us all believe."

"Whatever do you mean?" Anger flashed in her eyes along with something else. Madness?

Chapter Twenty-Nine

I set down my untouched teacup and faced Mrs. Jørgensen. "Just because you're in a wheeled chair doesn't mean you cannot walk. Or climb two flights of stairs to talk to Greta. That must have taken all your strength. She must have made you very angry."

"I had to use my cane and the railing to climb the stairs." She shook her head, an amazed smile on her face. "I don't remember striking her, I was so angry."

"With the cane." Cleverly disguised as part of the wheeled chair.

"Yes." I saw her eye my tea, but I had already determined not to drink it.

"The cane that looks as if it were a piece of your wheeled chair?" No wonder the police never found it.

"Yes. One metal tube looks just the same as any other metal tube." She took another long sip of her tea.

"But the top of it has a beautiful dragon's head for a hand grip."

"Yes. I designed it. I'm rather proud of it."

"You should be. It's lovely." Distracted, I needed to get back to what I really wanted to know. "How did Greta make you so angry? She was your maid. You could have just dismissed her."

"She'd seen me walking around the ground floor. She made me pay her extra for her silence, and she told me she'd tell everyone about my little deception if I fired her."

"You could have called it a miracle that you could now walk and it would have ruined her chance to blackmail you," I suggested.

"I couldn't do that. The only reason Olaf pays any attention to me is because I'm helpless. When we were young, he noticed me. Now, I'm old and invisible. He'd live in the laboratory if he could. I can't allow that. I refuse to be invisible, and that meant my little deception needed to continue."

"You could have killed Greta any day, on the ground floor, and saved yourself the risk of being seen walking. Why climb two flights of stairs in the middle of the night?" I asked.

"She knew we might leave in a few days and that would stop the money she was getting from me. So, she wanted one big payoff. Even as Katrine was trying to keep us at the institute."

"Who decided to have a meeting there at that time?"

"Greta did. She wanted me to come up while Braun was still with her, so he'd see me walk, too. I waited until I saw him leave by the front door." Ailsa smiled. "He left earlier than Greta had planned, and then I went upstairs."

"Had you intended to pay her?"

"Of course not." Mrs. Jørgensen sounded as if she found me dim. Why did the Danes all think that of me?

Maybe they didn't understand British understatement. "It was a large sum and she would have only wanted more. I had to stop that."

"She blackmailed you as well as being a thief? Golly, she was a foolish child." So foolish she didn't live to grow up and develop some wisdom.

"I should never have hired her. Mrs. Ulriksen felt sorry for her, but I should have paid more attention to my instincts."

"This is your business and no one else's. As I said, I won't tell anyone." British justice couldn't touch this. There would be time after the war to sort this out, and there was no statute of limitations on being tried for murder.

She smiled and sighed in relief. "I'm so glad. Would you care for more tea?"

"No, thank you." I hadn't tasted the first cup. Somehow, it didn't feel safe, taking tea with a poisoner. "I must be getting back to London to work."

"But we haven't had a proper visit. When do you think your husband will be able to come home on leave again? What is his name?"

"It's Adam, and I have no idea when he'll come back to London. Has Dr. Jørgensen made any further progress on his rubber experiments?" I asked as I rose.

"A little. You must find writing for a newspaper to be exciting. Your mother would have enjoyed doing that."

In spite of my determination to escape the house as

quickly as possible, I hesitated when she mentioned something about my mother I'd never heard before. "My mother enjoyed writing?"

"Yes. She had a couple of short pieces published in a ladies' magazine when you were a baby." After a moment, she added, "Sit down, have some tea, and I'll tell you all about your mother's articles."

Her offer was tempting, but she'd just admitted she'd killed two people. It didn't feel safe. I didn't know if she had more cyanide, and I didn't know where her cane was. "I really need to get back to town. My editor has an assignment for me this evening."

I took a step toward the door when she wheeled toward me. "I won't see you again, will I?"

"I'm glad you told me about my mother's life, but no, I don't plan to come back here. You have your life here, and I have my life in London. There would be no point, would there?"

"You understand I had no choice in killing Braun. He would have ruined Katrine if I hadn't. And Greta. Huh. That child." She brushed the air with one hand.

If she'd trusted Katrine with the truth, there would have been no need to murder Braun. And if she'd admitted to an ability to walk, at least short distances, there would have been no need to murder Greta or be blackmailed.

I knew she had justified her murders in her mind and there was no reason for me to argue. I bent over to pick up my bag and then walked toward the door.

A sound behind me made me turn to find Mrs. Jørgensen standing a few feet behind me, coming toward me with her metal tube of a cane raised in her hand.

"People know you invited me here. Don't be foolish," I said, backing up.

She took another step forward. She swung, and I easily grabbed the cane as I stepped to the back and side. I pushed the metal tube with its fancy dragon's head down past me, throwing her off balance. She collapsed on her hands and knees, the cane hitting the stone floor.

I hurried into the hall and out the front door. I did not look back as I pulled the door shut.

As I scurried back to the train station, the words "My mother's good friend tried to kill me" kept echoing in my head. I'd see that she wouldn't have the opportunity to try again. I didn't think she'd try to kill her husband, Katrine, or Andersen. Michelle seemed already to be on her guard.

There was no reason to report her actions. The voice in my head said, "No one would believe you."

* * *

Several days later, Germany invaded Belgium and the Netherlands, and Denmark was forgotten. I felt certain without anyone telling me that Adam was on the Continent, and if he wasn't already in danger, he soon would be.

Even on the features desk of the *Daily Premier,* we kept a close eye on the bulletins and the copy coming out of the news desk. My nerves were in tatters. I often wished

Adam had an army posting the same as James Powell, Esther's husband, that kept him based in England. I was living on weak tea and diverting my mind by working hard to make my articles letter perfect, which only succeeded in making me more irritable and my articles unreadable.

The telephone rang shortly after I returned home from the newspaper one evening in May. I grabbed up the receiver, hoping it was Adam. "Mrs. Redmond? Mrs. Olivia Redmond?"

"Yes." I didn't recognize the man's voice at the other end of the call. He sounded older, but vigorous.

"I'm Sir Reynold Tompkinson. I'm acting for Katrine Jørgensen in the death of her mother, Ailsa Jørgensen."

"What?" I squeaked out as soon as I found my voice.

"Miss Jørgensen has been arrested in connection with her mother's death."

"Arrested?" What was happening in Cambridge? I was feeling breathless and confused. Shocked and dismayed.

With a slight note of annoyance in his voice, Sir Reynold continued. "Miss Jørgensen tells me you are familiar with the family and her mother's condition and may be able to shed some light on details that may help Miss Jørgensen's defense."

"What does her father say?"

"Nothing. He refuses to say anything about his wife or his daughter." Sir Reynold cleared his throat. "He did, however, hire me for her defense."

"What do you want from me? I'm not sure how…"

"I'd like you to come to Cambridge and meet with me. Meet with Katrine too, if she'll allow it."

I doubted that. "When would you like me to come up there?"

"Ah, a former Cambridge student, are you?"

One went up to the university, down at the end of term or expulsion. Otherwise, one always went up to London, down to the rest of the country. He'd caught my wording and guessed correctly. "Yes."

"Would tomorrow suit? My office is on the far side of the market square from St. Mary's church." He then gave me detailed directions. "Say, ten o'clock?"

"Let me talk to my editor, but it shouldn't be a problem."

"Your editor?"

"I work for the *Daily Premier.*"

"I insist this not get into the national papers." Sir Reynold sounded quite firm for the first time.

"It won't go anywhere—yet."

As soon as I hung up the phone, I called Sir Henry and explained that I needed to go to Cambridge the next day.

"You need to visit that old friend of your mother's who's ill again? Why not wait until the weekend?"

"She's dead, and a solicitor wants to talk to me about the defense of her daughter, who's been arrested for her mother's murder."

"Good. Write it up as soon as you get back." Sir Henry always had his ear out for a good story for the *Daily*

Premier.

"Between Sir Malcolm and Sir Reynold Tompkinson, her solicitor, we may not be printing anything," I warned him.

"Well, keep your ears open for anything we can print."

* * *

The next morning, dressed in my sturdy gray suit that had survived any number of travels, dressed up with a plum blouse, I traveled on the smoky, lumbering train to Cambridge.

When I left the station, coughing, I walked to the center of town and noticed how few men were left in the university town. Most of them were past university age and in uniform. It felt strange. When I'd been a student, there were young men everywhere.

I found Sir Reynold's office without any trouble at a few minutes past ten and was immediately ushered in. "I was afraid you wouldn't make it," Sir Reynold said after asking his secretary to bring us tea.

"The trains are running so slowly these days they might as well run backward," I said to be polite. I didn't want to be there. It was only my curiosity that was driving me on.

After the secretary, a pinch-faced middle-aged woman, fixed our teacups, supplied us with digestive biscuits, and left, Sir Reynold said, "I suppose I should start with the basic facts."

"Please." I took a sip of tea. It was delicious. The secretary had fixed it exactly the way I asked. I suspected she was a very good secretary.

"On this last Tuesday morning, Michelle, Mrs. Jørgensen's maid, was taking her day off and left the house immediately after an early breakfast. You know of whom I'm speaking?"

"Yes."

"Dr. Olaf Jørgensen then had his breakfast and left for the laboratory, leaving Katrine still in bed and Mrs. Jørgensen upstairs where she'd been taken a breakfast tray by her husband. Katrine had taken a sleeping pill as she'd not slept well lately, and so we can only guess at this next. You understand?"

"Perfectly."

"Mrs. Jørgensen, after calling for Katrine several times and not getting any reply, decided to go downstairs on her own. It is not known if her slippers tripped her up, or the carpet at the top of the stairs slid first, but Katrine woke up to a scream and a loud series of crashes." Sir Reynold gave me a pointed look. "Katrine claims not to know her mother could walk, and we haven't yet found anyone who was aware of this."

I nodded. I could see where this was going. Did she fall or was she pushed?

"Half asleep, Katrine went out onto the landing and looked down to see her mother sprawled at the bottom of the stairs and a quantity of blood on the stone floor in the downstairs hall. She says she screamed, ran downstairs to the telephone and called, not a doctor, but her father."

"It doesn't sound as if a doctor could have done anything for Mrs. Jørgensen, and the family had only been in the country a short time. Katrine probably doesn't know any doctors."

"A sensible conclusion," Sir Reynold said. "Dr. Jørgensen's laboratory is only a few minutes' walk away from the cottage, and he rushed over as soon as he received his daughter's telephone call, accompanied by a Dr. Henrik Andersen, an assistant to Dr. Jørgensen. Do you know them?"

"Yes." I wondered what Andersen made of Mrs. Jørgensen's fall.

"A doctor was eventually called who telephoned the police, not being convinced this was a simple tumble down the stairs. Mrs. Jørgensen could easily have been pushed, there was bruising on her back, she was alone with Katrine, and they had had a terrible row the day before in front of witnesses. Katrine apparently threatened to either move out or kill her mother. Mrs. Jørgensen said she'd move out over her, Mrs. Jørgensen's, dead body."

"Did your witnesses tell you their fights were as nasty as that when they were still in Denmark? Who were the witnesses?"

"A Mrs. Hopper, their housekeeper, the maid Michelle, and Henrik Andersen. Mrs. Hopper was particularly forthcoming with evidence damaging to my client's position."

"Was all the argument in English, or was some in Danish? And does Mrs. Hopper speak Danish?"

"No, she does not. However, most of the argument was in English, and Michelle and Andersen told the police what little was in Danish. It didn't appear to add anything to what Mrs. Hopper said."

"Was anything in particular said during this fight that would make it more violent than any of the other arguments they had all the time?"

"Yes." Sir Reynold scowled before he continued. "Katrine accused her mother of killing someone named Braun, and her mother's response was 'So what? He'd never have married you.'"

Chapter Thirty

"You know Braun was already married," I said.

"No." Sir Reynold pulled out an elegant fountain pen and a crisp thick sheet of paper. "Could you give me his particulars?"

"Friedrich Braun, doctor of chemistry, German national, working in the Danish Institute for Theoretical and Applied Chemistry run by Dr. Jørgensen. His wife's name was Annemarie. I met her when I was in Copenhagen visiting the Jørgensen family."

When Sir Reynold finished scribbling, he said, "Why did Katrine say her mother killed him?"

"He died of cyanide poisoning while I was there. There was an investigation by the police who determined that Braun accidentally killed himself. Katrine never believed it. However, Katrine told me at the time she never planned to marry Braun. She only said that to stop her parents from pressuring her to marry anyone." Well, that was one version.

"Did they both know he was married?"

"They knew before they left Denmark."

"What else can you tell me?"

"I have no idea what you need to know," I replied.

"How active was Mrs. Jørgensen?"

I wasn't going to get caught in any traps set by Sir Reynold if I could help it. "What do you mean?"

"Would you be surprised if I told you Mrs. Jørgensen's wheeled chair was found in her room after her death? And that she could indeed walk."

"I'm not surprised. Just because she was in a wheeled chair didn't mean she was paralyzed."

"Did you ever see her walk?"

I remembered my visit to their Cambridge cottage just a few short weeks before. She'd risen from her chair, cane in hand, planning to strike me down. "Yes."

"Do you know of anyone else who had seen her walk?"

"Yes, a Mrs. Anne Bannacloss of London, an old friend of Katrine's, who saw Mrs. Jørgensen walk in 1937, before Mrs. Bannacloss married and left the country."

Sir Reynold studied me for a full minute before he said, "You've been investigating something to do with the Jørgensens, haven't you?"

"Yes."

"What?"

"Nothing that will help your client, and nothing I am free to divulge."

"What do you mean?"

"Ask Katrine. She was the one who first pointed this out to me."

Sir Reynold invited me to visit Katrine in the jail with him, and I agreed. I wasn't sure if she definitely knew her mother was a killer, and I didn't want to tell her lawyer without Katrine being able to refute my words to my face.

Also, she'd been so difficult that I wanted to see her stuck behind bars, if only for a few minutes. But I didn't want to see her hang, and I was fairly sure she didn't kill her mother.

The police station and its adjacent courthouse and jails were in lumpy brick Victorian buildings that were both ugly and formidable. We walked to them, the buildings not being far from the colleges where most of their business came from.

Had come from, when there were a great number of young men to get into trouble from pranks and brawls.

Katrine, in a plain dress and without makeup or anyone to do her bidding, looked downcast and pale. Her dress was thin, and I was certain she had to be cold in the chilled air of the prison. The walls and floor around us were unyielding stone, demonstrating Victorian attitudes to crime and sin.

As soon as she saw me behind Sir Reynold, she smiled. For once, it wasn't a smug smile. "Oh, Olivia, please tell them I didn't do it." She sounded desperate. I almost felt guilty for wishing her to spend a moment in this place.

"I don't understand why you were arrested." We sat across a table from each other. Sir Reynold pulled out his fountain pen and paper to take notes.

"It's all Mrs. Hopper's fault. She took our arguments seriously. Can you imagine anything sillier?"

"Why were you still arguing about Braun?" That made no sense.

"Because she killed him and she acted as if it made no difference. Even if we were never going to marry, and we weren't, he mattered to someone. His wife. His family. You can't just act as if no one matters except you."

"And Greta?"

"She was a slut, but she was just a child." Katrine looked at me and her shoulders slumped. "My mother killed her, too, didn't she?"

I nodded.

"She acted as if she was the only person who mattered. Everyone had to wait on her because she was in that dumb chair she didn't even need. And if you were too big a problem, she'd kill you. Yet I'm the one in here." She was nearly shouting now, and I thought she'd again become hysterical.

"You're here solely because Mrs. Hopper reported your arguments with your mother?" I looked from Katrine to Sir Reynold.

They both slowly shook their heads.

"There was bruising on her back, as if someone shoved her down the stairs. As if someone pushed her hard. And I was the only one at home."

"Were you really completely asleep until you woke up to the sound of someone or something falling down the stairs?"

"Yes. I had been having trouble sleeping, so I got

something to make me sleep. Even the sound of someone falling down those steep stairs only halfway woke me up."

"And the doctor who prescribed this drug?" I asked.

She shook her head. "I didn't get them from a doctor."

"You bought them on the black market? Oh, Katrine, that's dangerous. You don't know what you're getting."

"Could you have possibly walked in your sleep under the influence of this drug?" Sir Reynold asked.

"No. The drug leaves me limp and barely able to move. If that had been the case, my mother could have easily pushed me down the stairs and you'd be having a different sort of talk," she told him.

"It sounds dangerous. Don't take any more of it. It could become addictive," I told her. I didn't know, but I thought I ought to warn her.

"They won't let me have it in here and I get to lie awake at night listening to the crying and shouting and mice scurrying about. Horrible place." She rubbed her hands up and down her arms.

"Is it possible someone else was in your house when your mother fell?" I asked.

She thought and then shook her head. "No. I rose quickly and stumbled out into the hallway. From there you can see the front door. It was shut and locked."

Then she sat up straight. "I just remembered. I nearly tripped over the carpet at the top of the stairs. It was half on the hall floor and half lying over the top two stairs. I had to step around it very carefully or I would have gone down the stairs and landed on top of my mother."

"Who decided to put that carpet there? It was a loose carpet, a small carpet, you found at the top of the stairs?" I asked.

"I don't know. I hadn't paid any attention to it."

"How long had it been there?" asked the solicitor.

Katrine shrugged. "Not long. My father complained about it a day or two before my mother fell. I don't remember it before then."

"Something I must ask your father about," Sir Reynold said, making another note.

"It sounds as if there was a new carpet at the top of the stairs. Your mother didn't expect it, slipped, and fell. I can't explain the bruises on her back, but could they have been from a massage? Michelle might have been using massage and exercises to make your mother more comfortable." I looked from Sir Reynold to Katrine.

"I'll talk to the officer in charge and the court and see what might be done. Don't give up hope," Sir Reynold said, rising.

"By the way, what is Michelle doing these days?" I asked.

"Oh, she was taken on by a hospital almost immediately after Mother died. It turns out she had sent out letters to friends looking for a hospital position as soon as we reached Cambridge."

"And she had an alibi for when your mother fell?" I asked.

"The best. She was interviewing at a hospital fifty miles away."

I was glad of that. Otherwise, Michelle might have found herself in the dock.

"Livvy, did you know my mother could walk?"

"I found out the day I visited your cottage in Cambridge. Did you know?"

"No." Her voice came out nearly as a wail. "After I called my father, I glanced around the hallway looking for her wheeled chair. It wasn't there. It made no sense."

"She didn't tell you?"

"No one told me. Well, my father told me after she was dead that he suspected." She wrapped her arms tightly around her waist.

"Is there anything I can do for you, Katrine?" I asked.

"You already have. You've given me confidence."

* * *

The war progressed, but not the way we might have liked. Belgium and the Netherlands fell, and France was in serious trouble. Churchill became our prime minister, nearly giving my father apoplexy.

Everyone you saw on London streets now was in uniform. Men and women both, in the uniforms of the army, the navy, the ARP, the nursing services, and if they weren't in uniform, civilian dress was certainly designed to look like a uniform. And everywhere you looked, the piles of sandbags seemed to grow.

I was crossing central London one day on the way

back from a Ministry of Information meeting when I saw Katrine coming toward me on the pavement. She looked the same as the Katrine I had seen in Denmark, fashionably dressed, hair stylishly done, and energetic.

"Katrine," I said as I reached her. "It's good to see you in London."

"I'm living here now," she said as a smile crossed her face. She appeared satisfied, happy even. "Sharing a flat with three other girls at the Ministry of Information. I'm helping to design the artwork on posters for the 'Don't waste food' campaign."

Apparently, she didn't have a job that required signing the Official Secrets Act.

"So you're living in London now. Are you enjoying it?"

"Yes. My father wanted me to stay at home, but I convinced him to let me try to make it on my own. And I am! My roommates and I go dancing a few evenings a week, I'm involved in art, well, sort of, and I'm learning my way around London."

"Good for you. Are your roommates your age?"

"Yes. Two of them went to university in London and graduated in my year, and the other is a friend of one of them from her home town. Carlisle, I think it's called. Now, has your husband been home?"

"No. I get the occasional letter, but I'm sure he's busy."

"You must miss him."

"I do." I was amazed at the insight Katrine displayed.

Perhaps her recent experiences had made her grow up. "Do you miss Denmark?"

"Yes. Not our life at the institute so much as the look and sound of Copenhagen, the cooler weather, hearing my language, the life there. I'm sure it's changed now, under the Nazis."

I nodded. There wasn't anything I could say.

"Have you seen Mike Christiansen?"

"No. Have you?" Neither of us had shown any interest in seeing the other again.

"No, but I want to. I'd like to thank him for his role in helping us get to England. And I'd like to thank you for your role."

"You're very welcome." Saying thank you? She certainly had grown up.

"If I hear from Mike, we'll see if we can all get together."

"If you do, would you have Henrik Andersen come down from Cambridge?"

"Now that I've escaped him and my parents, why would I? He and my father practically live in that laboratory now, and they seem very happy. I hope they find a way to make synthetic rubber from vegetable matter after all the work they've put in."

"Did they ever solve the mystery of the carpet at the top of the stairs?" I asked.

Katrine frowned at me. "Mystery?"

"How a small piece of carpet ended up at the top of

the stairs shortly before your mother fell?"

"Yes." Katrine shook her head. "It was Mrs. Hopper. She found it in the bottom of the airing cupboard two afternoons before and put it there because she thought it looked good. My mother died because Mrs. Hopper decided to redecorate."

Probably a better ending for her than at the end of a hangman's noose. I hoped Katrine and her father didn't miss Ailsa Jørgensen too much.

We made promises to get together for an evening of dinner and dancing before we parted, but even as I said it, I didn't believe it would ever happen. There was six years of age between us. I was married, she was definitely single. She wanted to dance every night, while I'd rather spend my nights at home with Adam.

That night after work, I went home to listen to news of the war on the wireless and to write Adam another letter telling him how much I missed him. I missed the Phony War, but what I really wanted was peace. I wanted an end to the war in Europe and to have Adam home.

However long it might take, I was willing to wait as long as I got Adam home again.

I hope you've enjoyed Deadly Rescue. If you have, please be sure to read the rest of Olivia's adventures in The Deadly Series. And go to my website www.KateParkerbooks.com to sign up for my newsletter. When you do, you'll receive links to my free Deadly Series short stories you can download from BookFunnel onto your ereader of choice. If you want to let others know if you found Deadly Rescue to be a good read, leave a review at your favorite online retailer or tell your librarian. Reviews and recommendations are necessary for books to be discovered and to get good ratings. Thanks for your help for all good books.

Notes and Acknowledgements

The inspiration for Deadly Rescue must go to Admiral Wilhelm Canaris, head of the Abwehr, or German military intelligence during World War II. Canaris himself was executed on Hitler's orders near the end of the war for not agreeing with Hitler going back to the invasion of Poland. Canaris felt the German military was attacking too many civilian targets when Hitler wanted the Poles wiped out. Hitler wasn't as keen on wiping out the Danes or the Norwegians, so Canaris didn't get into trouble for warning both countries of their imminent invasion.

That much of Deadly Rescue is true. Canaris did notify the Danish and Norwegian governments on April 4 of the April 9 invasion. And the ships that traveled to Copenhagen and to Norway from northern Germany did set sail early on April 8 to arrive at their assigned locations on the morning of April 9.

Germany was dependent on Swedish iron ore, and the only way to move it from northern Sweden was through Norwegian ports and by sea to Germany. This was too exposed to British attack as long as Germany didn't have any bases or ports in Norway, so Hitler decided to take over the country. And since Denmark was in the way, he'd take that country over as well.

The character of Dr. Jørgensen was loosely copied off of the physicist Niels Bohr's life who was a famous Dane who had to escape Denmark during WWII. However, while others left in 1940, he stayed until 1943 when orders went out for his internment. Before that, he was under house arrest at his institute.

The synthetic rubber mentioned in the story was a very real necessity, since war kept natural rubber from reaching any of the combatants. A synthetic version was first perfected in the mid 1930s, but it required petroleum, which was almost as hard to obtain during the war years as natural rubber. A rubber made from waste products or locally grown products would have been welcome, however, I'm afraid it was only in my imagination.

I'd like to thank my first reader, my daughter Jennifer, my editors, Eilis Flynn and Les Floyd, my proofreader, Jennifer Brown, my formatter, Jennifer Johnson, and my cover artist, Lyndsey Lewellen. Their help has been invaluable in making this book as good as it can be. All mistakes, as always, are my own.

I thank you, my readers, for coming along with Olivia on this journey. I hope you've enjoyed it.

About the Author

Kate Parker grew up reading her mother's collection of mystery books by Christie, Sayers, and others. Now she can't write a story without someone being murdered, and everyday items are studied for their lethal potential. It had taken her years to convince her husband she hadn't poisoned dinner; that funny taste was because she couldn't cook. Her children have grown up to be surprisingly normal, but two of them are developing their own love of literary mayhem, so the term "normal" may have to be revised.

For the time being, Kate has brought her imagination to the perilous times before and during World War II in the Deadly series. London society resembled today's lifestyle, but Victorian influences still abounded. Kate's sleuth is a young widow earning her living as a society reporter for a large daily newspaper while secretly working as a counterespionage agent for Britain's spymaster and finding danger as she tries to unmask Nazi spies while helping refugees escape oppression.

As much as she loves stately architecture and vintage clothing, Kate has also developed an appreciation of central heating and air conditioning. She's discovered life in Carolina requires her to wear shorts and T-shirts while drinking hot tea and it takes a great deal of imagination to picture cool, misty weather when it's 90 degrees out and sunny.

Follow Kate and her deadly examination of history at www.kateparkerbooks.com

www.Facebook.com/Author.Kate.Parker/

and www.bookbub.com/authors/kate-parker